# Acclaim for *PERPETU*
## Winner of the 2009 Next-Ge
### Award for Best Short Stu̓ɾ

"These are big stories, not afraid to venture into ruined cities and ruined hearts . . . stories bold to tackle big themes with perfect detail. I expect we'll hear a lot more from James Nolan."

—Tom Franklin, author of *Hell at the Breech* and *Smonk*

"The real deal. . . . The city's long conversation with itself has never been louder or more insistent than in these stories, with all their exuberance, despair and wit."

—Susan Larson, *The Times-Picayune*

"Call me a gusher, but this is a standout collection, one of the best I've read in years, and it deserves a place in the most august company."

—Garry Craig Powell, *Arkansas Review*

"A fine debut collection. . . . Nolan's prose is both languid and biting. And he's wildly inventive in how he launches a tale."

—Michael Upchurch, *The Seattle Times*

"In the tradition of William Faulkner and Flannery O'Conner . . . dark humor abounds in this literary menagerie of Southern grotesques. Do yourself a favor: read this book."

— Terry Dalrymple, *American Book Review*

*"Perpetual Care* stands in accomplishment with *The Loved One*, *Miss Lonely Hearts*, *Wise Blood*, and *A Confederacy of Dunces*. The stories here are apt, disturbing, and funny."

—Wyatt Prunty, Director, Sewanee Writers' Conference

# HIGHER GROUND

## ALSO BY JAMES NOLAN

### Fiction

*Perpetual Care: Stories* (Jefferson Press)

### Poetry

*Why I Live in the Forest* (Wesleyan University Press)
*What Moves Is Not the Wind* (Wesleyan University Press)

### Poetry in Translation

Pablo Neruda, *Stones of the Sky* (Copper Canyon Press)
Jaime Gil de Biedma, *Longing: Selected Poems* (City Lights Books)

### Criticism

*Poet-Chief: The Native American Poetics of Walt Whitman and Pablo Neruda*
(University of New Mexico Press)

### Essays

*Fumadores en manos de un dios enfurecido: Ensayos
al caballo entre varios mundos* (Madrid: Editores Enigma)

# HIGHER GROUND

A NOVEL

JAMES NOLAN

UNIVERSITY OF LOUISIANA AT LAFAYETTE PRESS
2011

This novel is a work of fiction. Names, characters, places, and institutions either are the product of the author's imagination or are used fictitiously. Any resemblance to actual persons, living or dead, is coincidental.

Cover image: *Louisiana Suite: Mardi Gross*, 2000 by Warrington Colescott, courtesy of the artist; photographed by Greg Anderson

"Higher Ground" lyrics © James Nolan 2011
"Chain Reaction" lyrics used by permission: pgs. 24, 26, 167, and 271

http://ulpress.org
University of Louisiana at Lafayette Press
P.O. Box 40831
Lafayette, LA 70504-0831


ISBN 13 (paper): 978-1-935754-06-0

Library of Congress Cataloging-in-Publication Data

Nolan, James, 1947-
Higher ground : a novel / James Nolan.
p. cm.
"Winner of the William Faulkner-Wisdom Gold Medal in the Novel."
ISBN 978-1-935754-06-0 (pbk. : acid-free paper)
1. New Orleans (La.)--Fiction.  I. Title.
PS3564.O36H54 2011
813'.54--dc23
                                2011022470


Printed on acid-free paper.
Printed in Canada

in memory
David MacMillan:
*the best audience in the world*

*Blow, winds, and crack your cheeks. Rage, blow.*
*You cataracts and hurricanoes, spout*
*Till you have drenched our steeples, drowned the cocks.*
*You sulph'rous and thought-executing fires,*
*Vaunt-courriers of oak-cleaving thunderbolts,*
*Singe my white head. And thou, all-shaking thunder,*
*Strike flat the thick rotundity o' th' world,*
*Crack nature's moulds, all germains spill at once,*
*That makes ungrateful man.*

–Shakespeare, *King Lear*

Caller: *We're up on the sofa in the front room. . . .*
911 Operator: *You need to go to the, um, do you have an attic*
*inside your home?*
Caller: *No.*
911 Operator: *You don't have an attic?*
Caller: *Uh-uh.*
911 Operator: *OK, well you need to get to higher ground, OK?*
*Even if you have to get up to the, uh, to the roof, but I need you to get*
*to higher ground.*

–911 Call, New Orleans, August 29, 2005

*You take a chance the day you're born. Why stop now?*
–Barbara Stanwyck in *Golden Boy*

## Saturday, January 28

THE LONE WORKING STREETLIGHT in the 1000 block of Dauphine Street was wincing off and on like a migraine. Even five months after the hurricane, the air still smelled sweet and fetid, as if some large hairy animal had died nearby. Although the police curfew recently had been lifted, the neighborhood felt deserted, and the shotgun doubles and wrought-iron balconies remained shuttered along the darkened French Quarter street. Suspension springs squeaking, a low-riding black Chevrolet kept circling the block, cutting off its headlights every time it turned the corner. The night was dank and chilly, and yet the air bristled, as if waiting for something to happen.

Or for someone to appear.

With an insouciant skip to his walk, Marky Naquin veered around the corner at Tony's Superette and then rapped on the peeling green shutters at 1023 Dauphine.

"Hey, little mama," he called out. "What you got cooking?"

Then he banged on the shutters at 1025 next door, shouting "Nicole."

No answer.

He slung a tattered red backpack over his shoulder and approached an almost new Maytag refrigerator wrapped with duct tape and abandoned on the curb. Something was painted on the door in a wild, loopy scrawl. He jumped back, obviously shaken. The letters were still sticky.

"Hey, man, you seen Gary Cherry?"

Marky pivoted around. The teenager standing behind him was small-boned and light-complexioned, the wisp of a mustache cultivated over a fleshy mouth. The boy licked his lips, as if thirsty or nervous.

"I'm waiting for Momma and my sister, who live up front here," Marky said. "Gary's place is in the courtyard, and they'll know where he is."

"I come by twice before and ring his bell," the young man said. "You see Gary, tell him Latrome looking for him." His lidded eyes studied the scruffy white man with the graying ponytail. "He'll know what it about."

The low-riding black car rounded the corner and then slid up to the front of the shotgun double. The tinted back window slowly lowered. A dark face framed by a white T-shirt appeared at the window, observed what was painted on the refrigerator, and then aimed a snub-nosed chrome pistol.

"At last," somebody whispered inside the car. "That him."

Three shots popped.

Then a fourth one echoed.

Both men standing in front of the house crumpled to the pavement. The tinted window slid up again, and the car creaked off, bouncing over potholes, until it melted like a cat into the night.

A pale moon rose above rooftops as blood pooled on the sidewalk.

On the balcony next door, a light flashed on. "Lord have mercy," said a voice from above.

2

# Higher Ground

It wasn't until both squad cars arrived half an hour later, and the ghostly street pulsed with revolving blue lights, that anyone noticed the fresh graffiti painted on the Maytag.

"Shine that flashlight over here," said Sergeant Jurvis Brown. "'As above, so below,'" he read. "What the hell that supposed to mean?"

# I

# Chain Reaction

# One

THAT SATURDAY AFTERNOON, WHEN Nicole rammed her navy-blue Saturn into a FEMA trailer, she was driving on new meds with a tombstone in the back of the car.

In the morning she'd borrowed a dolly from Tony's Superette at the corner and hired Hunter, the tattooed delivery boy, to meet her at the cemetery to help load the damn thing into her car. Naquin. Hers was a common New Orleans surname, and six generations of almost illegible inscriptions were crowded onto the cracked marble tablet, now stained nicotine-yellow by the floodwaters. Her father's name and dates were carved in the second-to-last space. Nicole had mentally reserved the next place on the tombstone for her seventy-six-year-old mother. At the moment, Nicole couldn't imagine who else could possibly take that last slot.

Before the end of the day, she would find out.

But now, on top of everything else that would go wrong today, she was stranded with a flat at the only gas station left open in Lakeview. The lone attendant was rolling the punctured tire toward her, holding up a squat silver nail. Stoop-shouldered, he dragged his feet like someone working on a chain gang.

"Lady, you picked up a roofing nail," he crowed, as if he'd discovered a tumor. "Another little present from FEMA."

Nicole grimaced. She never told people where she worked, unless she had time for an hour-long tirade against the government. She felt like someone in the French Resistance secretly working for the Nazis, or a Creole collaborating with the Union army in occupied New Orleans. But the job with FEMA was the only one she could get. "How long will it take to fix it?" She glanced at his name badge. "Hewitt."

Hewitt spat, pink gums flashing in his tire-blackened face, then gestured to a mountain of rubber in the corner of the garage, next to the Pepsi machine. "You see all them other tires what got roofing nails? They lying all over the road now. Use 'em to tack up the blue tarps so it don't rain in people's houses." He eyeballed her Texas license plate. "This city is a crying shame."

"You don't have to tell me, Hewitt." She was relearning how to get things done in her torpid hometown: mention your mother, tell an interesting story, and call the person by name. "During the storm my momma lost her house in Lakeview where she'd lived for fifty years and now she's camping out in the French Quarter and driving me up the wall, as if my crazy brother weren't enough. Now if I don't get this tombstone back to her—"

"Tombstone?" He shaded his eyes with stubby fingers covered with grime to peek into the back of the SUV.

"During the storm the slab fell off our tomb in Lafayette Cemetery like a broken oven door." She pointed through the tinted hatchback window. "My daddy is buried in there."

He stared farther into the car. "Look, lady—"

"Call me Nicole," she said. "I grew up here in Lakeview. My momma has been coming to this station since Bienville landed. You must know Gertie Naquin, a sweet, yacky old

8

lady with gray corkscrew curls." Nicole belonged, one of the few pleasures left to her in this town. She had a past here, if not a present. So fix the damn tire already.

"Miss Gertie. Sure I know her." He screwed up his face, catching Nicole's eye. "So how'd you do?"

This was the question on the tips of everyone's tongues. She had figured out that it didn't mean *how are you?* but rather *how much of your life did you lose in the hurricane?* "Momma's house got eight feet of water," she said, taking a deep breath, "and the day after the levees broke, the Coast Guard rescued her from the second floor, then they bused her to the Astrodome in Houston, and she came to stay with me in Austin while I was breaking up with my husband. So then three months ago we both moved into this shotgun double in the Quarter, you know, her on one side, me on the other—"

"Mean you moved here *after* the storm. For *what?*" He rolled his eyes. "Kicks?"

She let out a shrill laugh and turned red, shaking her head like a ragdoll. "Yeah, after twenty-eight years away, I picked now to come home. Smart, wouldn't you say? And if you don't fix my tire I'm going to break down crying and won't stop until I rust every scrap of metal in this place."

"Okay, I'll put the spare on, and you can come back next week for this thing." He bounced the flat tire. "Only don't run over no more roofing nails, hear?" With a weary whistle, he swung open the hatchback, yanked out the spare, and crouched next to it.

"Hewitt?" Nicole couldn't stop herself. When she was little, that was how Uncle Alfonse, a tug boat mechanic, used to whistle whenever he'd come over to fix an air conditioner, and while he worked he'd let her hand him the tools. She knew her question might take all afternoon, but she really wanted to know.

"Yeah?" Hewitt's sky-blue eyes blinked up at her from a smudged face.

"How'd you do?"

He blinked again, shaking his head.

"In the storm, I mean," she said. "Did you get much water?"

"Lemme show you something." He hoisted up his turnip-shaped body.

Without uttering a word, he led her to the back lot of the gas station, where a rusted Impala was parked on a weedy patch of cracked asphalt. When he popped open the door, Nicole peered inside. The back seat was made into a bed, piled with pillows and blankets, and the front seat was a nest of dirty clothes. From the dashboard he retrieved a violet velveteen slipper caked with mud, resting next to a toothbrush and tube of Crest.

"My mama was in that nursing home over in Chalmette they didn't bother to evacuate," he said, handing Nicole the slipper. "She was tied into her wheelchair account of her bum back, so she wouldn't slide out. The night before the storm I told her, 'Mama, come with me, we'll drive to Picayune to stay by cousin Ferrel's,' but she was worried about her dialysis. When the National Guard let me in that place two weeks later, this was all I could find of her. Still have nightmares about brown water inching up over her face."

Nicole looked at the moldy slipper in her hand, and then back at Hewitt. Tears welled in her eyes. "I don't know what—"

"That's okay," he said, taking the slipper and placing it back on the dashboard. "Not much anyone can say at this point. Tell Miss Gertie that Hewitt over by the gas station is still kicking. Told me she had a daughter somewhere off in Texas. Welcome home."

# Higher Ground

As Nicole swerved onto West End Boulevard, the crumbling tombstone shifted behind her, and she reached back to steady it. Barreling along past a thicket of picket signs advertising "roof repair" and "house gutting" and "mold abatement," she felt giddy and lightheaded. She wasn't sure if it was because the tire was changed or because the Zoloft was finally kicking in.

She never thought she'd need antidepressants here in festive New Orleans. But the divorce had been like flossing her teeth compared to coping with this broken city, an ashen expanse of dark, abandoned streets lined with boarded-up houses and patrolled by Humvees filled with National Guardsmen shouldering M-16s. Most of these decaying shells still had the ominous red $X$ of the rescuers spray-painted next to their doors, as if the biblical Angel of Death had passed over them, marking the number of the living and the dead. Only a third of the former residents had returned, mostly to the historic neighborhoods perched along the sliver of higher ground that banked the Mississippi River. The bowl of reclaimed swampland that made up the modern city was now a tundra of phantasmal ruins. It was as if Nicole's blue Saturn were spinning around inside the grainy black-and-white war footage of bombed out Dresden. Suddenly turning a corner, the sight could make her heart stop.

Leave it to her gynecologist ex-husband to demand a divorce the day after the most destructive storm in American history slammed into New Orleans, precisely at that moment when she'd had one eye glued to the CNN coverage while with the other she was searching the Internet for her mother's name posted among the thousands on refugee lists.

"Can't you see I'm busy, Buster?" That was the only response she could muster at the moment. After she located her mother and flew her to their house, what Buster had told her sank in. In a nutshell, he was kicking her out. While her mother spent the morning in the bathroom soaking her weary old bones in all the hot water the state of Texas had on tap, the couple had it out.

"So who is this skanky twat you've been seeing?" Nicole sputtered, slamming down the coffee pot. "Don't you get enough of that during office exams?"

"Pam and I are going to be married as soon as I can disentangle myself from—"

"And how long have you been sneaking around screwing Miss Cuntley?"

"About as long as you and I snuck around while I was married to my first wife."

That did it.

Nicole had blamed herself. She just didn't feel sexy or pretty anymore. Whenever she studied herself in a full-length mirror, what she saw was Mrs. Frump, no matter how much she moisturized or waxed or spun like a manic hamster on the stationary bicycle in her Austin garage. Her spiky hair was tinted bronze—she could never get the color right—and her porcelain complexion webbed with fine lines like antique china. Sure, her plump, wide-hipped friends told her she was the original "Heroin Chic" model, so gaunt, wispy, and flat-chested. But look at them. She felt most herself dressed in teenage boy's clothes from off the rack at the Gap, like a ragamuffin David Bowie with Orphan Annie eyes. Now there she was, forty-six, childless, and snake-bit, just another middle-aged ex-Mrs. Doctor from the Texas burbs.

"Boy, I thought I had problems," her mother had said, toweling the hair that hadn't been washed since the day her kitchen flooded up to her second chin. "Sorry, but I couldn't help but overhear." Nicole and Buster had been screaming at each other in the breakfast nook for an hour.

"Momma, don't. . . ." Nicole was melting into a puddle, sobbing from every pore.

"Just throw out the no good bum and redecorate." Gertie Naquin dried her daughter's face with the damp bath towel.

"It's *his* house. And I signed a prenup, remember? According to which, even the goddamn Cuisinart is his." Her wheezing sobs turned into a screech. "After fifteen years, all I've got is the clothes on my back."

"That makes two of us."

All Nicole kept from her marriage was the Saturn, in which she was now bowling along past the mounds of fetid debris on Mouton Street on a final Saturday errand, to look for Momma's potting trowel and watering can. Her mother had discovered these rusted treasures in the wash shed the last time she went to visit the ruins of her house. Of all things, her momma was starting a garden. Mrs. Naquin had lost her antique furniture and, what was worse, the albums with family pictures going back to the 1880s.

"If I can't have my old memories back, looks like I'll have to grow me some new ones," her mother had told her this morning, trellising a potato vine up a post on her side gallery. She was dressed in Salvation Army clothes, camping out alone in three sparsely furnished rooms with her crippled dachshund, Schnitzel. Never ever during Nicole's booze-fueled, teen-aged daydreams while ratting the Quarter, could she have pictured that one day she would live next door to her mother on Dauphine Street. That some day she might live close to her brother Marky, maybe.

But poor Marky, now that was another story.

So far, hardly anyone in her mother's Lakeview neighborhood had come back, although occasionally Nicole spotted the white breadbox of a FEMA trailer squatting in a driveway or in front of a house, mounted on six cinderblock pillars. If you asked her, the Federal Emergency Management Agency was a government bureau dreamed up in some lost chapter of *Alice in Wonderland*. But the job was all she could scrounge up in a city where few businesses had reopened. So from 8 a.m. until 4 p.m. every weekday, she was now a Debris Removal Monitor. That meant she counted the dump trucks hauling the mountains of trash from the sites where people were gutting their houses. Bored out of her gourd, watching the parade of trucks lumber by heaped with bulging plastic sacks, she dubbed herself Miss Glad Bag.

What a perfect job for somebody thrown away.

She was suddenly grateful to be back on four solid wheels and couldn't wait to get home to her mother's oil-cloth covered kitchen table. She didn't know what to say to Hewitt or to anyone else in this city. When she heard their hurricane sagas, she'd fight back tears, her mouth would flap open, but no words would come out. And the stories were everywhere. Hewitt's was now roiling around in her mind with Momma's and her own Job-like tales of tribulation. You worked hard, paid your bills, ate plenty of fiber, drank eight glasses of water a day, and then in a flash, everything you once recognized as your life was gone.

Vanished.

*That makes two of us.*

A whole city of us.

As her car lurched though the open crater of a pothole, the dolly rattled in the back of the SUV and the marble slab shifted again, sliding from its position propped between two boxes. Then the massive stone toppled, crushing the boxes and crashing against the dolly. At that moment, she was sucking from a plastic water bottle in her right hand. These new pills made her so thirsty. And when she lifted her other hand from the steering wheel to reach back and steady the stone—for just one second—she felt the jagged edges of the two splintered fragments. Her mother would throw a fit.

Then before she knew it, the car veered toward a FEMA trailer parked at the curb, slamming to a sudden halt with a resounding crash.


KELLY CANNON USED TO HAVE A great sense of humor. He really did. Everybody said so. That is, until his Lakeview house flooded with five feet of water and his wife Lena decided to stay put in their FEMA apartment in Houston. Now he only communicated with her by cell phone and had just moved into the FEMA trailer parked in front of what was left of their house.

"Yeah, Lena, the trailer is finally set up," he barked into the cell. "Even have the key. Call the Pope, it's a miracle."

While Kelly wrestled with crumbling sections of Sheetrock, he shouted into the cell cradled in his shoulder. "I finally moved out of the Star Lite Motel, and in a few minutes I'll take my first shower in the trailer. Now I'm not gonna try and fool you, babe. Place is a stinking mess. But you know something? Boy, it's good to be home."

Lena now had a part-time job in Houston and showed no signs of wanting to help Kelly claw his way through the muck. "Get a grip," was what she had to say. "New Orleans is over."

Kelly was dressed in a smudged orange T-shirt and black cargo pants, yellow rubber gloves rolled up to his elbows. With his graying carrot top, freckled pumpkin face, and gauze mask yanked over his forehead so he could talk on the cell, he looked like an overgrown trick-or-treater costumed as a septic-tank cleaner. Moving through the house, he crunched underfoot what had once been the layer of slime covering the carpeting, now dried and cracked into a surface resembling

15

elephant skin. It was the end of January and the weather had stayed cool, but the leaf-mold stink was more suffocating than ever. Several times this afternoon, he gagged and ran coughing outside for gulps of fresh air. With its blackened walls and moldering furniture, the house was a seething compost heap, a sty of bacterial sludge and rampant fungi blooming in jazzy pastel patterns. Jackson Pollock couldn't have done a better job with the kitchen. But Kelly was adamant about rebuilding. This was their home, for Christ's sake, where they had raised their two kids. He couldn't just leave it to rot. That would be like letting his mama die of gangrene in a ditch.

"The trailer really is comfortable," he said, dragging a mound of Sheetrock shards toward the door on a plastic tarp. "It has a built-in double bed, and the cutest kitchenette, like a doll house. I feel like the Jolly Green Giant knocking around inside, but—"

A crash resonated from outside, as if a truckload of empty steel drums had hit the pavement all at once.

"Gotta go," Kelly spit into the cell. "Something just collapsed."

He spun around and raced out the front door.

And then couldn't believe his eyes.

The front end of his trailer had been knocked off its cinderblock pilings and was now jutting at a forty-five degree angle into the air, one whole side wrinkled like cellophane. The hood of a blue Saturn was buried halfway into the buckled wall of what was going to be his bedroom.

Kelly stood there paralyzed, his mouth hanging open in a cavernous O.

"Holy shit," he muttered.

A skinny woman with a blondish pixie cut stood frozen next to the SUV, shaking her head and rubbing her slumped shoulders as if she were freezing. Slowly a stark paraffin face, melted into a mime-like grimace, turned to meet his glare.

Then the two figures floated toward each other like dissonant dancers.

"That your car?" Kelly demanded.

"No. I mean yes. Actually, it belonged to—"

"May I fucking inquire why it's rammed into my trailer?"

The woman slid down onto the sidewalk next to a heap of mildewed carpeting and then curled up on her side into a ball like a doodlebug.

"What kind of nut case? Look, I just got that trailer set up and was about to take my first shower, and. . . ."

Kelly dropped to the sidewalk beside her and swiped his eyes with gloved hands, as if trying to wipe away the vision of the wreck in front of him. When he looked up, the crumpled trailer was still there. The loopy dame was still there. And he felt as if he were back under the floodwaters, a primordial ooze against which it seemed pointless to fight. I'm going under, he admitted to himself.

Big sink hole ahead.

For five minutes they said nothing.

Early evening shadows thickened around the two figures facing each other on the sidewalk, a bird twittered in the weeping willow overhead, and the air grew close and humid as low clouds rolled in. Nothing and no one stirred on the ghost-town street, except for a cockroach scampering across the sidewalk, disappearing under the pile of foul carpeting.

"If one more thing goes wrong," the woman moaned, coming up for air, peering out of her trance through red-rimmed eyes. She jerked her head from the pavement with a decisive nod and sat up.

"You telling me, sister."

"I just reached back for one split second to steady the tombstone—"

"The *tombstone?*"

"—but it broke and now my mother is going to kill me."

"I waited three months to get this trailer from FEMA," Kelly said, peeling off his rubber gloves, finger by finger. "And another month to get the key. The government shitheads brought me three different trailers without keys, can you believe it? I just got this one connected, I'm gutting the house where my family lived for twenty-two years, and I'm about to settle into my cozy toaster oven, make myself a cup of goddamn joe and finally feel at home for the first moment since the storm, and along come you and your *tombstone*, and *splat*, back to square one." He slapped the gloves down on the sidewalk. "Goddamn."

"I work for FEMA so maybe I can—"

"Oh, ain't that cute." He jumped up, flailing his arms. "You work for FEMA. Do they pay you by the hour to go around knocking down the trailers soon as people get them set up? Wouldn't want the locals to get too comfy now, would we?"

A plaintive bird trilled above in the weeping willow.

"You look familiar." She knitted her brows, studying him hard.

"So do you." He squinted, trying to place the face of the woman who had just upended his life. "Don't sound like you from here."

"I went away for a long time." A bit of color seeped into her cheeks. "Where did you go to school?"

"Warren Easton." Of course, he knew she meant high school. This was the inevitable question that popped out when natives first met and tried to identify each other.

"Did you know Marky? He's about your age, maybe a few years older." She actually smiled. "Marky Naquin?"

"Know him? I dated his sister."

"Wait a minute, I *am* his sister."

"You Nicole Naquin?"

"I don't believe it," she squealed. "Are you . . . Kelly, Kelly Cannon?"

"Can't believe running into you like this."

"Don't forget," she said, "I'm the one who ran into you."

For the first time in five months, Kelly threw back his head and laughed.

During the next twenty minutes, it was 1975 and they were both teenagers again. There he was on the dance floor in his shiny wide-collared shirt cranking his elbows to Linda Rhonstad's "Heat Wave," Nicole with her hair poufed up into a perfumed nimbus, shaky as a newborn colt in strappy platform shoes. All of the old crushes, jokes, embarrassments, gossip, hopes, and dreams came hurling back to him from that lush, distant planet, along with Miss Violet, the eleventh-grade art teacher who had inspired him to paint. He could smell the crushed peanut shells on the floor of the beer dive in the Quarter where they hung on weekends, hear Bob Dylan wailing about being "Tangled Up in Blue," feel pert nipples under tight bras, see the waves of bright, acned faces filing up and down the pea-green staircases while bells shrilled mercilessly and something deep inside of him stretched its wings and soared for the first time.

How, in the meantime, had he managed to get so old?

God, it was Nicole after all, restored to her pubescent splendor, a fresh-faced girl crawling out of the shriveled cocoon of that ditzy old bitch who crashed into his trailer. Kelly had lost touch with crazy Marky and had last heard—was it twenty years ago?—that he needed to be hospitalized again. Marky, a savvy senior when Kelly was an impressionable sophomore, had been the first guy to bring him to the Quarter and turn him on to pot, Salvador Dalí, and art galleries. But when

Kelly brought up her brother, Nicole stared into the distance and then changed the subject.

"So," Nicole asked with a sigh, "what have you done for the past thirty years?"

With a sweeping gesture, Kelly pointed to the brick ranch house, its blown-out windows gaping like skull sockets. "A wife, two kids, a job, a life." He caught sight of the faux Doric pillars he had attached to the carport, a twentieth anniversary surprise for Lena, who bragged about being from an old plantation family. "Gone with the wind."

Nicole nodded. He saw that she understood exactly what he meant.

"What about you?"

"I worked as a secretary in New York, did the whole stupid glam scene at Studio 54, then ran off with a divorced Texan. Actually, he wasn't divorced when I met him." Nicole stared down at her cuticles. "That should have taught me what to expect. Now I'm the one who's divorced."

"Any kids?"

"His," Nicole murmured. "To them, I was Nicky the babysitter. Do you still paint?"

"Mostly on weekends. Funny, but accounting and cubism don't seem to mix. But I carry my sketchbook everywhere." Kelly was too embarrassed to admit that he hadn't finished a single painting during the past ten years.

"I was always in awe of your talent."

"Well, what Picasso needs now is a shower." Kelly stood up, flapping the armpits of his rank T-shirt. "Back to the No-Tell Motel."

"You can take a shower at my place if you give me a ride home. Just try to get a taxi these days. I'll have to call a tow truck in the morning. As it is, I was driving on the spare. Thank goodness I kept up with the car insurance."

"Deal. Where you live?"

"The Quarter."

"First time I ever went to the French Quarter to get clean."

Kelly finally managed to put Nicole's car in reverse, and after he backed out his own car, they pushed the Saturn into his driveway. He decided not to chance crawling into the wobbly trailer to get a change of clothes—the entire mess might topple over with him inside. Besides, he remembered, he still had that one canvas bag stuffed with clean clothes stashed in the trunk of his car. Wait, one last thing. He patted the pockets of his dusty cargo pants, looking for the house keys. Then he burst out laughing.

"What's so funny?" Nicole asked.

"Was just going to lock up the house," he said, cracking open the driver's door of his car. "Force of habit. But after twenty-two years of working my ass off, I don't have a damn thing left to steal."

# Two


GARY CHERRY TILTED THE SHOEBOX lid until the seeds rolled down into a corner. Like candle making, composting, and tie-dyeing, cleaning pot was one of the ancient hippie skills he maintained from mother ship San Francisco before it crashed decades ago into a high-tech desert of yuppie real estate and New Age puritanism. He had been a refugee in New Orleans ten years before he was turned into a refugee from New Orleans. Five days after the storm, he was hoisted into a helicopter from the rooftop of his flooded Bywater shotgun dressed only in a Speedo, clutching a glossy of himself and Mick Jagger with their arms around each other. But the hurricane wasn't the first disaster he had survived.

During the eighties in San Francisco, half of his friends had dropped dead with AIDS. Like his favorite heroine Blanche DuBois, after several long years of emptying bedpans for the sick, Gary arrived penniless in New Orleans one sweltering afternoon, frantic to wash away the rancid stink of death with booze, a whole Mississippi River of booze. Then a few years ago, when the alcohol itself started to taste like dying, he gave that up. But only because it got in the way of his high. Travel light, as he always told himself, and keep on trucking.

# Higher Ground

Only dead fish float with the current.

Nobody in their right mind was returning to live in New Orleans, which was why Gary was here, back from the dead and ready to party. Now he had the pot and pill trade sewn up among white folks in the French Quarter, and through his friend Sweet Pea, a.k.a Lionel Jackson, a.k.a. Miss Nida Mann, he was reaching out to black folks on North Rampart Street and in the Tremé.

"Mexican," he said, sticking out his bottom lip in disgust. "That's all we have coming through the pipeline these days. California sinsemilla too high-priced for this crowd." He scooped the fragrant green marijuana into a plastic baggie and placed it on the scale.

"Girl, why you messing with them seeds?" Sweet Pea adjusted a towering afro wig on his shaved bald head. "Raggedy-assed queens buy from you don't know the difference between salt and pepper." Sweet Pea was a cocky peanut of a man, and his gravely baritone could shoot into shrill falsetto in a heartbeat.

"To keep them coming back for more." Under a frayed Marilyn Monroe poster, Gary shook out his own curly mane, which he dyed with tea bags to cover the encroaching gray and washed in Tide to make it frizz. Although now paunchy and barrel-chested, he moved with the androgynous grace of the fawn he had been for most of his life. He was still everybody's sweet kid brother, the one who crashed the family car on the way home from a rock concert and was pulled from the wreck playing delirious air guitar. The tentative slightness of his presence had always allowed him to go anywhere, to slip unnoticed past doormen, ticket-takers, and border guards. Drawn to the spotlight, for almost twenty years he had drifted directly to the epicenter of every major scene: he was with Allen Ginsburg marching on the Pentagon, with the Rolling Stones at Altamont, with Iggy Pop at the Fillmore, and with

William Burroughs at the Bunker in New York. The sixties weren't over as long as Gary Cherry was alive. The chords may be distant, the needle skipping across a scratched LP, but he was still with the band.

Sweet Pea swung around from the mirror, fluffing the wig and sticking out his chest under a T-shirt that read "FEMA EVACUATION PLAN: Run like hell, mothafucker." Then he sashayed over to put on his rehearsal CD.

"Diana," Gary screamed, pumping his fists in the air. "Diana."

A blast of throbbing Motown shook the two-story slave quarter on Dauphine Street. On bare feet, Sweet Pea swirled along the tile floor, doing jerky kicks with his shaved, caramel-colored legs. Then clutching a carrot from the fridge as if it were a mike, he stretched his meaty lips around the lyrics like a mollusk:

> You took a mystery and made me want it
> You got a pedestal and put me on it
> You made me love you out of feeling nothing
> Something that you do . . .
> I'm in the middle of a chain reaction . . .

Gary sang chorus, waving his arms every time Sweet Pea batted his sultry lashes, looked him in the eyes, and mouthed "chain reaction." The doorbell buzzed, but Gary couldn't be bothered. Nothing interrupted Sweet Pea's act. Although he couldn't sing or dance or play an instrument or write, as anyone who ever stood under a spotlight in San Francisco or New York could tell you, Gary Cherry was the best audience in the world.

Sweet Pea's hands were slicing through the air as if parting endless beaded curtains, exploding all over the small room where cracked plaster walls exposed splotches of crumbling brick. At the insistent rapping on the windowpane, Gary leapt up, annoyed, to swing open the French doors that led to the courtyard. The powdery face of a gray-haired old lady peeked in, smelling of talcum and peppermint.

"Y'all having a party in here?" she asked, planting herself in the doorway.

"Say whaaaa?" screamed Gary.

Sweet Pea switched off the boom box and stood there, hands on hips.

"I said looks like y'all having a good old time," the old lady said.

"Hey, Miss Gertie," Gary said. It was Marky's mom, who four months ago had moved into one side of the shotgun double in front of his slave quarter, and her daughter into the other. Marky Naquin, his old boyfriend from the commune in San Francisco, was the first person he'd run into when he landed in the French Quarter. Gary knew that Miss Gertie wasn't there to bitch about the noise. After all, she and Nicole had found their reasonable rentals through Gary, and so they never complained about the all-night foot traffic and his midnight broadcasts of the Rolling Stones. "Guess what? Sweet Pea is rehearsing his number for the big Mardi Gras drag contest next month," he said with the moppet glee of little Mickey Rooney hawking Shirley Temple.

"I love shows," Gertie Naquin said, clapping her hands. "Did I ever tell y'all I used to sing songs on the radio my daddy wrote for commercials?" She then belted out a chorus. "At the beach, at the beach, down at Pontchartrain beach." Gary and Sweet Pea applauded.

"You and that weenie dog want to come in?" Sweet Pea asked. "Cause let me tell you, Miss Nida Mann just getting her batteries plugged in."

Gertie stepped in, followed by an ancient dachshund with a withered hind paw lifted off the ground by two rusty wheels fastened like a chariot to its haunches. Schnitzel creaked over to lick Sweet Pea's toes.

"How you feeling, Miss Gertie?" Gary asked.

"So so. The arthur-itis in my knees acting up."

"Let me see what I have." Gary went through a grocery sack of Ziploc baggies until he held up one to the light. "I can turn you on to half a Percodan."

"That what I had last time?"

"No, last time you had a whole OxyContin."

"That's when I couldn't get up out the damn bed." She held her belly when she laughed.

"This is the other half of the Percodan I turned you onto on Monday."

The old lady's palm shot out. "How much I owe you?"

"This isn't business, it's trade," Gary said.

"I got some red beans on the stove. With sausage. I'll bring it over soon as I see the show. By the way, I come over to ax you, you seen Nicole? She was supposed to be back from the cemetery three solid hours ago."

"She out on a booty call," Sweet Pea said, switching on the boom box. "I been teaching that girl a thing or two. Now y'all take a seat, cause Miss Nida Mann gonna show you something you ain't never seen before." He slapped the rump of his blue-jean hot pants, bumping his heart-shaped butt to the left and right.

Gary lit a joint, Miss Gertie popped her Percodan, and they positioned themselves on the paisley love seat like an old married couple.

Then Sweet Pea really cut loose.

> We talk about love, love, love
> We talk about looove . . .

# Higher Ground

Miss Gertie clapped her pudgy hands to the Motown thump, tapping her orthopedic oxfords as Sweet Pea vogued the length of the room, snapping his remarkably long fingers over his head.

The doorbell rang again, but Gary ignored it.

"Wait till y'all see this number with my new tits and the red feather cape," Sweet Pea said when the song was over. "Miss Nida Mann gonna turn that place out."

"One thing, sugar," Gertie said, "when you get to that part about the 'chain reaction,' you should flutter your hands down over your head, wiggling your fingers like. . . ."

"Molecules exploding?" Gary offered.

"Yeah." Gertie beamed. "Like all the molecules in the universe was exploding."

"Looks like I got me a choreographer. What about that part where I shake—"

An insistent rap rattled the windowpane.

The French doors swung open as Nicole stuck her head in, eyes wide and frantic.

"Momma," she said. "Thank God Almighty. When I got home, I let myself into your apartment, and you weren't there, and I thought what if she's out walking Schnitzel with all those bullets flying."

"What you talking about, honey?" Her mother stood up, yanking down the hem of her rayon housedress.

"Don't you know? Some people were just shot in front of our house. The cops are all over the place."

"Lord have mercy. And here I was, watching Sweet Pea's show."

Nicole looked around the room, sniffing. "What are you people having in here, a pot party?" She shot her mother an accusing glance. "Momma?"

Kelly's kinky auburn curls loomed over Nicole's drawn

face framed in the doorway. Schnitzel charged yapping to the door, chariot wheels squeaking behind.

"This is Kelly Cannon," Nicole said, standing to the side. "He and I dated in high school."

"Good evening." Kelly shot a gap-toothed grin around the room, tipping an imaginary hat over the grimy face mask still strapped to his forehead.

"Told you she out on a booty call." Sweet Pea yanked off his wig.

In a hospitable gesture, Gary extended the lit joint in his hand in the direction of the doorway. Nicole grimaced and shook her head, while Kelly reached past Nicole and sucked on the pot like a surfacing scuba diver gulping for air.

"Really needed that," Kelly said. "Y'all didn't hear the gun shots back here?"

"Who got killed?" Gary asked, eyes sweeping the room. The fuzz could be back here any minute.

Kelly opened his mouth and then glanced at Sweet Pea. "They say some young black dude. And an older white guy who just happened to be standing there. We drove up after it happened, and the bodies were already in the ambulances. Like gangbusters out there. I'll bet it was a drive-by."

"As if we don't have enough problems," Gertie said, sighing. "First the storm, then FEMA, and now crime is back. Come on, Schnitzel. Time to go beddy-bye."

Gary wondered if the murder victim could have been Latrome, the kid who called to say he was coming by for a quarter ounce at nine o'clock. The doorbell had rung twice while Sweet Pea was performing and could have been his client. Gary shook his frizzy head, kicked the scale under the loveseat, and grabbed Ziploc bags to store in the freezer.

"I'll be back in a few minutes with y'all's dinner," Gertie told Gary, hobbling toward the door. "I loved your little show," she said to Sweet Pea. "Now remember that part about the chain reaction. By the way, maybe you two big boys can help move our tombstone out of Nicole's car."

"Your *what?*" Gary asked, giggling. This old dame was a hoot.

"It's not safe outside the gate now," Nicole said. "Momma, we need to talk—"

"About what? What you gonna fuss at me about now?"

"It's not about—"

"Don't be such a stuffed shirt." Gertie turned her back on Nicole. "These are my friends," she said, squeezing Gary's and Sweet Pea's hands.

The doorbell buzzed, sending Gary into a panic. Finally, could that be Latrome, his nine o'clock, but with the fuzz still out front? Maybe they were already gone. He hated to lose the business. Gary touched the talk button of the intercom with his pinkie. "Who's there?" he chimed in a singsong.

"Sergeant Jurvis Brown," came the staticky reply, sounding as far away as ship-to-shore. "They been a coupla shootings out front your house, and a neighbor cross the street say one of the victims be hanging outside, like he waiting for someone in this building to come home. I rang the other two bells out front, but no answer. Need to ask you a few questions."

"Not right now, officer. I'm . . . taking a bubble bath." God, Gary thought, what a bummer. It must have been Latrome. "Who is it you think I might know?"

"Older male, Caucasian. Wait a sec, here the ID. Name of Marc. . . ." Static chewed up the last two words.

"Say what?" Gary shouted into the speaker.

"Name of Marc Rousell Naquin." The words rang clear as trumpet notes. "Know him?"

Gertie Naquin pivoted around to stare bug-eyed at her daughter, who turned to her high-school sweetheart, who caught Gary's eye, as if he alone could explain this ridiculous mix-up. In the kitchen, a faucet dripped, one, two, three drops plinking into a pan full of water. Through the opened French doors, banana tree leaves rustled in the breeze, scraping against the brick courtyard wall.

Next door a dog was barking at the empty sky.

Gary glanced around. The only person who looked unfazed was Sweet Pea, who didn't know any of his white druggy friends. Sweet Pea glanced at his watch, pursed his elastic lips, and then turned to the suddenly pallid faces in the room.

"Okay, any y'all wanna see me do 'Chain Reaction' again?" he asked, fluttering his fingertips through the air as if all the molecules in the universe were exploding.


WHO THE HELL WOULD SHOOT somebody like Marky Naquin, a diagnosed schizophrenic and street character beloved by every shopkeeper and dog-walker in the French Quarter? That was what Lieutenant Panarello wondered as he parked his unmarked car on Dauphine Street, near the corner of Tony's Superette.

Vinnie was a squat, olive-complexioned man with a beaked nose and jowly face that looked like it should have been beaming on the label of a marinara jar. Only now he wasn't smiling, and the scowl lines etched on his forehead showed that he hadn't for a long time. After all, he was a homicide detective currently under arrest for murder. As he scooted into a spot in front of the Little Debbie Snack truck, a girl with pierced eyebrows and a tousled green mane emerged from the corner grocery to stand staring at him with a menacing glare. The side of the truck read "Little Debbie Has a Snack for You." I bet she does, thought the cop, scratching his ass as he locked the car.

"Hey, I saw you on the news," the green-haired girl shouted, approaching Vinnie with a loaf of French bread under her arm.

Here goes, he thought. This girl looked like Little Debbie on the rag.

"You the same cop shot that poor deaf man in the Walmart parking lot after the storm," the girl snarled. "That's pretty low. Even for a cop."

"Look, lady, you don't know the facts." Vinnie's eyes crinkled, trying to draw a bead on this wacky dame.

"The TV said he was some guy trying to escape the flood with his cousin and worried about his dogs."

"Yeah, but the cousin had a gun—"

"That you assholes probably planted." The green-haired girl raised the loaf of French bread over her head.

"Are you threatening an officer?"

"Yeah, with a soggy baguette." The girl burst out laughing, wagging the bent end of the loaf toward the policeman. Then she scurried around the corner.

After Vinnie's grand-jury indictment last week, the District Attorney had reduced the murder charge to negligent homicide since the shooting happened while the cop was on duty. The lieutenant shook his balding head whenever he considered the charge, punctuating his disbelief with a hiccup of a laugh. Under any other circumstances, he would have been assigned to desk duty until the case came to trial. But after the storm, the city needed every cop still walking on two legs.

Right after the drive-by shooting last night, he was assigned to the Naquin-Batiste case and now was on his way to speak with Naquin's mother, who apparently lived in the house facing the sidewalk where the crime took place. He had met Marky several times before the storm, at a poetry reading joint he used to frequent during an off-duty murder investigation. He could remember the hand-rolled cigarettes, the long, greasy ponytail, how Marky rocked back and forth at the podium to the rhythm of his words, and the rousing cheers he received when he had finished reading one of his outrageous poems. The guy was out there—no doubt about it—a collector of stray dogs and people who rented a bathless room over a dry cleaner's. When he was off his meds, he could be spotted holding midnight conversations with the Joan of Arc statue at the French Market. In French, no less. A long time ago he had been committed to St. Vincent DePaul's, the Uptown loony bin, but his chart indicated that he'd been released after he wound up running the kitchen and starting a literary magazine among the patients. The shrinks were coming to him with their own problems, and the staff threw him a going-away party the day they signed him out.

Obviously, Naquin had been in the wrong place at the wrong time. Walking the streets was dangerous now in New Orleans. That was why the cops hid inside their cars. Whole flooded neighborhoods had been taken over by feral kids holed up in abandoned houses, dealing crack and shooting each other. Vinnie suspected that Marky had no relation at all to Latrome Batiste, the high-school student also shot. Marky was probably hanging on the stoop, waiting for his mother, when Latrome happened by. Maybe they exchanged a few words under the street lamp, maybe one of them asked the other for a cigarette. No drugs were found on either corpse, and nobody saw the drive-by car that did the shooting.

Latrome lived with his mother and two brothers just six blocks away in the Tremé, and this morning Mrs. Batiste had told Vinnie that her son went to St. Augustine, the Catholic prep school, and spent his free time practicing the clarinet with the marching band for Carnival parades. He was a purple-and-gold Creole kid, not a lowlife gangsta. Although these days all the black kids wore those white T-shirts down to their knees, and from a distance you couldn't tell which was which until you talked with them. For some the baggy tunic was a cool MTV fashion statement, but others wore it so that the pistols stuck in their waistbands didn't show.

Vinnie dodged the reeking refrigerator wrapped with duct tape that was parked on the cracked banquette in front of the shotgun double on Dauphine Street where Naquin's mother lived. Somebody had scrawled graffiti on the refrigerator door: As Above So Below. This was a pro-forma, day after visit to the family, and Vinnie wasn't expecting to gather much information. The mama probably wouldn't know what happened to her son.

Marky had lived in another world, one in which the street voodoo eventually would get you.

When the lieutenant rang the doorbell, a rail-thin dame with crepe-paper skin and long yellowed teeth swung open the peeling green shutters. She was dolled up in a tailored hounds' tooth tweed suit with a red Hermès scarf tied around her withered neck and splayed open across one shoulder. She looked like one of those salesladies at the Godchaux's perfume counter.

"You Gertrude Naquin?" Vinnie asked.

"Naw, I'm Dixie, her big sister. Dixie Rosenblum," the old lady croaked in a raspy baritone. "You the cop called and said he coming over?"

"Detective Vincent Panarello, Eighth District Homicide."

"Come on in. Gertie's laying down with a washrag on her forehead. Let me tell you, she taking Mawky's death hawd, hawd, hawd."

Vinnie stepped into a high-ceilinged Victorian parlor

furnished with aluminum patio furniture. Cardboard boxes were stacked in one corner and suitcases in another.

"That stuff is what's left out of Gertie's house in Lakeview. I told her, girl, you in this for the long haul, better go by Hurwitz-Mintz and get yourself a new living room set. Somewhere decent to put your behind. But she got her a hawd head, that sister of mine. What can I get you to drink?"

Vinnie pointed to the glass of water in Dixie's hand.

"This is Gordon's. We got that and water. That's what I live on, gin, tap water, and Kents."

"Water will be fine. Listen, I can come back later if Mrs. Naquin not feeling up to it."

"I'll go get her." Dixie pointed to the aluminum chaise. "Take a load off."

Vinne closed his eyes, rubbing the bridge of his nose, hoping that this family wouldn't bring up the Walmart parking-lot shooting like the Batistes did this morning. The story had made the Channel 4 news two days in a row this week. If people could only understand what the cops had gone through after the storm. He wasn't a murderer.

"She'll be up in a minute," Dixie said, thrusting a glass that smelled like gin into Vinnie's hands.

She lit a Kent. "Me, I could never live like this. My home on State Street stayed dry, and all I lost were a few shingles. How'd you do?"

"We live in Terrytown and had a few feet of water. But they let the West Bank people come home early, so we mucked it out and saved the house. Although it's not what it used to be. Of course, the whole city isn't."

"Tell me about it," Dixie said. "I'm eighty-one years young, and this the worst I ever remember it. Although I had a hawd time growing up."

"We all did. Where I seen you before?" She looked like one

of those socialites who came to fox trot with the commissioners at the policemen's ball.

"I seen your face before, too. Think it was on TV, something about Walmart. Maybe you know me from Harvest House. That's the home for unwed mothers over by Rampart Street. I'm president of the board, and go to all the fundraisers."

"You run Harvest House?"

"I don't actually run it, but I twist the arms of rich people Uptown to support it. See, officer, I got knocked up at sixteen, and I'm not ashamed to say it. By somebody I met at a Momus parade. He kept catching glass beads for me, and boy, did I catch something later from that mister. The next thing I knew, my stomach swole up and my daddy was yelling at me. So they put me in the Home for Wayward Girls. Remember that?"

"Sure," Vinnie said with a slow smile. He was used to it: people in this town would spill their life stories to you in the supermarket check-out line.

"That place sure turned my giddy little head around. I put the kid up for adoption, then went to Soulé Business College and became a secretary. Then married my boss, a fine man name of Abe Rosenblum. And now that I'm a respectable old widow," she said, draining her tumbler of gin, "I wanted to do something to help girls starting out life on the wrong foot, like I did."

"So why isn't your sister staying with you?"

"Lord, don't get me started. She got some notion in her noggin she wanted to live next to her daughter Nicole who just moved here from Texas. And Nicole decided to live near her brother in the French Quarter, where she used to rat the streets while she was in high school. But I told my sister, 'Gertie, why you want to live down there?'" Dixie cupped a hand over her mouth and whispered. "'It's nothing but queers and niggers.' But after this awful thing with Mawky, I'm putting my foot down. She's coming to live with me."

"Oh, no, I'm not." Gertie Naquin stood leaning against the partially closed pocket doors to the parlor, a washrag in her hand. Schnitzel creaked in behind her, then rolled on chariot wheels toward Vinnie, yapping.

"Shut up, Schnitzel. Honey, this is Officer—"

"I heard what you said, Miss Mouth. And I'm not." Gertie threw the damp rag, and it landed in her sister's hounds' tooth lap. "She was all the time trying to boss me," she told the policeman, "even when we was little."

Vinnie jumped up, moving away from the lunging dachshund. "Maybe this isn't the best time—"

"Can I put a head on your drink, officer?" Dixie swooped up the cop's untouched glass and trotted past the pocket doors into the kitchen, giving the lame dog a surreptitious kick on the way out. "Like I say, all we got is gin and tap water."

Gertie collapsed into an aluminum armchair. "I wish she'd go home."

Vinnie sat back down and scrawled "neurotic family" in his notebook. The old lady reminded him of his own mother. He could smell the onions and garlic under her fingernails, and admired how, buried in grief, she managed to put on a good face for company.

"How often did you see your son?"

Gertie sniffled and yanked a lace handkerchief out of her sleeve. "I lost my house after the storm, and since I been living down here in the Quarter, he come by all the time. Never called, just rapped on the shutters screaming, 'Hey, little mama, what you got cooking?'" Gertie giggled, and then started to sob. "I had some red beans simmering on the stove for him last night. . . ."

"I know this is hard." Vinnie wished he could just hug her and skip the questions. "Did you know any of his friends."

"Just that precious boy Gary Cherry in the back slave

quarter. That's how my daughter and me got these apartments for cheap, through Gary."

Must be the clown that Sergeant Brown told him was taking a bubble bath last night. Vinnie wrote "Gary Cherry— bubble bath—drugs?" in his notebook.

"Was Marky involved in drugs?" he asked.

Gertie shot the cop a suspicious look. "Oh, officer," she said, swatting a hand in front of her face, "you know how these young people are. He was a good boy, but had mental . . . problems."

"I'm aware of that."

"I always said he had too much imagination."

"Imagination!" said Dixie, sweeping into the room with a tumbler of gin in one claw and a cigarette in the other. "I'll tell you about that imagination of his. Last time he dropped by to see me, I was entertaining Bitsie Landry, you know, the senator's mother. And I was serving coffee in these adorable little Art Nouveau seashell cups. And he said, 'Auntie Dixie, these cups look like they were blown out of the ass of Marcel Proust.' He said that right in front of Bitsie. I don't know where that boy got his ideas."

"He told me he was a surrealist," Gertie said, glaring at her sister. "How did he ever pick up that kind of stuff in New Orleans?"

"Momma." Nicole appeared pale and red-eyed between the pocket doors. Must be the daughter, Vinnie thought. Looked like an anorexic or a junkie. "Excuse me, I didn't know you had company. Look, Kelly and I just brought the tombstone back in his car. Where do you want to put it? It weighs a ton."

"Officer, would you mind helping my daughter's friend Kelly bring our tombstone from out his car. The tablet got blown off our crypt during the storm."

"Why, no, I'd be. . . ." Vinnie jumped to his feet, delighted with any excuse to get out of this room.

"Oh, Momma," Nicole said, rushing with heaving sobs to embrace her mother.

"Now don't get me started again. Your brother—"

"It's not Marky," Nicole said, breaking away from her mother. "It's me. I'm in love."

"I just got me a swell idea," Dixie said, tugging Lieutenant Panarello's sleeve toward the door with an exaggerated wink. "You boys bring that tombstone up through the alley and around to the back door. We can lay it on top of that utility cart in the kitchen and use it for a bar."

# Three

NICOLE HADN'T MEANT FOR ANY of this to happen. Her brother was dead, she was living in New Orleans again, next door to her mother, and the first guy she had ever slept with in her whole life was now lying pink and naked beside her on the Beautyrest mattress, snoring like a leaf blower. She stared at the elaborate plaster medallion over the bed, watching early morning sunlight play along the ribs of the white Japanese lantern that dangled from the light socket. Okay, what if she had married Kelly Cannon when she was sixteen, she wondered, as she was supposed to do with the man who took her virginity? What if they had moved into a bungalow around the corner from her parents' house, as young couples were expected to do in those days, raised two or three children, and had been lying side by side like this for the past thirty years? What if she'd never taken LSD or run away to the Lower East Side or mooned around the dressing room doors of rock stars after concerts? What if everything that happened to her between high school and now had been a bizarre dream, and she were just waking up?

She fished around on the nightstand for her pill bottle and water glass and popped a Zoloft. Then she buried her face in the curly auburn down on Kelly's back, taking in the musky smell barely disguised by Lifebuoy. After the shooting on Saturday night, he had spent an hour in the shower while she lay curled up in a ball on the bed. Gary Cherry had been antsy to get out of the house to avoid the cops and insisted on driving her mother to identify the body at the morgue in St. Gabriel, the only one open after the storm. And there, among the drowned still waiting to be claimed by the displaced, her brother had spent his last night in New Orleans. Nicole was used to getting tipsy phone calls from friends passing through town, announcing *it's my last night in New Orleans* and dying to make plans with her.

"It's always *somebody's* last night in New Orleans," she would tell them. "Hope it's not mine."

The night before last had been her brother's. She wondered if Marky had finally been happy when he died, or if not happy, at least stoned or drunk. With her mother-hen social worker instincts, on every visit home she had tried to help him, to sign him up for mental health outpatient services at Charity or locate a support group for those living on antipsychotic meds or at least make sure he had clean clothes and something to eat. But after the storm she'd given up. There were no more social services, and besides, he had never wanted her help. What he wanted was for her to listen while he explained his complicated visions. What he craved was to be understood.

Nicole had only been to his room once, the airless box he rented with his S.S.I. check, and had to leave almost immediately. The smoke-smudged walls were covered with a mosaic of broken mirrors, surrounded by columns of spidery handwriting and the Egyptian hieroglyphs he'd been studying. Every few minutes he would jump up, as if he just remembered something of enormous importance, and turning his back to her, would scribble with intense focus on the crumbling plaster.

"I'm almost finished," he'd told her. "It's a record of my journey through the underworld." Then he would sit back down and cuddle Anubis, a scrawny stray dog he picked up at the French Market. Even then, with those dimples and twinkling hazel eyes, he was still so handsome, in spite of the greasy ponytail.

"What's wrong with this world?" Nicole asked him. "The one above ground."

"As above, so below. And this," he said, gesturing to the walls, "is a map to the secret correspondences between the two lines. Change at Jamaica." Then he chortled like the mechanical clown that had ushered them as children into the amusement-park ride at Pontchartrain Beach, the one called Laugh in the Dark. Marky was always laughing at his own esoteric jokes that nobody else ever got.

Nicole wondered how her mother was getting along on the other side of the bedroom wall, the one Gertie pounded with a fist whenever she wanted her daughter to come over to her side of the house. Her Auntie Dixie had insisted on coming over Saturday night right after the shooting, and Nicole feared that the unsettling quiet was because the two bickering sisters had finally killed each other.

A lizard scampered across the window screen and peeked in. Pulling the sheet up around herself, she searched in vain for the familiar feel of a Monday morning, but it felt as if the world had come to a screeching halt.

Kelly rolled over and flung his meaty, freckled arm around Nicole's hips. His eyes creased and then opened, staring directly into hers.

"Hi," he said.

"Hey."

"What time is it?"

"Later than you think."

# James Nolan

The sheet was tenting between his legs with an exclamation point. He reached over to kiss her full on the mouth with stale morning lips and then licked around her nipples and down to her navel to finally dive between her legs. She tensed with an automatic *oh no you don't, Buster,* but her lower body finally got the message from her brain that it wasn't her ex-husband, it was a warm and funny Kelly tongue that belonged to her teenage heartthrob, Marky's friend from down the block, the redhead who did wheelies on his bike in front of her house. She relaxed into the slurping and moaning, picturing a thirsty Schnitzel lapping from his pink plastic water bowl and then did some groaning of her own.

God it had been so long since anything felt that good.

Yet this wasn't supposed to be happening. Following the shooting, Kelly had refused to leave, or she insisted he stay—Nicole couldn't remember which—but after they held each other in a chaste embrace on the patio, he made up the sofa bed in the front room while she collapsed in her bedroom. Later that evening, shivering and weeping, she crept in to perch on the sofa bed, then curled up quietly beside him, needing to be close to anything alive and breathing.

When he rolled over it started—she hadn't meant it to—was shocked really, and resisted. Her brother was lying in the St. Gabriel morgue, for God's sake. But she wasn't used to being touched, not like that, not down there, and this led to something else. Nothing was being demanded of her, not like with Buster, who she often accused of just jumping on top to jerk off inside her. She wanted to give Kelly something, and so what did Sweet Pea call it—a hum job? Sweet Pea claimed to be an expert on how to get and keep a man and had coached her in the courtyard laundry room while her clothes were going through the spin cycle that nothing will keep a man coming back for more like a hum job. So while her mouth vibrated with a Strauss waltz, she sucked Kelly to satisfaction. Then they both cried some more, and she led him to her bed by one finger.

This morning Kelly was returning the favor. What were those lips plastered to her under the sheets humming? Was it "Do You Know What It Means to Miss New Orleans?" Don't stop now, she prayed, not yet. And he didn't, and what happened next brought her back twenty-five years to the hotel room of Mick Ronson, David Bowie's lead guitarist, time itself exploding in ripples of black satin sheets and a shower of silver glitter. It was like kicking off leaden diver's boots that had weighed her down forever. As she lay there panting, Kelly bobbed up for air with a devilish gleam in his viridian eyes, then climbed into the saddle and slipped it in so smoothly she thought it had always been there.

At that moment, Gary Cherry was rubbing his eyes, cracking open the green shutters of the slave quarter, and cranking up his stereo as "Wild Horses" filled the courtyard:

> Wild horses, couldn't drag me away,
> I say wild, wild horses,
> We'll find them someday.

Nicole's and Kelly's horses reached the fence together, and airborne in a flurry of whipped manes and flying hooves, leapt over it at the same instant, to land spent in a tangle of sheets on the Beautyrest mattress. Nicole's tears turned to giggles as Kelly shot up, following his bobbing red knob toward the bathroom.

"Gotta take a leak."

"Take one for me, too," she said, not wanting to move a muscle for the next two weeks.

Yesterday afternoon, bleary-eyed and dazed, she and

Kelly had moved the tombstone to her mother's kitchen and then stepped around each other for the rest of the day, finally falling asleep on opposite sides of the bed. Embarrassed, Nicole dismissed what happened between them as something friends in New York called "terror fucking" after 9/11, when complete strangers, numbed by the attack, grabbed each other in delis and elevators, only to screw their way back to normal, using sex as a defibrillator for hearts frozen in panic. Five minutes later, blinking away tears, Nicole decided no, she wasn't just numb or needy or out of control. She was in love. Had always been in love with Kelly Cannon. He seemed in no hurry to leave, and his moony gaze followed her everywhere. What in the world were they doing?

A cell phone bleated on the nightstand and Nicole groaned, leaning over languorously to pick it up, not sure if it were his or hers.

"Heelloooo," she purred, like someone who had been doing exactly what she'd been doing. "Yes, ma'am, he is," she said, suddenly the secretary. "He'll be with you shortly."

The toilet flushed, and then Kelly let loose a loud chorus of "Wild Horses."

"Shush," Nicole whispered, crooking her finger to beckon him to the cell in her outstretched palm. "A woman," she mouthed.

"Lena!" Kelly said, sinking down to sit on a corner of the bed, back to Nicole. "Where the hell do you think I am? I'm at our house, working my butt off. . . . That lady? Just someone from FEMA here to do an appraisal. . . . Oh, I see. You're at the house. Look, there was an accident this weekend I didn't want to tell you about. Some dizzy dame rammed. . . . Okay, so you see the trailer. . . . No, the car in the driveway belongs to the woman who ran into it. . . . I'm still sleeping at the Star Lite Motel. . . . Yeah, you right. I did check out on Saturday morning."

Kelly cradled the phone between head and shoulder, punching at the air in front of him. "When did you blow into town? . . . In the French Quarter, if you want to know the truth. . . . With an old friend, Marky Naquin. . . . Oh, you've seen the news. . . . Yeah, he was murdered night before last. . . . No, I'm not mixed up in any monkey business in the Quarter. . . . Actually, I'm staying with his sister. Did I ever tell you about Nicole Naquin from high school?"

"Son of a bitch." Kelly threw the cell down on the bed. "Called me a goddamn liar and hung up."

"But I am a lady from FEMA." Nicole lunged toward Kelly's chest. "And before I leave for work, I'm going to give you a big wet grant."

"Babe," Kelly said, holding her bony shoulders at arms' length between two huge paws, "this has been the best thing to happen to me since the storm, since way before the storm. But my wife is madder than a wet hornet, so I better hightail it over to the house to sort his out. The gas station must be open this morning, so I'll ask Hewitt to tow your car."

"Don't go."

"I have to—"

"Don't."

Nicole threw herself onto the bed and then scrunched up under the sheets, back to feeling like Miss Glad Bag. After Kelly left, she lay there scanning the empty room, wondering what sort of phantasmagorical incubus had taken the form of her high-school sweetheart to visit her on the night her brother died. It seemed as otherworldly as one of Marky's visions, until she spied the canvas bag packed with Kelly's clothes, perched like a love note in a pool of sunlight on the damask chair.

# James Nolan

IT HAD STARTED OUT INNOCENTLY enough, as far as Gary Cherry could remember. He didn't want his house to get too hot, for the neighbors to notice druggy people coming and going day and night through the front gate. That always drew the pigs like roaches. So he'd talked Miss Gertie into diverting some of the traffic—not the pot but the script stuff like Valium, Vicodin, and Xanax—and eventually wound up giving her 30 percent off the top.

That was how, finished with housework forever, Gertie Naquin had started dealing dope.

But Gary certainly didn't plan to bother her today, only four days after her son was murdered. She was probably still crying her heart out. So as thick raindrops pelted the French-door panes, he sat huddled in a blanket, filling slim envelopes with Valiums and Vicodins to bring to a few steady customers. The church-offering envelopes made him smile. They had been Miss Gertie's innovation. She'd complained that the Ziploc sandwich bags "showed everybody your business," so she sorted the pills for her own clients into the collection envelopes she found inside pew racks at Mass. Soon Gary was buying them in bulk at a religious wholesaler's on Camp Street.

At first, Miss Gertie claimed she was just doing Gary a favor, meeting with his friends at her booth at the Laughing Buddha and slipping them a church-offering envelope marked with their names, then sticking the cash into a zippered pouch in her square vinyl pocketbook. She always ate a late lunch at that Chinese joint in front of the gay bar recently rechris-tened the Aftermath Lounge. The Kitchen Goddess Special was what she would order—sweet and sour soup, an egg roll, and shrimp lo mein—for $5.99, and then she'd linger in a back booth sipping a beer while she read *The Times-Picayune*.

Miss Gertie told Gary that after her house flooded, she

surely wasn't going to spend all day dusting aluminum patio furniture. "When I think of those years I wasted waxing hardwood floors and antiques until they shone, taking down winter curtains and putting up summer ones, polishing silver, soaking lace tablecloths in Woolite, just for it to wind up a heap of stinking trash piled in the street, I could croak."

This arrangement wasn't putting Miss Gertie in any real danger. Gary made sure of that. He wouldn't touch the heavy stuff like smack and blow, no matter how much money he could pull in selling them. Years ago, he had watched too many friends OD on these drugs and knew they carried bad karma, involving bloody cartels, wars, and dictators. He didn't discuss this sinister side of the drug trade with Gertie, introducing her to the cold cuts, not the abattoir. She made her rent money, and then some. And all she had to do was sit there, sip her brew, and read the paper.

"I came up during the Depression," she'd explained to Gary one evening while counting out his cut of the money. "Dixie and me used to collect newspapers in our little red wagon to sell to the junk man and return soft drink bottles to the corner store for the two-cent deposit. What they call that now, recycling? I always worked, me. I don't know what else to do with myself."

Gertie seemed delighted with her new sideline, almost as if she'd become an Avon lady peddling beauty products at card parties. Sometimes Gary gave her pills for her arthritis aches in exchange for feeding him. This was what she called "trade," and the sales at the Chinese joint she referred to as "business." She was meticulous about not getting trade mixed up with business and kept detailed accounts in a flowered memo book with a gold clip-on pen.

Gary's friends kidded him about using an old grandma as a drug runner, but she obviously grew on them. And although she sometimes complained that most of the scraggly lot needed a bath, a new dye job, or a teeth cleaning, she called them "my boys." Sometimes they would invite her across the street to the Aftermath for a beer or two. Often the only woman of any age in there with the hunky happy-hour crowd, she was the belle of the ball and started wearing makeup—too much, in Gary's opinion—and what she called her "sporting" jewelry. Eventually she started doing her "business" with the customers right there in the bar, and that got her in trouble. So Gary had been called in to straighten things out, and "business" was again confined to her booth in the restaurant across the street, where Gary could see that the owner loved her.

"Miss Gertie, what your secret?" Mr. Wong always said. "You draw customers like lucky charm. Wonton soup on the house."

Gary stood up, stuffing a handful of filled offering envelopes into the elastic of his sock. He hadn't left the apartment since the shooting and didn't feel like doing business at the Chinese joint today. But the problem with this job was you could never take a day off.

Hustle, hustle, always a hustle.

He stuck his head out of the French doors, inhaling the damp brick smell of the winter courtyard. The rain had slackened to a drizzle under a leaden February sky. Next to a blooming camellia bush, Miss Gertie was standing with folded arms under the balcony overhang, staring down mournfully at the weeds sprouting between wet bricks. He hadn't heard from her since her daffy sister Dixie showed up on Saturday night. When he and the old lady got home from the morgue in St. Gabriel, Dixie was already there, mixing a drink in the kitchen.

"Miss Gertie, how you feeling today?" he whispered.

Wrapped in a baggy cardigan sweater, the old lady was

wearing fluffy pink house slippers. Gary couldn't believe how shriveled up she looked, her radiant smile reduced to a wan pucker.

"I gotta get out that house," she shouted, rushing past Gary and into his apartment. "Dixie driving me bananas."

"I was just on my way to the Laughing Buddha. Business."

"Can I come with you? I'm starving. Haven't cooked anything in four days. Alcoholics like my sister don't eat, you know."

"Is she staying long?"

"Not if I can help it. Who does that woman think she is, Uptown royalty? Like Miss Priss can just sweep in to take over my life. First she makes our broken family tombstone into a bar in the kitchen to hold her gin bottles, and now she's trying to get me out of what she calls 'this hole' to move in with her on State Street. I don't want to go back to polishing furniture—especially her matchy-matchy store-bought stuff—and sit around having coffee with Bitsie Landry all day. I like it beaucoup right here."

"So stay."

"By the way," Gertie said, "a detective name of Panarello came to talk with me on Sunday. Nice man. Says he knew Marky from the poetry readings, and he's real sorry."

"So what's he going to do?"

"He don't have a clue. Says that colored boy who got killed was from a good family in the Tremé and went to St. Aug. Now who would do a thing like that? All these people being killed are somebody's children."

Gertie plunked down on the love seat, right in front of the impromptu altar Gary had set up on the coffee table, where photos of Marky were balanced between lit candles and vases of red camellias. At the center lay a book by Aleister Crowley and a Tarot deck.

"My little boy," she moaned, reaching over to bring one of the snapshots to her lips. Then she just sat there, staring into space.

Gary didn't think this was the best time to mention that Latrome had been one of his pot clients, or that Latrome's Uncle Oscar, a church choir director, had been Sweet Pea's first husband. Sweet Pea said that the whole family was just beside themselves.

"My son have any enemies?" Gertie leaned forward, as if ready for the truth.

"Well," said Gary thoughtfully, "some people thought Marky was a magician."

"Like with rabbits and top hats?"

"One who could put spells on people."

"Marky?" Gertie shook her head. "Oh, come on."

"Marky was known to dabble in the magical arts. An occult bookstore on Rampart Street called Minerva's Owl is run by an old organization called the Mani, and before the storm he used to go to meetings there, sometimes with a character named Bob White. Marky was always ranting about how the Mani was practicing black magic and getting people to do destructive things. The owner might have a word or two to say on the subject. Maybe we should go talk to him."

"If anybody's going to solve this murder, it won't be the cops." Gertie pounded the arm of the settee.

"Don't worry. You and me and Sweet Pea will catch them. I'll put the word out on the street. That's how this town works. Marky was a Quarter character, and everybody loved him." Gary plucked a camellia out of its vase on the altar and handed it to the bereft old lady. "We'll find the killer."

# Four

As Gary bounced down rain-slickened Dauphine Street, Miss Gertie hobbling a few steps behind him under her red umbrella, he wondered how he could possibly explain to her Marky's involvement in magic. Say something that would make any sense to her. Gary's friends in San Francisco thought that New Orleans was a real low-chakra place, about nothing but eating, drinking, and screwing. But those airy-fairy people were Gemini-city potheads, their mercurial minds permanently fogged-in while their feet never touched ground. Like Tangiers and Amsterdam, New Orleans was ruled by Scorpio, a sign of dark, stagnant water. After the storm, when the city was 80 percent flooded by a toxic gumbo from the lake, Gary finally understood what the place really was. As he was being hoisted up half-naked from his roof into the Coast Guard helicopter, he peered down at the miles and miles of swamped houses and saw the city as if for the first time, a fleeting mirage shimmering over the surface of the coffee-brown water. People here had it backwards: water was the reality, dry streets the illusion.

Sure, New Orleans was about sex and death, just like other Scorpio cities. Open the newspapers here or walk down any street, and you'd get your fill. The city's first cemetery was three blocks from the steamy back room at the Aftermath. But that Scorpionic serpent twisted up the spine from the ass to the scalp like the yogic kundalini, transforming the baser energy from below into higher spiritual purpose. "As above, so below," as Marky always said. That was why New Orleans was home to the snaky loas of voodoo, to fortune-tellers and Tarot readers, mediums, and hauntings. Gary could feel himself undergoing a regeneration beside the dark waters, from the bottom-feeding scorpion of a drug dealer into a soaring white dove that communed with the saints. Marky had taught him that.

"Watch out, boy." Gertie caught up just in time to push Gary out of the way of a noxious plop that hit the pavement next to his shoe. "That pigeon almost pooped on you."

He glanced up. An iridescent gray pigeon perched on a balcony railing overhead took off in a muffled flutter of wings.

"You gotta watch where you going in this town," Miss Gertie said, shaking out her umbrella, "if you don't want to get all dirty."

"Oh, no," Gary said, "here he comes."

Limping across the street toward them was a chocolate-colored lizard of a man, a single crutch tucked under one shoulder, dragging a dead foot behind him. One hand waved a greeting while the other hung palsied at his side. He planted himself on the curb in front of Gary and Gertie, eyes darting back and forth between them.

"Want to hear a poem?" he asked.

"Not now, J.J.," Gary said. "Catch you later."

"Who's the lady?" J.J. asked.

Gary rolled his eyes and grabbed Miss Gertie's elbow, steering her toward the corner.

# Higher Ground

In every sleazy port city Gary had ever visited in Latin America—Veracruz, Barranquilla, Guayaquil—he had always spotted a crippled man who limped between the café tables selling cheap watches, a withered reptile with milky eyes who said he could get you anything you wanted: coke, sex, emeralds, or stolen native artifacts. Gary learned too late that those snitches, like J.J., were how the police controlled the street.

"I think J.J. was the guy who set me up for that pot bust a few years back," Gary said, once out of earshot. "He insinuates himself into your life with his street poems, but he's really an informant for the pigs at the Eighth District. But he works both sides, and sometimes fences hot goods, or is a watchdog for crack dealers, or pimps black drag queens. He's just another one of the fly-by-night con men drawn to this place. Everybody thinks he's someone else."

"I didn't want to hear his poem," Gertie said, closing her umbrella. "Probably would have been dirty."


THEY HAD NO SOONER OPENED THE menus in Miss Gertie's back booth at the Laughing Buddha when Gary looked up into the hairy nostrils of a huge beaked nose hovering over their table. The sweaty guy smelled like the fuzz.

"Mrs. Naquin?" the man said.

"Oh, Lieutenant Panarello," Gertie blurted out, looking up, "what a surprise."

"I was just having some chow mein over by the other booth."

"Lieutenant, this is Gary Cherry, my neighbor in the back slave quarter. He was a good friend of Marky's."

"Oh, so you was the one Sergeant Brown said was taking a bubble bath on Saturday night when Naquin got shot?" the cop said. "You kinda hard to get a hold of."

Gary hadn't answered either the phone or his doorbell since the murder. He didn't want to talk to the cops, especially now, while he was carrying.

"I was back there, too," Gertie chimed in, "when it happened."

"I get it. You two was taking a bubble bath together," the lieutenant said, studying Gertie's face with a scowl. "Ain't that cute."

"Of course not." Looking flustered, Gertie stared down at her menu.

"Need to ask you a few questions, Mr. Cherry, soon as I finish my chow mein."

"I don't feel like answering any of your dumb-ass questions, so take your time with lunch. *Bon appétit.*" Gary rose halfway inside the booth, jar jutting out. The cherubic smile gave way to the fierce mug of the street-fighting man he'd become while dealing to hookers and hustlers in San Francisco's Tenderloin. He wondered what would happen if he sprinted to the door. Would the pig shoot him?

"In that case, I'll have to take you for a little ride until you change your mind."

"Where to?"

"Tulane and Broad."

"You mean Parish Prison?" Gertie gasped. "Look, officer, Gary is my good friend. He hasn't done anything wrong. What's the charge?"

"Public drunkenness."

Gary burst out laughing. "Everybody can tell you I haven't had a drink in five years." He was calculating the distance between the booth and the door, but the cop blocked his path.

"If you want to arrest someone for public drunkenness,

go get my sister," Gertie screamed. "You saw the way she carried on. She's the lush, not Gary. Book Dixie Rosenblum for disturbing the peace."

"Come on," the lieutenant said, grabbing Gary by the arm. "Let's go. This will teach you to play games with the law."

Think fast, Gary told himself. You're one hair short of a drug bust. "Can I go to the bathroom first? I'm about to pee myself."

Gertie locked eyes with the cop. Her look said *don't you dare.*

Vinnie backed down from her stare. "Should have my head examined, but okay, make it snappy."

When Gary returned to the booth, the lieutenant was explaining to a seething Gertie that this was the only way he could deal with an uncooperative witness who he suspected was withholding information.

"But he wasn't a witness," Gertie shot back. "He was with me."

"Yeah, I know. Taking a bubble bath. Come on, let's go."

Gary swung around to wrap Gertie in a bear hug. "Go get the envelopes at the bottom of the trash bin in the men's room," he whispered through clenched teeth into her plastic pearl earring. "Empty my freezer and stash it at your house."

Then he backed away from the embrace. "Tell Nicole to come pick me up in two hours at Parish Prison," he boomed, "Will we be finished by then, officer?"

"If you cooperate. Or else we book you till your jaw thaws out."

"Lieutenant," Gertie said, rising, "I'm a seventy-six-year-old widow who just lost her son to a drive-by shooting and her home to a hurricane. I can't take any more of this rough stuff. I'm going to call my congressman right now if you take that boy off."

"You do that," the cop said, slipping handcuffs around Gary's wrists behind his back. "Feds just caught your congressman with $90,000 in bills marked by the FBI hidden in his freezer." He steered Gary toward the door. "Maybe him and this joker can be roomies at Parish Prison. Y'all could take bubble baths together."

Gary jerked his head back to shoot Gertie a snaggle-toothed smile, pointing with his chin toward the men's room door.

Gary slumped in the back seat of the squad car for five minutes while Lieutenant Panarello ran his ID through the radio and filled out a report. This wouldn't be Gary's first trip to Tulane and Broad, and he doubted it would be his last. When the cops in this town didn't like the looks of you, they sent a neighborhood snake like J.J. to wiggle his way into your life until they got the goods on you. During the pot bust, Gary had smelled them coming and got rid of his stash at the last minute, but wound up spending five days in the queens' tank anyway for "disturbing the peace" by standing on a street corner. On the other hand, that was where he'd met Sweet Pea, and a good number of his clients came through contacts made in jail. If they did book him, he'd just think of it as a business opportunity to network. Wasn't that what the slammer was designed for?

As the police car pulled into the street, Gary turned around to gaze through the raindrops glazing the rear window. Miss Gertie was shuffling across the street in her fluffy pink slippers. He waved at her, but the old woman didn't see him. She glanced nervously to the right and to the left, and then rushed into the Aftermath Lounge, the blackened glass of the bar door swinging shut behind her.

# Higher Ground

THIS SECOND-FLOOR CELL HADN'T flooded after the storm, and not much had changed since Gary's last visit. He glanced around. Rickety bunk beds were fastened to the cracked cement floor, fluorescent tubes blinked overhead, and the seatless toilet in the corner still reeked to high heaven.

"They ever take your sorry ass to Parish Prison, ask to be put in the queens' tank," the bartender at the Rough House had told Gary. "Or else you ain't going to come out in one piece."

Within twenty-four hours of landing in New Orleans, a one-eyed bartender gave him this sage advice. Today was Gary's second stay in what he thought of as the Lady Chablis Memorial Detox Clinic, and he knew the ropes. The first time, he'd never forget, he was booked on Monday, September 10, 2001, and the next day, after he and his jail mates had stared bug-eyed at the Twin Towers collapsing over and over in a terrifying tape-loop on the cell TV, they finally broadcast the mug shots of Mohamed Atta and his swarthy accomplices.

"Oooh, they cute," purred the queen sitting next to him. That was Sweet Pea. They had been friends ever since.

Now moans were coming from behind the thin faded blanket tied across a creaking lower bunk, where evidently one of the girls was entertaining her husband from another cell down the corridor. Five drag queens were crowded onto a bunk watching a blaring Ambien commercial and painting their toenails flamingo pink from a single bottle. A threatened-looking white boy with a cowlick was huddled on an upper bunk, buried in a Stephen King novel.

"Who she?" one queen asked another, pointing at Gary.

"I seen her on the streets over by the Aftermath," another answered. He pinched two fingers to his lips and sucked in air. The others nodded and went back to squabbling over the toenail-polish brush.

Gary threw himself onto a lower bunk, studying the metal mesh above. He had spent two hours with Panarello, and the grilling still echoed in his ears. The lieutenant had played good cop, bad cop, mama, and then daddy, but there wasn't much Gary could tell him. Okay, he dropped the bubble-bath bit, and said that he and Gertie had been scared shitless when they heard about the shooting. Sure, he used to deal a little weed—his record said so, why lie?—but he gave that up. He said his income came from a trust fund, which, in fact, he used to have, until his parents showed up at the Chelsea Hotel years ago with a court order and dragged him off to a detox clinic. Yeah, he was good friends with Marky, who he first met at a commune in San Francisco during the seventies but, no, he had zero idea who would want to off him.

Panarello kept insisting drugs lead to murder, so Gary had to be involved in this up to his eyeballs, didn't he? But no, Gary insisted, Marky didn't do any drugs other than pot, and sure, if you must be nosy, his friend was bisexual but didn't pick up trade or hang in the bars. No, Gary had never heard of Latrome Batiste. Well, maybe a little white lie, but who would ever find out they'd met through Sweet Pea and that Latrome had become a steady nickel-bag customer. He figured that pretty soon the fuzz would be searching his apartment and told Gertie during his first phone call to let the assholes in. Good luck, boys. They'd never guess it was the grandma who was holding.

It felt late, and he was dying to take a piss, an aspirin, and a snooze, in that order. Breathing through his mouth, he stumbled over to the toilet and unzipped. A huge molasses-colored queen tapped Gary on the shoulder with a menacing look in his eye. Traces of mascara, blush, and foundation were smudged across his baby-smooth face, and a topknot of fried red hair was caught up in a plastic yellow barrette.

"What you doing, girl?" Topknot demanded in a rich contralto, hand on hip.

"What does it look like?"

"You pull them pants down and squat like the bitch you is," he said, burying a long scarlet fingernail in Gary's arm. "Only the mens stand up to use the commode in my cell."

"You tell her, Big Mama," squealed one of the toe-nail painters. "Who that old white ho think she be."

"It's okay, Big Mama," Gary said with a broad grin, lowering his pants and sinking down onto the stained porcelain rim. "I forgot. I'm Gary Cherry, Sweet Pea's friend."

"Oh, child, what you doing in here?"

"Public drunkenness. Only I don't drink."

"Ain't got nothing on me. I in for soliciting on Rampart Street, and I ain't had no dick since last Tuesday. And that a fact. Pretty sure J.J. set me up." Big Mama rolled up the tight peach stretch pants bunched under his belly and rattled the rainbow of plastic bangles along one arm. "You come sit by me. We got some catching up to do."

Big Mama, Gary recalled, ran the queens' tank, only the big mamas kept rotating, depending on the weekly catch the police brought in. The cops never locked up two big mamas in the same tank, afraid of the fur that would fly when queens collided. The Big Mamas kept the prisoners in order and arranged for the conjugal visits of their jailhouse husbands from the cells down the corridor. That was called "entertaining," as in "tonight Luscious entertaining Jamal." Big Mama kept the peace and was in charge of visitations, sanitation, and recreation. When he screeched "stop working my nerves," the place fell silent. The last time Gary was in, the Big Mama had shown the queens how to use a Sprite bottle to douche standing up. You could learn a lot if you paid attention in the queens' tank.

This Big Mama's street name was LaTusha, and his bunk was made up with a chenille bedspread. A gold-framed picture of a rouged, wavy Breck-blond Jesus hung from the post. A worn New Testament lay open between two tattered velveteen animals of indeterminate breed, next to a half-eaten bag of Oreos. Big Mama must have been walking the streets with an overnight bag packed, but then again, Big Mamas had perks.

"Big Mama, you don't have an aspirin, do you?" Gary asked, perching gingerly on the bedspread, as if he were visiting his aunt in assisted living.

"Oh, I think I does." His face softened with a maternal look.

Big Mama pulled a train case from under his bunk, a square piece of luggage like the one in which Gary's mother used to store her cosmetics on car trips. Several pairs of pressed striped pajamas were folded inside among Ziploc bags bulging with makeup, an array of hairbrushes and picks, some Life Style condoms, and a family-size tube of K-Y.

Out came a tiny tin of Bayer.

"Much obliged," Gary said, swallowing the pill dry.

"How is Miss Nida Mann?" Big Mama lounged back on the bedspread, combing a plucked eyebrow with the curved talon of his pinkie nail. "I entering that contest on Mardi Gras, too, and that bitch don't stand a chance. You should see my shiny pink gown. By the bye, I hear Oscar Batiste's nephew Latrome got shot. Sweet Pea don't talk about nobody but Oscar, her first husband. Course she only had but three, the poor thing."

"That happened right in front of my house on Dauphine and is really what the cops pulled me in to talk about. My friend Marky Naquin got killed, too."

"He dead?" Big Mama sat up. "That man *sooo* sweet. Looked like the big actor what wore the dress in that Marilyn

Monroe movie." He rapped the side of his head. "Oh, you know who I mean. That my all-time favorite movie."

"Yeah, Marky did look like Tony Curtis in *Some Like It Hot*. Chicks found him irresistible. And so did men, even after he got sick, when he let himself go."

"First met him over by the Dragon's Den at that open-mike thing they got there. He wrote me a poem saying how I just like Maya Angelou. I gave it to my mama, and she keep it in her Bible. Oh, child."

A muscular young man with a heaving chest tattooed with a striking scorpion emerged from behind the blanket, yanking up his baggy orange prison-issue. Big Mama bolted from the bunk and stuck his topknot under a corner of the blanket. "Clean yourself up, girl," he spit. "Then you can eat." Big Mama winked at Gary, then beckoned Baggy Orange to the other end of the cell and, arms folded, spoke in whispers.

"Where you stay by on Dauphine?" Big Mama hollered to Gary. "In the Quarters?"

"Yeah," Gary shot back. "Dauphine near Ursulines."

The lovebird behind the blanket probably was sampling the delectables that her husband just brought. Gary had learned during his first stay that the so-called "straight" men from the other cells—really bi tops on the down low—courted the queens by re-cooking their own food over Bic lighters in homemade tin-foil ramekins. The dishes they offered their jailhouse dates were lovingly prepared and truly original: miniature mashed potato pies in a crust of crumbled Cheez Whiz drizzled with Tabasco; hamburger nuggets wrapped in melted cheese, speared on a toothpick with a pickle garnish; pound cake soaked in sugared nondairy creamer, studded with M&Ms and glazed with Bosco. Many of these men had worked at one time or another as cooks. The turnkeys who escorted the butch tops to the queens' tank usually snacked on the hors d'oeuvres along the way, Big Mama got his cut, and the more generous queens passed the leftovers around to the others after they'd eaten their post-coital fill.

A curlicue of smoke streamed from behind the blanket, and Gary knew it soon would be time to chow down. Big Mama strode back to the bunk as the turnkey was ushering Baggy Orange out of the cell with a rattling of keys.

"I doing this for Mama and for my sistah Maya Angelou. And for Oscar Batiste, who come sniffing round my kitchen door more times I care to count. And not for that raggedy-ass ho, Sweet Pea. That hot number I just talk to give me an earful," Big Mama said, re-clasping his barrette with a sigh, "but I too old for him."

"What did he tell you?" At last they were getting somewhere, Gary thought.

"Say a guy in his cell talking big-big about some job he done in the Quarters gone bad. Somebody pay him a roll of benjamin to do a drive-by, but some little brother run in the way and get his self killed, too."

"Must have been about drugs." A benjamin was a hundred note, Gary calculated. A roll must be a few thousand.

Big Mama shook his head. "Nothing to do with drugs."

"Who paid him then?"

"Ever hear of a shop over by Rampart called the Nervous Owl?"

"You mean the occult bookstore, Minerva's Owl?"

"That what I say. The Nervous Owl. Some creepy dude there mighty interested in seeing your friend Marky get plugged. Know who I talking about?"

"I think so. Did you get the name of the guy who did the shooting?"

"Honey, I wouldn't tell you if I did. Then he shoot me soon as I turn my back. These children just as soon plug you as look at you. Think that make them real mens. But mark my words, the killer be coming through here entertaining himself sooner than later, and I find out who the big shot is. That who you want." Big Mama wagged his long red fingernail extension in Gary's face. "The big shot that pay, know what I mean? Don't be fooling with no two-bit fly boys just trying to score a rock. Not if you wants to live."

The five drag queens clopped over in pastel flip-flops, ten sets of flamingo-pink toenails gleaming in the fluorescent glare of the cell. One of them, shaved bald but with a tank top wrapped around his head like a *tignon*, sashayed straight over to the blanket still covering the bunk and ripped it down.

"Get up off your fat ass, bitch, and give us something to eat. We hongry. Last night I give you three of them little weenie things Luther brung me."

Gary knew he had no right to share in the goodies since he wouldn't be doing any entertaining. Nobody wanted old white-boy booty, not with all these hot young pralines to choose from. He found a bunk and stretched out, relieved to be back in a make-believe world that made so much sense. Some boys played at being girls, others pretended they were men, and nobody ever stepped out of line or went hungry.

The Nervous Owl, Gary thought with a wry chuckle. Just what he'd suspected all along.

# Five

"WHAT IN THE WORLD IS WRONG with you?" Nicole asked, leaning her mother's head of stiff gray curls over her kitchen sink and wetting it. "You never used to let your hair get this dirty."

"Every Friday I used to go by that beauty parlor on Canal Boulevard and let Angela do it. She fixed it nice." Gertie squinted, straightening the towel around her shoulders, then sat back in a chair as Nicole worked in the shampoo. "But Angela's shop blew away in the storm and she's in Atlanta. Everything is so different now."

Yes, different and strange, Nicole was thinking as she massaged shampoo into her mother's hair. She'd just woken from a short nap after work, and the dream she had was still so vivid. She and her mother were trudging through the desert. Gertie, dressed in a billowing kimono, decided to veer off along a narrow green path that ran like an oasis toward the horizon. As Nicole continued on alone through the sand, a flock of birds came darting at her overhead. She tried to swat them away. As they got closer, she saw they weren't birds at all but schools of fish swimming directly at her head. I'm at the bottom of a primordial sea, she realized, digging her toes into the sand.

"That warm water sure feels nice," Gertie said.

"I'd be glad to fix your hair from now on," Nicole said, lathering up the shampoo. When she was little, her mother used to wash her hair on Saturday afternoons. She had adored the fruity aroma of the candy-colored shampoos and the caressing fingertips that made her skin tingle, one of the few times she ever felt close to her mother.

"So much I miss about the way things used to be." Gertie started to sniffle. "Pink camellias would be blooming in my garden about now and I'd float them in crystal bowls around the house. Had to throw those bowls on the street with the warped china cabinet. They were caked with black goo. Of course, you never appreciated a lovely home, so you wouldn't understand."

"I've been meaning to ask you," Nicole said, squirting on another dab of strawberry-scented shampoo, "why did that cop car take you home Wednesday afternoon?"

Nicole had been waiting for the right moment to bring this up. She suspected it had something to do with Gary and drugs but couldn't put her finger on it. Lately her mother had been popping a lot of what she called "arthritis pills," but since her doctor at Memorial Hospital had been flooded out of town, Nicole wondered where she was getting them. Besides, arthritis medicine didn't make you act the way her mother was, paranoid and obsessive. Could Gary be dosing her mother with those club drugs she read about, Special K and Ecstasy?

"Who told you about the cop car?" Gertie asked.

"I'd just come home and peeked—"

"Was hoping nobody saw that." Gertie barked out a laugh. "Neighbors are gonna think I'm some big crook."

"Was it that lieutenant what's-his-name investigating Marky's murder?" Nicole rubbed the shampoo behind her mother's ears. Easy does it. She was worried sick.

"Like I told you, that knucklehead Panarello was the one arrested Gary. I was so shook up I went across the street from the Chinese place to have me a few drinks."

"Across the street?"

"Yeah, to the Aftermath Lounge."

"That wild gay bar? With all those balloons out front?"

"They said I had one too many—"

"My mother got kicked out of a gay bar for being drunk?" This couldn't be the woman who dragged Nicole to Mater Dolorosa every Sunday morning for fifteen years, the same one who once walloped her with a missal for showing up at Mass in a tube top and mini-skirt.

"Sweetheart, it wasn't exactly like that. I had a little set-to with the bartender, but the cops were real nice, and told me how sorry they were about Marky."

"Time to rinse. Stand up and lean over."

This had gone too far, Nicole decided, sluicing Gertie's hair. She needed to speak with the bartender at the Aftermath. Why in the world would he call the cops on a seventy-six-year-old woman? What could she have been doing, lifting wallets, groping customers, or stealing tips from the go-go dancers' jockstraps? Losing the house was just too much of a shock for her mother, not to mention those days she spent marooned alone inside the sweltering second story with nothing to eat but Ritz crackers and sardines. And then imagine being put on a plane and not knowing where you'd land. This must be the delayed post-traumatic shock disorder that the TV psychologists said everybody in town was suffering from, causing people to self-medicate with alcohol or drugs. Perhaps it was time to help her mother with an intervention, like when they had to force Auntie Dixie to dry out.

"Maybe you need to talk to someone," Nicole said, lathering up her mother's hair again. Extra gentle.

"I *am* talking to someone." A sharpness crept into Gertie's tone. "*You.*"

"I mean professionally."

"Professionally?"

"A nice doctor who can help you adjust—"

"Look, honey, let me tell you something," Gertie said, swinging around a headful of peaked suds to face her daughter. "All my life other people bossed me around. First it was Dixie when I was little, then Mama after Dixie got put in that home, and then along come your daddy. And now it's not going to be *you*, hear? And I'm sure not going to pay some stranger to tell me what to do. Gosh darn it. I got soap in my eyes." Gertie bolted out of the chair and stuck her head under the faucet. "Rinse me."

"I'm concerned about you," Nicole said, splashing water around Gertie's eyes. "I called FEMA again yesterday, and it doesn't look like your trailer is ever going to come through."

Months ago her mother had requested a trailer that hadn't been delivered. On the other hand, FEMA had called Nicole three times to offer *her* a trailer. In the French Quarter. She explained that her mother, right next door, had lost her house and couldn't supervise the repairs until she had a trailer installed in Lakeview. Couldn't she have it?

"Excuuuse me," came the nasal reply, "but the government is trying to help you. Isn't there anywhere at 1025 Dauphine Street where you could park this trailer?"

"Yeah, but it would break my chandelier."

Nicole was tired of being put on hold at the trailer office. "Momma, I've really tried. Ever thought of selling the house and starting over again, like across the lake?"

"After all I've done for you, now you trying to get rid of me?" Gertie sat back down, vigorously toweling her hair. "Sure I thought about it! But Allstate just jacked up my house insurance 400 percent. I can't afford to pay that on a place where I ain't even living. And rent, too. But I'm not selling the house for peanuts to some developer who would just tear it down, not just to please you."

"Didn't you and Daddy know Lakeview could flood?" Nicole asked, working in the coconut-smelling conditioner.

"We moved there for you and Marky, even though everybody said the land was real low. The place was empty, and I was stuck out there till I learned to drive. What we wanted was to fix up an old raised house Uptown by my mama's. Ever hear of the GI Bill?"

"Sort of."

"The soldiers coming home after the war got help to buy them a house. But the government told your daddy it had to be 'new construction,' like one of those slab-foundation houses in the cypress back-swamp by the lake. Then the government put up levees in Lakeview and New Orleans East, swearing it wouldn't flood any more. Ain't that rich?"

"Especially since those are the levees that just broke. So do you think the feds were in league with the developers?"

"They all in cahoots." Gertie stood up and leaned her head over the sink. "But in those days we did what we were told. *Go to war*, we went to war. *Buy a new house in the swamp*, we bought a new house in the swamp. *Get a car*, we got a car. Thought we was being mod-ren, but was just a pack of darn fools. Me, oh I was always so, *so* good, doing what everyone expected of me. Little Gertie was the perfect daughter and the perfect USO belle and the perfect mama and wife. Guess I would have been the perfect grandma, too," she said, craning her neck around to meet Nicole's eyes, "but that never gonna happen now. Although I would've felt some sorry for your kids, if you'd had any."

Okay, rub it in, she forgot to have a baby. By the time she got around to marrying, Buster already had two kids who lived with their mother and didn't want any more. Nicole wondered why she and her mother always felt compelled to keep punching the same old numbers on their jukebox, having the identical conversations over and over again. She knew the hurtful words by heart but was tired of singing along.

"Sorry to disappoint you," Nicole murmured, biting her lip.

"You're pushing fifty, and life is passing you by."

"I know, Momma."

"For all his flaws, that Buster was a good catch, your last chance for a decent life."

"Don't you think Kelly—"

"Another married man, and don't think I can't smell what's going on from a mile away. You're like a cat in heat. One day Kelly is gonna two-time you the same way your husband did, because men don't respect home wreckers like you."

Nicole flinched. Yes, it was a pattern. Maybe, as her mother claimed, she was damaged goods, a serial "other woman."

"No man gonna stay long with a woman who looks like a whisk broom," Gertie said. "If only you'd put some flesh on those bones and let that spiky hair grow back out, soft around your face like it was before you ruined your life."

"*Ruined my life*! I was waiting for you to play that oldie-but-goodie." Nicole slung the shampoo bottles into a drawer then turned to face the window. "Look, it's hard watching you ruin *your* life, the way I did when I was young."

"Like what?" Gertie asked, cutting her eyes at Nicole's back.

Nicole swiveled around. "Hanging out with drug addicts and drag queens, for starters. You know, drugs really were a

69

bad experience for me. What's going on with you?" Her voice shot up, and she wanted to grab her mother, peel back her wet scalp, and peek inside. "Now that Marky's dead, you're all I have left."

"So why did you throw me away like a rag doll after high school, when you ran off to New York thinking *oh, she's just my mother, she don't count*." Gertie yanked the towel from around her shoulders and wrapped it into a tight turban. "Sure, we thought of coming up there to get you. But you said, 'Momma, I just need to do my thing.'" Gertie burst out laughing. "I didn't have the faintest idea what a *thing* was."

"Not sure I did either."

"Only now I got a *thing*, hear?" Gertie bolted up, eyes flashing.

"So what's your thing, Momma?" Now that the shoe was on the other foot, Nicole felt backed into a corner. What could she do about her mother running wild in the French Quarter? Ground her? Monitor her phone calls? Slug her with a missal?

"My thing is if a bunch of stupid old men sitting around a table in Washington says I can't have my life back, I'll just have to start a new one."

"By getting drunk in some gay bar?"

"I wasn't drunk," Gertie said. "It was something else."

"What?"

"That's for me to know and you to find out."

NICOLE HADN'T SET FOOT IN A GAY bar for the past twenty years, so she felt self-conscious cracking open the blackened doors of the Aftermath Lounge. Even on a rainy Tuesday afternoon, she was expecting the manic festivity of those evenings she'd spent dolled up in vintage frocks, slinking around Studio 54 and

Max's Kansas City. But the exhausted air in this place smelled like an ashtray, and the five or six men sitting around looked like a bowling team, identical in baseball caps and football jerseys. Where was the glitter and glamour she remembered? Now all the gorgeous guys were probably off getting married to each other, and these were people like Miss Glad Bag, the leftovers.

Nobody smiled or made eye contact. Two video monitors were mounted in opposite corners of the dim room, one mutely showing two gym bunnies getting it on in color, and the other blaring a black-and-white episode of "I Love Lucy." Everyone was watching Lucille Ball instead of the blow job, and no one was laughing.

Nicole took a seat at the bar and looked up. Lucy and Ethel were bobbing up to their necks in water, trapped inside a flooded shower stall, accompanied by a raucous laugh track. Nicole understood why nobody in New Orleans would find this scenario amusing. Not in the least.

"What can I get you, sweetheart?" asked the bartender, bald and beefy as Mr. Clean.

"Just a Sprite." Nicole wasn't about to follow in her mother's besotted footsteps. "And may I ask you a question?" Her lips twisted into a tight smile. "About my mother?"

"Love her while you can," said the bartender, plunking down a plastic cup of Sprite on a napkin. "She won't be around forever, especially at your age."

Nicole bristled. "I'm not looking for advice."

"Then exactly what are you looking for?" The bartender cocked an eyebrow at the only woman in the place.

"My mother is Ms. Naquin, an older lady who comes in here frequently."

"Miss who?"

"Gertie."

"Oh, her." The bartender rolled his eyes.

"I want to know why on Wednesday she came home from this place in a police car."

Lucy belted out her classic *whaaaa*, trying to climb over the shower door.

"Look, we love your mom in here, and anytime she waltzes in, I'll stand her to a drink. She lights up the place, especially when she sings along to Judy Garland videos. But fact is on Wednesday she was in here peddling her pills. I already warned Gary she couldn't do that."

"What kind of pills?"

"Got me. All I know is she takes out those church-offering envelopes, and the queens line up like they're at communion."

"It cuts into the bartender's sales." The pock-marked face of a man perched next to Nicole leaned into the conversation with beery breath. "These guys can't make it on tips alone after the storm."

"Button your lip, bitch," the bartender said, "or you'll be making friends back at the bus-station toilet."

"You called the cops on Momma because she's a drug dealer?" Nicole's head spun. This must be some kind of joke. "Are you sure we're talking about the same old lady?"

"Miss Gertie said Gary had just been popped and she was trying to make his bail." Mr. Clean's eyes softened. "So I told the cops she was drunk and to take her on home. I know she lost her house and her son got shot, but lemme tell you something, honey. The next time she pulls a little stunt like that in here, she'll get slammed with a felony that means more years in jail than she's got in her. So tell her to push those pills on the street like everybody else."

"And don't compete with the house," slurred the man on the next stool.

"Out!" roared the bartender, slapping down his rag. "You've had enough."

Everyone's eyes swiveled to the other screen to watch the money shot and then back to Lucy. She and Ethel were standing drenched in a flooded bathroom, water up to their knees.

"Ricky's going to be so mad," Lucy wailed, followed by the laugh track.

Pale and stiff as a mannequin, Nicole turned to leave, shoulders hunched with the weight of what she'd just learned.

"We feel real bad about Marky," the bartender called after her. "But your mom is mixed up in something way over her head, and I'd hate to see her get hurt."

# Six

"LET'S CARRY OUR BURDENS DOWN by the riverside," Kelly told Nicole, emerging from the shower in a cloud of Lifebuoy-scented steam.

Lord knows he had enough of them. The latest was that his wife was suing for divorce and, to be closer to her lawyer, had moved in with a maiden aunt in St. Francisville. He and Lena would never understand each other. Even during their engagement, Lena Ludlam of the Sundown-Plantation Ludlams had let it be known that in taking up with Kelly Cannon, that devil-may-care, red-headed kid from the Irish Channel, she would be marrying down. Now Lena didn't mince her words about his sleepovers with an old girlfriend in the French Quarter.

"This is the last straw," she had shouted when Kelly arrived at Mouton Street last Monday. She was pacing the sidewalk under the weeping willow tree, cradling a stack of moldy daguerreotypes rescued from over the mantel. "First we lose our home, then you lose your job, and now you've lost your mind. Bottom line, either come start a new life with me somewhere sane or it's over."

# Higher Ground

True, what Kelly assumed was a temporary lay-off after the storm from his accounting job with Macy's had become permanent when the department store chain decided to cut its losses and pull out of Louisiana for good. It seemed that just yesterday he had been merrily tooling home from work to barbecue ribs with his wife. Then *boom*. The winds blew, the water rose, and suddenly, no home, no work, and now no wife.

Sitting on the damask chair in Nicole's bedroom, Kelly dried his hair, wondering what came next. Actually, the more he thought about it, he had grown to loathe his job and didn't give a flying fuck whether Macy's increased its profit margin during the third quarter or not. The house seemed too large, now that the kids were gone, and he could count on one hand the times he'd had sex with Lena during the past few years, or even a memorable conversation. Recently, what Kelly had wanted to do was to dabble with the unfinished paintings in his studio and to grow tomatoes and zucchini in the backyard. Yet any day he'd expected Lena to sprout a mustache after she went back to work as a go-getter real estate agent with Latter & Blum. While she spun around in a cell-phone tizzy spearing lawns with "For Sale" signs, all he could think about were washes and mulch.

Maybe—just maybe—he decided while slipping into one of the three pairs of pants he had left to his name, he'd taken a wrong turn at some juncture many years back, and all-knowing Mother Nature had intervened by blowing to hell the life that no longer fit. Now here he was, back to square one, in the French Quarter of his misspent youth, sleeping with the same woman he had been with when he was eighteen, living out of a duffel bag like a camper, as if the past thirty years had been a waking dream. Suddenly, he was smoking pot again that he scored from Gary—let Lena add that to the growing list of his aberrations—and seeing colors and textures he hadn't noticed in years. If there was one anchor, one thing from the past he wanted to save, it was his house. Every day he attacked the marinated strips of Sheetrock like a pit bull, trying to put some discernible order into this shambles of a life.

Even though the mold had given him a hacking cough. Nicole said that even before he reached the front door, she could hear him coming down the street. *Hack, hack, hack.*

Kelly sat studying Nicole. She was changing out of her FEMA threads—black jeans, white blouse, spongy sneakers—into a striped fisherman's sweater and suede boots. Changing. She was always changing. At some moments she seemed a middle-aged lady under siege, shoulders slumped, groping for her glasses. And at other moments, particularly in bed, she was the identical sophomore he met years ago with schoolbooks balanced on her hip. Sometimes he would sneak up behind the old fussbudget, grab her around the waist, and a young girl would twirl around into his arms, giggling.

"Your mother heard any more from Gary?" Kelly asked.

"He calls collect from Parish Prison," Nicole said, turning to adjust her skirt in the mirror. "The calls cost ten dollars a pop. It's been a week now, and he says they can't hold him much longer without seeing a judge. Momma says they raided his apartment yesterday morning with a search warrant but claims they didn't find anything. Wonder where he stashed those drugs."

"The whole thing stinks. We know he was in his apartment when those shootings took place. But the cops will pick up anybody for anything and, bingo, crime solved."

"I've never seen Momma this freaked out, not even after Daddy died. She claims she's doing her *thing*, which appears to be peddling barbiturates in gay bars. I've got to stop her before she lands in jail but don't know how to accuse my own mother to her face of being a drug dealer. Hey," Nicole said, grabbing Kelly's arm, "thought we were going to lay down our burdens down by the riverside. Before it gets dark."

"Just remember," said Kelly, studying the dying light in the courtyard, "what Chairman Mao says: it's always darkest just before it turns totally black."


ALONG THE DESERTED MOON WALK, the tourist steamboats hugged the dock, moored in shadows. Staring across the muddy expanse of the Mississippi, Kelly fell silent. Who would want to live with a waterfront view in this town? These days he couldn't so much as look at water without imagining hideous scenarios. There he was again, baking half-naked on his rooftop in Lakeview, waving his T-shirt at swooping helicopters. Now even a fish aquarium made him nervous. He felt more threatened than comforted by the swelling river, kept on an artificial course as it flowed through the city. Nature will have the final say-so on this, he decided, not the Levee Board. He had looked it up: in the city's 289 year history, it had flooded twenty-seven times because of hurricanes or the river. That was an average of once every ten years. After all, water's job was to seek its own level, and people's job was to stay the hell out of the way. At the moment, New Orleans seemed as damned by geography as Venice, and any engineering feat to the contrary was just a sandcastle waiting for the tide to wash in.

All the popsicle sticks in the world wouldn't stop the sea.

Nicole broke the leaden silence. "Let's go have coffee at Café du Monde."

"Sure," Kelly said. "If I can ravish you afterwards."

A lone sax player was standing in front of the café, horn lifted into the opalescent sky of early evening, blowing an upbeat version of "Just a Closer Walk with Thee." On the other side of the café railing, four hefty ladies in pastel T-shirts with matching baseball caps tapped their feet, gathered around one of the few occupied tables on the terrace. A clown with a basketful of unsold balloons slouched against a streetlamp, counting his change.

"Thought you wanted some coffee," Kelly said as Nicole quickened her pace to cross the street. After gutting his house all day, he just wanted to sit down.

"It's that fat blonde in the pink T-shirt," Nicole whispered, "just behind the railing. She's from Indiana and works at my FEMA office. She told me this morning she had friends from home visiting. Quick. Let's cross here." Nicole pulled Kelly's hand across Decatur Street toward Jackson Square.

"So I guess the only people in town," Kelly said, glancing around at the eerily empty Square, "are the jokers who have come down here to save us. FEMA. Red Cross. Halliburton. And out-of-town contractors." He didn't mind. The French Quarter sure beat the foul-smelling streets of unlit Lakeview, which he left every day the minute the sun sank below the top of the weeping willow tree in his front yard.

Two of the street lanterns on the Square flicked on, emitting an unnerving hum. The rest stayed unlit, swallowed by the darkness engulfing the flagstones. Six months ago, the President of the United States stood under klieg lights at this very spot, promising to rebuild New Orleans. Then the lights went out. And stayed out.

They sank onto an iron bench in front of the three towering spires of St. Louis Cathedral. The only fortune-teller on the Square tipped her plumed hat, pointing at her Tarot cards. When they waved her away, she slumped back into her lawn chair behind the fringed card table and picked up a tattered issue of *Time*.

# Higher Ground

"Don't need a fortune-teller to predict the future of this town," Kelly said, pounding on his chest after a coughing spell. "All we know how to do any more is throw parties. And guess what?" He cleared his throat. "The party's over."

It hadn't been this way when he was coming up. He and his family always managed to have a good time, with highball-soused barbecues, Carnival parades, and cutting it up at all-night dances. But back then people had real jobs, too. His family had moved to Lakeview from the Irish Channel after his old man got that good job at the shipyards, and Mr. Naquin had worked for Shell Oil. Yeah, they probably drank more than people in Ohio—damn straight his dad did—and they certainly ate tastier food and listened to funkier music. But in those days fun meant free time, not full time. Now, of course, the city had lost both the downtown port and oil, not to mention cotton and shipbuilding. He recalled that the real change came as late as 1984, during the World's Fair. That was when fun became obligatory—the cornerstone of the economy—because the city didn't have anything else left to sell. Ambitious natives soon followed the real jobs out of town, and boozy civic boosters moved in, pretending that crime, poverty, failing schools, and the oil bust were just one big second-line parade.

"So, what are you going to do?" Nicole asked.

"About what?" Kelly had been avoiding this conversation.

The cathedral bells tolled six times, each *bong* resonating with a soul-shaking finality.

"About work," she said.

"Keep gutting the house," he said, coughing, "until my unemployment runs out."

"And when it does?"

"Look for another job."

"In this town? There's nothing, unless you want to wait tables or tend bar." She opened her arms in a wide gesture. "And you can see all the customers you'll have. Fifteen percent of nothing is nothing."

"I have savings. You know, retirement."

She gave him an impatient look.

"But it's going for mortgage payments," he said. "The kids' college. And to Home Depot for building materials."

"You could always just sell the place."

"Will your mother ever sell her house?"

"No way," she said. "Besides, what could she get for a wreck on a floodplain?"

"Bingo. Besides, it's my home. I want to leave it to our children."

"Do they plan on moving back after college?"

"You kidding? Both got big-ass plans. Grad school. Internships."

"But like I keep asking Momma," Nicole said, "what if the city doesn't even reopen Lakeview as a neighborhood? Because of the jack-o'-lantern effect, you know—a couple of houses on each block surrounded by ruins—they may leave it as green space."

Kelly shrugged. "I'd live there anyway."

"All by yourself, without any streetlights or stores or garbage pickup? It's up to Mayor Blinger, which doesn't inspire a lot of confidence."

He held out his palm. "Got an extra Zoloft?"

"I have a better idea." She stood up. "Let's go by the store and pick up something for dinner. Momma's not cooking tonight, and since the storm, the store closes at 6:30."

The door of the A & P still had plywood covering the glass shattered by looters after the hurricane. Inside, only three grizzled alkies waited in line, each waving a quart of malt liquor. And the store was out of onions, garlic, and eggs.

"How can a supermarket be out of eggs?" Kelly demanded of the checkout lady.

"Don't worry," the lady said. "Truck be in next Thursday."

"Next Thursday?"

"We still having delivery troubles."

"I could lay the damn eggs faster than that."


OUTSIDE ON ROYAL STREET, KELLY heard live music blaring from up the block. A crowd was milling around a long row of white linen-draped tables lined with covered steam trays and silver tureens. Bow-tied servers were just setting up. Signs indicated that the buffet came from the best restaurants still open in the city: Tujacques, Bayona, and Arnaud's. Other tables were already dispensing plastic cups of wine and champagne, and another station had a machine spurting out frozen daiquiris.

"What's this?" Kelly asked a server.

"It's the Mayor's Art Party!" the bouncy blonde chirped. "Like to try our crab meat *au gratin* or shrimp remoulade?"

"How much?" He plunked down his sack of wilted lettuce, Velveeta cheese, and milk long past its expiration date.

"It's free," the young blonde said, uncovering the steaming food.

Kelly was hit in the face with the overpowering aroma of why he could never leave New Orleans. While Nicole balanced Styrofoam bowls of shrimp and crab, Kelly went for two cups of champagne. The drink table was set up in front of an art gallery—a real hole in the wall, not one of the fancier venues—filled floor-to-ceiling with glossy photos of a beaming man with a shiny, caramel-colored dome. A homemade sign advertised a Bourbon Street titty bar, and scrawled under a crude drawing of a Hurricane cocktail was the slogan: "Roy Blinger, Strongest Mayor in the Nation."

Kelly stood there with his mouth hanging open.

Roy Blinger was the leader in charge of the city during the two weeks of unmitigated hell that followed in the aftermath of the hurricane, and as far as Kelly was concerned, the mayor royally blew it. While hospitals, nursing homes, and jails flooded, and tens of thousands were trapped without food or water in the Superdome and Convention Center, he hid on the twenty-seventh floor of the Hyatt Regency waiting for a call from the President on a telephone that didn't work. Kelly wondered how the mayor could dare set foot in the city again.

But here was Blinger, putting on an art opening in the French Quarter that consisted of nothing but cheesy photographs of himself. Kelly glanced around at the crowd. He didn't recognize a soul from the neighborhood. Everyone looked like a tourist or FEMA worker scrambling to get at the free daiquiris and gourmet grub. Blinger probably figured he was going to rub elbows with the artsy set in the Quarter. That was how out of it he was.

"Can you fucking believe this?" Kelly asked Nicole, handing her a cup of champagne. "The only grocery open within miles is out of eggs while our mayor is dishing out shrimp remoulade from Arnaud's to celebrate an exhibition of his own damn self."

"Here he comes now," Nicole said, spearing a shrimp with a toothpick.

A Pharaonic profile emerged above the crowd. The tall figure did a loping camel-walk past the food tables, shooting the French cuffs of his starched white shirt as he reached out to grab the hands of wide-eyed gawkers with their mouths full. Two squat bodyguards followed in his wake, ebony faces glistening and muscles straining under the tight shoulders of their polyester suits. Then Roy Blinger positioned himself under the spotlight in the gallery doorway and clasped both hands above his bald head, bathing in an adulation that wasn't there. After a polite patter of applause, everyone went back to scarfing up free crawfish ravioli and daiquiris.

"Who's that clown?" asked the guy standing next to Kelly.

"Our mayor." Kelly tried to keep a straight face.

"Jeez." The guy drained his glass. "Thought he was some big TV actor. I'm from New York, see. Our mayor would be meeting with engineers or directing bulldozers. I mean, after what just happened here."

"Bingo. Welcome to the Caribbean," Kelly said, raising his glass. "Just think of Baby Doc visiting his poor subjects before he splits to his château in the south of France."

"Yeah?" asked the New Yorker. "But who's paying for this? That asshole?"

"Washington," cut in Nicole. "I work for FEMA. See it every day. By the time the money trickles down to the ones who need it, nothing's left. Enjoy," she said, spearing another shrimp. "You're eating our recovery."

Blinger raised his index finger toward the brass band assembled at the corner, which began to parade down the crowded street, drowning out any conversation in a crescendo of screeching syncopation.

"One more?" Kelly mouthed to Nicole, pointing at her drink.

One more led to three, and they were among the last to leave. They trailed Mayor Roy Blinger and his bodyguards down the emptied street, kicking their way past plastic cups and Styrofoam bowls under a blinking streetlight that couldn't decide whether it was on or off. The music was over, the booze gone, and their footsteps echoed through a city of hungry ghosts.

"Sad," Nicole said.

"What?"

"Oh, I don't know. Blinger, New Orleans. He's like that character in *The Great Gatsby*, my favorite book from Miss Arceneaux's class. Remember Jay Gatsby, the insecure guy from the poor background trying to impress rich people with his bootleg money? But then Prohibition is over and he keeps giving parties but nobody comes. Meanwhile, he's alone in his mansion and. . . ."

"The city rots," Kelly said. "While we're waiting for the Great Blinger to feel good about himself." Kelly grabbed Nicole around the waist and kissed her. "It's all about him."

"It's all about him," she sang in clear soprano to the tune of "It Had to Be You," staggering along the darkened, garbage-lined street. "All about him. . . ."

WHEN THEY REACHED THE SHOTGUN on Dauphine, Nicole rapped on her mother's shutter. What Kelly wanted was to take her directly to bed, but while he was purring in her ear, she was batting his hands away from her butt.

"Just want to scheck up on her," she slurred.

When there was no answer, she let herself in with a key. They crossed the unlit parlor, rolled open the pocket doors to enter the bedroom, and headed for the crack of light under the kitchen door.

Startled, Gertie swung around when they pushed open the door. She was emptying the contents of her freezer into a brown grocery bag.

"You like to scare the daylights out of me," Gertie said, slamming the freezer shut. Schnitzel jumped up from his wicker bed in the corner, growled unconvincingly, and then creaked over to sniff at whatever gamey smells Kelly brought in on his shoes.

Gary was seated at the kitchen table, a beatific smile plastered on his face and a joint burning between his fingers.

"Welcome home," Kelly said, slapping Gary on the back. "How was the slammer?"

Gary squinted, red-eyed, and waved the joint at Kelly. He reached over to grab it, steadying Gary, who seemed about to tumble out of the chair any second.

"Momma, what's going on here?" Nicole scowled at Kelly, who was coughing up a storm. "What's in that bag?"

"Just some chicken thighs I was saving for Gary," Gertie said, rolling up the top of the bag and placing it out of reach. "Where y'all been?"

"You'll never believe," Kelly said, not believing for a hot minute that the old lady chose this moment to deliver frozen poultry to the stoned jailbird in front of him. According to Nicole, they were standing in the secret lair of a powerful French Quarter drug cartel, run by a hippie pothead and a pill-pushing granny. "The Mayor's Art Party."

"Awt pawty my behind," Gertie hollered. "Why don't he get the darn lights fixed in Lakeview or the Lower Nine?"

"Your hair looks pretty," Nicole said, walking over to pat her mother's clean do. "But if you're not consherned about schecond-hand marijuana schmoke, I am." Hiccupping, she waved a hand in front of her face. "I don't want to drop dead from inhaling all this . . . substance abuse."

"Gary's just unwinding after a rough time in jail. But it sounds like you need a cup of coffee, Miss Smarty Pants. So you went out and got yourself drunk, and now you come home to fuss at me. Just like your daddy."

Gertie turned around to the stove and filled the filter of

the white enamel French-drip pot. The tombstone still topped the rusted utility cart salvaged from Lakeview, but the gin bottles had disappeared with Dixie. Now an aluminum urn rested on the cracked marble slab: Marky's ashes. No funeral parlors were open in the city, and the cemetery had only one employee left, a wizened geezer who hobbled on his one good leg to open and close the gates every day and took a long nap in between. Rather than keep Marky's body on ice for months, Gertie had decided to have him cremated and to place the ashes in the crypt, as she put it, "once things get back to normal." Kelly savored that phrase with a rueful chuckle every time he heard it.

"Besides," Gertie said, thrusting a wooden match into the gas burner and stepping back from the soft blue explosion, "Gary found out puh-lenty in jail."

Gary wobbled in his chair, head bobbing. Kelly wondered what silent guitar rifts he was grooving on behind those puffy pink eye slits.

"Like what?" Nicole asked, crossing her arms.

Smoking match in hand, Gertie whirled around from the stove to face her daughter.

"Like who killed Marky," she said. "That's what."

# Seven

YOU CAN FIND ANYTHING YOU WANT here, Lieutenant Panarello thought as he crossed Rampart Street, especially if you don't plan on living long.

Glancing over his shoulder, Vinnie made his way past the rusted balconies and fly-by-night bars. Rampart Street had always been a dividing line, a border between worlds, separating the swamp from the early settlement, the dead from the living, and the whores from the wives. These days the wide avenue was a no-man's-land between the touristy Quarter and the gritty ex-city left to rot after the storm. During the day, people along the treeless street scuttled like cockroaches from the glare. But at night, they mingled in dark corners along this honky-tonk boulevard of hookers, con artists, and horn players, where history repeated itself in clandestine transactions, the primal swamp rising like bile in the throats of people who thought they just wanted to have a good time. Everybody got fleeced on Rampart Street.

When Vinnie was a boy visiting his grandparents above their corner grocery on Decatur Street, Nonno let him run wild with the other kids but forbade him to cross Rampart Street.

Once he did, and five minutes later Nonno came looking for him, whipping off his belt when he spotted the boy. As punishment, he had to sit next to the dusty antipasto jars on the counter at Angelo's, under Nonno's watchful eye for a week. When Vinnie was a kid, the Quarter was alive with Italian eyes. Word traveled from balcony to balcony, stoop to stoop, and shop to shop faster than a text message. A dago kid couldn't get away with anything, and Lord knows Vinnie tried.

Even now Vinnie felt watched in the Quarter, both by the living and the dead.

He felt watched this afternoon, crossing Rampart Street to duck into the vaulted interior of the Our Lady of Guadalupe, where his grandfather used to drag him to the St. Jude shrine. The saint of impossible cases had been Nonno's patron saint. The old man, born aboard a ship sailing from Palermo in the final year of the nineteenth century, felt cursed by the evil eye and carried his myriad woes to the St. Jude statue in the rear nave of the oldest church in New Orleans, once known as the Mortuary Chapel, where pestilent cadavers were stacked during the yellow-fever and cholera epidemics.

Years ago, Vinnie had come here on his own to beseech St. Jude while his first wife Janice lay dying in the ICU after a bloody car crash. She had been the real love of his life, a blond poet he met at Tulane night school, and he still caught glimpses of her dreamy green eyes staring down at him from iron-lace balconies. But that filigree of first love had since hardened into the steely resolve of duty, remorse, and a Mediterranean sense of fate.

After the storm, to downplay his role in the alleged negligent homicide, Vinnie had been transferred from the Sixth to the Eighth District—his nemesis—the fucking French Quarter. Once upon a time he had been happy here, as a boy shooting marbles on the brick banquette in front of Angelo's, and then as a young man courting Janice over candle-lit patio tables. Yet these days his vision of the Quarter was so blurred by his own history that he couldn't separate the ghosts from the shadows, or sort out the young criminals he was supposed to catch from the retired ones who raised him. Back when he was coming up, the neighborhood had been a slummy port filled with sailors and whores, and in the sixties the city wanted to raze the whole stinking dump to build an overpass along the river. Too bad they didn't, as far as Vinnie was concerned.

Now tourism and real estate had replaced foreign freighters and the mob, and the Quarter had gone cutesy with weekend condo-dwellers trying to make these rotting façades and slave quarters—what was their phony baloney word?—"upscale." Even though Vinnie had turned into a suburban dad down to his bones, he could relate better to the weirdos and winos, the street walkers and two-bit hustlers hanging onto the long-gone glory days of Quarter vice, rather than to the whiny condo people from away who dialed 911 every time a pigeon shit in one of their color-coordinated window boxes.

He was happy to stick with murder, thank you, and dreaded being demoted to Quality of Life.

Today Vinnie had a particularly urgent prayer in mind as he lit the fat, three-day novena candle and found an empty holder in the wall of flickering votive tongues pulsing in the dark. He had killed a deaf man—possibly an innocent man— or at least that was what the family's lawyers were claiming. Unfortunately, because the gunshot victim was black and most of the policemen white, the case was being championed as a civil rights cause. But nothing could be farther from the truth.

When he and the three other officers were called from their storm headquarters to the gunfight in a Walmart parking lot, none of them had slept since the hurricane ripped through the city and the levees breeched. When they arrived at the scene and learned that two cops had already been shot at, they zoomed into the parking lot to find the perps. There hundreds of half-drowned residents were milling around, desperate people who had waded from their flooded homes in Central City to higher ground through a poisonous sludge bobbing with corpses. The parking lot had become a nightmarish concentration camp filled with shrieking children and dying grandmothers, piles of shit, pools of blood, and mounds of refuse. Nobody was in their right mind. The sun had baked the cement into a griddle and the reflected glare was blinding. Here Vinnie's memory became a woozy blur.

Gunshots popped in the distance. Some asshole pointed to two guys with dogs and screamed, "It's them over there."

Then one of the guys, a fifty-three-year-old named Chief, came racing in his direction, and Vinnie ordered him to step back. The guy kept lunging toward him, something shiny and metallic flashing in his hand, as if about to attack. "Stop!" Vinnie shouted, but he didn't, so the cop drew his revolver and fired. Chief slumped to the pavement, hit twice in the chest. An empty aluminum water bottle clanked to the ground, and a mutt named Wigwam bounded over to lick the wounded man's fingers. Powwow barked at his side. "He couldn't hear you," insisted the man's cousin, Wardell. "He deaf. All he wanted was water for his dogs." Six teenagers in long white T-shirts were scampering in the opposite direction. The two dogs got their water, and their owner died an hour later. Chief and Wardell appeared unarmed, or were they? Did Wardell throw their gun into a dumpster, as the police report stated? Or was the gun recovered from the dumpster a "ham sandwich," one of those unregistered, wiped-cleaned pieces that some cops carried to plant on unarmed victims of their own gunfire. Was there an official cover-up that Vinnie didn't know about? Had the provoking shots come from Chief and his cousin, or was it from the teenagers?

What really happened that day in the Walmart parking lot?

Vinnie bent down to kiss the hem of the statue's robe, and then fingered the plaster feet worn to stubs by generations of impossible cases. He glanced up at the flame shooting from the top of St. Jude's head and—just like that—had an idea.

Why not plead temporary insanity?

Two days after the storm he was out of his mind with fatigue and stress. He should have just bolted along with the hundreds of other cops who abandoned the force, some looting Cadillacs as they hightailed it out of the city, others lodging bullets in their brains after trying to maintain order in those hellish scenarios. Yet day and night Vinnie had stayed on the job, napping in his squad car, crapping in alleys, and suctioning gas out of flooded vehicles. He could still taste the gasoline, smell the vomitous stench of rotting corpses, and feel the sour sweat streaming down his grimy face. He hadn't even known where his wife and three children were. But out of loyalty he stayed, going through the motions of enforcing the law in that Wild West free-for-all, while Blinger and the big monkey-monks at City Hall stared at dead BlackBerries, heads up their butts.

This morning Vinnie had given yet another deposition. But, thank you, St. Jude, now he knew what he should do. He'd go to a shrink and amend his testimony with a psychiatric evaluation of temporary insanity. Of course, he couldn't continue as an officer after pleading insanity, temporary or otherwise, but he could always take an early retirement from the force at age fifty-five. The family could scrape by with private eye and security gigs if his wife went back to work full time. Marky Naquin's would be his last case for the New Orleans Police Department.

If only he didn't have to do time. That was what he came to ask St. Jude.

Funny that he should decide to retire at the official shrine of the police and fire departments, a church where cops and firemen stopped between shifts to pray for their safety. Vinnie sank onto his knees in a pew facing the statue and mumbled the prayer he knew by heart, as if still a bambino walking in Nonno's footsteps. "Most holy apostle, friend of Jesus, the Church honors and invokes you universally as the patron of hopeless cases, of things almost despaired of. Pray for me, I am so helpless and alone. . . ." He repeated the prayer three times, as Nonno always did, then threw in three Hail Mary's for the repose of his first wife's soul, and, for good measure, a couple of Pater Nosters.

When he rose, he noticed a corpulent man with a pointy beard and piercing blue eyes sitting two pews behind him. The man was watching him. Dressed in a flowing purple tunic, the weirdo had a chalky, half-dead complexion. He hadn't been seated there when Vinnie knelt down, and he didn't hear the man come in. The creep just appeared. The bronze amulet around the fat man's neck flashed in the light reflected from the walls of votive candles, a dog-headed Egyptian figure holding scorpions by the tails in either hand. What kind of nut? Vinnie wondered. Unnerved, he stumbled out of the pew, shooting the big fruit a dirty look. The bearded man stared back with a knowing smile, his magnetic sapphire eyes boring into Vinnie like a laser. Vinnie genuflected, crossing himself, and then scampered down the aisle. On his way out of the church, he glanced up at the statue of St. Expédite, the voodoo saint of immediate results.

*Get this over with quick*, he prayed.

# Higher Ground

As THE LIEUTENANT SLIPPED ON shades and adjusted his vision to the bright street outside, a figure limped around the corner and caught his eye. It was J.J., who turned up at the station every Friday evening to collect his envelope of cash. Vinnie didn't trust him, but the precinct was forced to rely on these neighborhood snitches, especially in the murky French Quarter.

"Hey, lieutenant," J.J. said, palsied hand shaking, "who that old white lady cross the street? I seen her before."

There they were, ambling down the other side of Rampart, toward Esplanade. That Gary Cherry clown with the frizzy hair trucked ahead, followed by a short black queen in hot pants with a mincing stride, blowing a stream of smoke into the air like Bette Davis. Behind him hobbled the old lady, Naquin's mother, wearing a flowered rayon dress, her wrinkled face screwed up with determination. Scrambling behind her on a leash was the lame pooch with the chariot wheels attached to its hind paws.

"She's Marky Naquin's mama," the cop said, "that guy got shot over by Dauphine Street."

"1023 Dauphine?" J.J. swung his crutch around, facing the cop. "The dealer she walking with live in back that house and the queen be Sweet Pea. She save my ass one day LaTusha try to cut me. Them two bitches don't get along nohow."

"Enough gossip," Vinnie said. "Now scram. We shouldn't be seen together."

"Bet I knows where they heading. That bookstore." J.J. directed his hooded eyes once more across the street, blinked once as if taking a picture, then gimped off in the other direction.

Intrigued, Vinnie decided to trail behind the unlikely crew on his side of the street, just to see where they were headed. At Parish Prison, he hadn't managed to get a peep out of Cherry about Naquin's death, nothing he didn't already know.

So he booked him for public drunkenness. A withholding-information charge wouldn't stick. Now, a week later, here he was back on the street—ain't that just like New Orleans?—prancing around pretty as you please with some homo homey. Vinnie felt sorry for the old lady and wondered how she ever got mixed up with a bunch like that. He even felt sorry for the spastic dog.

Near the corner of Rampart and St. Philip, the ratty Three Musketeers came to a sudden halt. Blue lights pulsing, two squad cars were parked in front of a shabby outfit called Minerva's Owl at 826 Rampart. The old lady stuck her head into a cop-car window and then went back to tell the two bozos something that apparently upset them, probably that the shop was closed. What could Minerva's Owl be selling that would interest these three? And why were squad cars out front?

Vinnie's cell chimed, and he fished it out of the pocket of his blazer.

Eighth District.

"Yeah, Sergeant, funny you should mention it," Vinnie said. "Right this sec that's where I'm at, the corner of Rampart and St. Philip. What the hell's going on over there?"

Sirens wailing, a third squad car came screeching to a halt in front of the building.

"Sure, sure," he spit into the cell. "The apartment upstairs, with the dormer windows, over that Minerva place. That where it happened?"

He yanked out a notebook and jotted down some information. Then he dropped the notebook and pen, and stood there on the forbidden side of Rampart Street, his mouth hanging open, unable to believe his ears.

"You kidding me? The officers found the gal dismembered in the oven?" he shouted into the cell. "Like the boyfriend was going to eat her?"

## Higher Ground

At that moment, Gary Cherry waved to him from across the street. Before Lieutenant Panarello knew it, the three of them were marching across the neutral ground toward him dragging the yapping wiener dog, their faces contorted like Halloween masks with shock and horror.

# II

# Skull in a Jester's Cap

# Eight

THE FRONT-PAGE STORY IN THE Friday, February 10, *Times-Picayune* held Nicole's full attention. The headline read: BOYFRIEND CUT UP CORPSE, COOKED IT.

How had her mother managed to get mixed up in *that*? It certainly was time for an intervention.

The story, Nicole noted with a shudder, began as a storm-tossed French Quarter romance. Deckie Hall spent the night the hurricane hit with a man named Hunter Finn, and a color picture of them smoking on a French Quarter stoop appeared under the headline. The Deckie girl had pierced eyebrows and a mane of green hair, and Nicole was sure she had run into her somewhere, probably over the cooler of wilted vegetables at Tony's Superette. She looked like one of those hard-living waitresses who jumped from restaurant to restaurant in the Quarter. Nicole squinted at Finn, buffed and shirtless, covered with tattoos.

She just couldn't believe it.

There he was, Hunter the delivery boy from Tony's Superette, the same one she'd hired to help move the tombstone from the cemetery the afternoon she ran her car into Kelly's

FEMA trailer. Hunter had been so helpful she tipped him five dollars for half an hour's work. He seemed to enjoy the cemetery, and pointed out the Rosicrucian and Masonic symbols on several tombs. After he loaded the tombstone into her car, he hopped back on his mountain bike. Index finger pointed to the sky, he told Nicole, "As above, so below." She wanted to run after the bike to ask him what in the world that meant. Marky was always saying the same thing. But the tattooed delivery boy was gone.

Nicole slammed the paper down on the sofa bed. Hunter cooked the green-haired girl?

She peeked again at the story.

A week after the murder, Hunter left a three-page suicide note tucked into a Ziploc bag in his pocket when he jumped to his death from the rooftop bar of the Royal Orleans Hotel, his body covered with twenty-eight cigarette burns, one for each year of his life. In the note, he explained how he couldn't believe that he strangled the woman he had been so in love with after the storm. They had been holdouts together—glorious, free-wheeling outlaws—refusing to leave the Quarter even when confronted by National Guardsmen waving M-16s. Hunter made a charcoal stove out of a bucket and traded booze from the bar he looted for food and water. Several neighbors were quoted praising Hunter and Deckie as heroes. The couple saw to it that any neighbors left behind had whatever they needed to survive camping out in the stifling heat of a month without electricity, running water, gas, or any open businesses. A blurry black-and-white snapshot showed them on a balcony at night, clinking wine glasses in the glow from a kerosene lamp.

"You could actually see the stars over the Quarter," Deckie had told her friends. "It was so romantic."

Obviously, it didn't stay romantic for long after the lights flashed back on. The suicide note led police to the grisly scene at the second-floor apartment the couple had just rented at 826 Rampart Street, over Minerva's Owl Occult Bookshop. The cops found Deckie's head wrapped in tinfoil inside the freezer, next to a bag of peeled carrots and potatoes. In the oven her severed arms and legs had been sprinkled with spices and baked in aluminum roasting pans. The bloody torso was stuffed into a garbage bag inside the refrigerator. In the note, Hunter confessed to dismembering the body in the bathtub. Then he said something mysterious. That he wasn't ready to become an initiate, which was followed by some gobbledygook about crusades and ceremonies. The note was signed with a skull and crossbones.

The police found the bathroom gleaming and spotless. Quite an efficient little homemaker, thought Nicole, that Hunter Finn.

She put down the paper and counted on her fingers. Hunter must have strangled his girlfriend just six days after he moved the tombstone and was probably plotting the murder even while speaking to her. No wonder he liked the cemetery so much. She shuddered. What in the world was she doing in this hell hole? She pictured her quiet, suburban home on Caribou Lane in Austin, the yellow dahlias blooming like pumped-up suns and the collie racing across the St. Augustine lawn. Now it was Buster's collie and Buster's home. Buster's and the new Mrs. Doctor's, that is. She could make out Buster dressed in Bermudas, seated at the glass table on the patio downing a margarita. A Jerry Jeff Walker song was pouring onto the patio through the sliding glass door, and a large slab of meat was grilling on the barbecue pit.

Could the slab on the grill be the new Mrs. Doctor?

Nicole sniggered and went back to the paper.

Neither Hall nor Finn was originally from New Orleans.

Both had arrived here within the past few years, part of a migration of disaffected young people who moved to the city before the storm looking for some lost Bohemia, rotating between gigs in bars and restaurants, renting cheap digs in the Quarter, Marigny, or Bywater. Marky's generation dropped acid and went to San Francisco with flowers in their hair. Her own generation ran away to New York to wear glitter and snort lines at Studio 54. Hunter's generation got tattooed and moved to New Orleans to become alcoholics. At this rate, Nicole wondered if the next generation shouldn't just stay home and play golf.

A grief counselor suggested that the horrendous crime was yet another example of the post-traumatic shock disorder that everyone in New Orleans was undergoing. A friend of Hunter's pointed out that he had spent two years deployed in Baghdad, and that the National Guardsmen who treated Quarter holdouts like Iraqi insurgents filled him with seething anger. Hunter kept protesting, "But I'm a Christian and an American citizen."

The final page of the story featured a color photo of the building's owner, Duffy Bordelon, the gay candidate running for mayor against Roy Blinger in the March primary. Standing next to him was Eliphas Labat, the proprietor of Minerva's Owl, a fleshy, bearded man in a purple tunic with sky-blue eyes. "Hunter was a higher being," Labat said. "I wonder what made him snap."

Nicole pondered the photograph. So that was what Labat looked like. Wasn't he the one who Gary said ordered the drive-by to kill her brother? To her, he looked so nineteenth century, more like one of the Wright brothers than a devil worshipper or murderer. But what did she know about judging a murderer? That afternoon in the cemetery, Hunter Finn had struck her as boyish and spacey, some mother's milk-fed son living out the wild life in the French Quarter before he settled down with two kids and a mortgage in River Ridge.

Nicole folded the paper. An approaching cough grew closer and closer on the sidewalk outside, and suddenly Kelly's dirt-smudged face was framed inside a pane of the French doors before they swung open into the living room. He was covered with plaster dust and stank like a drainage ditch. "That Lakeview look," Nicole called it. She didn't jump up to kiss him as she usually did.

"Hey, hey, hey," he chanted. "How many dump trucks did you count today?"

Nicole held up the newspaper headline.

"Today Thursday?" he asked.

"No, Friday."

"Thought Thursday was when the food section of the paper came out."

"That's sick. The guy who ate his girlfriend was the delivery boy I hired to help me move the tombstone." She bared her teeth in a silent scream. "Remember?"

"He didn't eat her. News on the car radio just said they tested his guts for human remains, and no dice. Must have just been trying out the recipe."

"Momma is somehow mixed up in this, you know." She reclined back onto the sofa bed to luxuriate like an odalisque, one nipple peeking out of her half-unbuttoned FEMA blouse.

Kelly coughed, stripping off his shirt. "So who she fixed for dinner tonight?"

"Sounds unlikely, but Momma said that Gary found out in jail the guy who runs Minerva's Owl is the one who hired the drive-by to kill Marky. Now she's not only dealing drugs but talking crazy about murder and black magic. Look," she said, flipping through the paper to Labat's picture. "That's him. And the other one owns the building and is running for mayor."

"Anybody can beat Blinger," he said, kicking off his cargo pants.

"So she and Gary and Sweet Pea walked Schnitzel to the bookstore just to snoop around but it was closed because the police had already arrived. Then they ran into that lieutenant what's-his-face, who questioned them about why they happened to be at the crime scene. They asked him about what Gary overheard the cops discussing—something about arms and legs in an oven—but he wouldn't reveal much."

Kelly was standing stark naked in front of Nicole, his rose mushroom tip rising to attention until it pointed straight at her. "Come here, babe, and gimme some sugar."

"Yuck. Go take a shower." Nicole recoiled. "You're all covered with Lakeview."

He lunged at her. "I could just eat you up."

"Help!" She glided off the sofa bed and ran screeching into the bedroom. "I'll see you in the bathroom. I need a shower, too."

He caught her from behind. "Okay, hot stuff, meet me in the bathtub," he growled into her ear. "First let me find my hack saw."

She shrieked, trying to wiggle free, and then they collapsed together onto the Beautyrest mattress in a writhing heap of giggles.

"Boy," said Gertie, collapsed into a lawn chair in her parlor. "You see that look on the lieutenant's face when the cop introduced him to Labat? Wouldn't even shake the fat man's hand."

Gary was feeling shaky after his run-in yesterday with Panarello in front of Minerva's Owl. The cop had glared at him like, *hey, every time somebody gets murdered in the Quarter, you pop up*. He was afraid that the lieutenant was going to run him in again. Then Gertie had her own meltdown, wringing her hands and moaning, "There ain't enough soap in the world, there just ain't enough soap in the world." Panarello acted like quite the gentleman and offered to drive them home. Of course, Gary and Sweet Pea were frequent fliers in cop cars and so declined the invitation. Besides, Gary was holding. He whispered to Miss Gertie not to breathe a word to the lieutenant about what he learned in the queens' tank. It would blow everything for the cop to stick his big fat nose into the situation, like chasing a snake with a machine gun. After a lot of noise, that slimy Labat would just slither away.

The phone bleated on the floor, and Miss Gertie reached down to answer it.

"Speaking. This is Mrs. Naquin." She sat up straight, brow furrowed, then covered the speaker with one hand and whispered to Gary, "A friend of Marky's. Bob White. Know him?"

Gary shrugged. Wait a minute, hadn't Marky mentioned that he used to take someone named Bob White to spiritual discussions at Minerva's Owl? In spite of his goofy name, this guy might know something about Labat.

"Yes, Dr. White. . . . So you saw the obituary in the paper?" Gertie said. "It came out late but we were in shock, too. . . . No, we have the ashes and my daughter is going to organize the memorial service after Mardi Gras."

They had postponed the service until sometime after Mardi Gras, now just a couple of weeks away. After Twelfth Night, when the Carnival season officially started, time split into two hemispheres, before and after Mardi Gras. When the first parades began to roll, even death and taxes were postponed until after Mardi Gras. Nobody could think straight about anything serious, much less a funeral.

"Where did you meet Marky?" Eyebrows raised, Gertie cupped the receiver again with one hand and mouthed to Gary: *says they met in the mental hospital.*

Gary twirled an index finger around his ear.

"You weren't his doctor? . . . Oh, so you two was locked up together. That's sweet." Gertie grimaced. "I see. So then you became a psychiatrist. Guess one thing leads to the other in this life, don't it? . . . Oh, you couldn't miss my boy more than me, Dr. White."

Miss Gertie was starting to choke up, so Gary stepped out into the courtyard, where he could still hear the murmur of her voice like some mournful fountain. Gregarious as she appeared, the old lady was an intensely private person. She was doing better, but occasionally broke down, spending whole days in bed on crying jags. Last week she confessed to him—after exacting the solemn oath to secrecy demanded by Southern ladies before divulging anything about themselves— that maybe she'd be better off in an old folks home. But then, a born saleslady, she bucked up, went out to clear fifty bills selling a new shipment of Percocet at the Laughing Buddha, and came home singing show tunes.

When Gary crept back into the parlor, Miss Gertie was slumped into her chair. "Bob White said he'd be in the Quarter this afternoon on some business, so we planned to meet. But you go see him. I'm some worn out after all that commotion yesterday."

"Where did you say you'd meet him?" Gary asked.

"Over by the Napoleon House around three. He invited me to his house in the Garden District for lunch on Saturday, but I couldn't get up there unless I drug along Nicole. And you know how whiny she can be. All she wants is to be in bed with that Kelly Cannon. She don't care if the world burns down around her."

"What about over here?"

"Honey, he introduced himself as Dr. Robert White. I can't ask some big doctor to come set down in these lawn chairs." Gertie's fist pounded the aluminum armrest.

"Marky told me he used to go to Mineva's Owl with someone named Bob White. Maybe he knows something about Labat."

"Said he and Marky was patients together at DePaul's, but looks like he couldn't stay away from the crazies. Told me he directs the Jung Center. Ever heard of it?"

"It's a far-out place Marky mentioned to me. They study the theories of Karl Jung, a psychologist into dreams and myths."

"Well, then you two will have plenty to talk about. I told him I'd bring along another one of Marky's friends. Thought you two could start planning the memorial service, or whatever y'all call it. Me, all I know about is wakes, where people get drunk and bawl. Excuse me, sweetheart, but after that Percocet, I got to lie down."

Gary rolled a couple of joints for this encounter, and flashing on the spiritual connection, put on his Tibetan mandala T-shirt. He felt like Nancy Drew setting off in her blue roadster to look for clues, in this case from a doctor on the patio of the Napoleon House.

# Nine

ONCE SEATED IN THE COURTYARD at a round wooden table, Gary didn't have long to wait. A trembling Mozart arpeggio was streaming through late afternoon shadows when Bob White emerged on the patio from the dank brick alleyway fronting Chartres Street. Under a flickering gas lantern, he swung around on creaking metal crutches to survey the tables. He was dressed in a pin-striped Oxford shirt beneath a rust corduroy sport coat with felt patches at the elbows. Balding, he wore rimless oval glasses and his whitish blond sideburns ended at a square jaw. As their eyes met, Gary sized him up: yeah, a shrink, but one who had probably dropped acid.

"Marky's mom couldn't make it," Gary said, standing. "But I'm Gary Cherry and was a good friend of his, so she sent me to talk about the memorial service."

Bob White seated himself, hoisting a prosthetic leg across his knee. He leaned his crutches against the peeling plaster wall and waved over the lone bow-tied waiter, who apologized that since the storm there was no food or menu. The doctor ordered a Pimm's cup, and Gary was already sipping a Nehi Orange through a straw.

# Higher Ground

Bob White took one look at Gary's frizzy hair and mandala T-shirt, and then the two immediately entered into a conversation as if they were old friends. Gary noticed that many people his age, now graying pillars of the community, responded to him as if he were a welcome time out from the tedious charade of being an adult. Like Clark Kent, they would rip open their mild-mannered, middle-aged disguises to reveal whatever might be left of a joyous hippie heart.

It turned out that while Gary and Marky had been hanging out together during the seventies at the Bodhisattva commune in the Haight-Ashbury, Bob White had been a student at Berkeley and then wound up tripping his brains out at the Esalen Institute at Big Sur, acting as a psychic lifeguard for spaced-out rich guests who tottered too close to the edge. It was there that Bob White became hooked on psychology in general and Jung in particular. He returned to New Orleans to enroll in Tulane Medical School and later trained as an analyst at the Jung Institute in Zurich. Now he was married with one grown son and lived in the house his parents had left him in the Garden District. Somewhat defensively, he claimed that he had seen little of Marky since the opening of "In the Shadow of the Shadow," an art exhibition that the doctor had curated several months before the storm at the Jung Center. Bob White, all milky complexion and social graces, was really into the Shadow.

"So why were you in DePaul's?" Gary asked. "Dope?"

"No. Parents," Bob White answered with a crooked smile. "My daddy was a King of Comus, and obviously I wasn't going to be. My room at home was filled with black-light posters and copies of the San Francisco *Oracle*. Drugs? Sure. But my parents drank like fish. They didn't care how I got high. What threatened them were my ideas," he said, tapping his temple. "DePaul's was a rite of passage for any Uptown kid who got out of line. But I figured if 'crazy' had to be my adult identity, I might as well be a shrink. It's like cops and robbers. Shrinks and crazies are the same people, only on two different sides of the power game."

"Don't need to tell me." Gary thought about the jailers and the jailed at Parish Prison, the so-called girls and their "straight" boyfriends in the queens' tank. The only reason he'd never stop being a criminal was because he was afraid he'd turn into a cop like Vinnie Panarello. Gary suspected that he had it in him, but that would be the day. "So why was Marky in DePaul's?"

"Back then he was misdiagnosed as schizophrenic, but everybody was. Now I'd say he had more of, let's see," Bob White said, fishing for the precise term, "an ego integration disorder. Marky had no boundaries, no stable development of the self, and just flowed until he became whomever he was with."

Years ago in San Francisco, Gary had noticed that Marky's chief fascination was how he could turn into a psychic mirror for those around him, one in which they could discern their own true faces. For Gary, Marky had always seemed something of a rebellious seeker and explorer, reflecting his own impulses. But now he could see that Kelly remembered Marky as a hell-raising wild man, Nicole saw him as damaged and fragile, needing constant care, and his mother spoke of him as a lonely little boy looking for home. With his chestnut curls, dancing eyes, and that pogo-stick energy, Marky was Mercury incarnate and seemed to sprout wings at his ankles as he walked. And like mercury, the liquid metal, he was always changing shape, reflecting light, merging. Meeting him was an instant personality test, and Gary always could figure out what made people tick based solely on what they loved about Marky.

"So what was Marky like back then," Gary asked, drinking in the doctor's face. "I mean, with you?"

"Crazy as a loon." Bob White threw back his head and howled. "At group therapy sessions, when his turn came, he would just chant in a singsong, 'I me mine I me mine.' Marky was so tired of thinking and talking about himself, he could puke. He said psychotherapy turned people into self-centered hysterics. Whenever I would obsess about myself, Marky would lead me into the kitchen to chop vegetables. So I was drawn to him." Bob White lowered his eyes. "We became lovers."

"Oh?"

"And continued to be, on and off, until six years ago, when Marky insisted we spend the final night of the millennium together. But then our bond grew even stronger."

"I thought there might be a faggot in the woodpile," Gary said. "He was my boyfriend, too, in San Francisco. They called us the Gemini Twins."

"He's the only man I've ever slept with," Bob White said, shaking his head. "I miss him so much. He was my brother, the holy fool I never let myself become. The other *me*."

It never failed: Marky the mirror. Yet Gary wondered if Marky recognized himself in the mosaic of shattered mirrors that covered the walls of his room. Did the fragmented reflections of everyone who loved him ever cohere into his own face?

"And what about your wife?" Gary asked.

"We're open."

"That open?"

"Margot didn't see Marky as competition. She also fell for the handsome devil and slept with him, too."

"This is starting to sound *sooo* Uptown," Gary drawled.

Bob White laughed through perfectly capped teeth. "Can

I buy you a drink?" he asked, draining his Pimm's Cup.

"I don't drink," Gary said. "But we can do this." He held up the joint.

"Not in the Napoleon House, man. Are you crazy?"

"Marky would."

"You're right," Bob White said, smiling. "Marky was always quoting Aleister Crowley: 'Do what thou wilt shall be the whole of the Law.' Except usually he did what he 'wilt' with other people's money. To tell you the truth, I really got tired of being hit up for cash every time I saw him, but I suppose that was part of his raffish charm. Waiter, another's Pimm's Cup. And an ashtray, please."

Gary lit the joint and passed it under the folds of the white table cloth. After one hit, the doctor turned dreamy and distant. "Marky terrorized people when we were in DePaul's. One day he found this big old rusted hook lying next to the high brick wall that separated us from Henry Clay Avenue. He scrunched up a hand inside his long sleeve, inserted the hook, then hung by the hook from the iron fence. Folks walking by freaked, thinking he was the hooked madman from the urban legend, you know, the one who escaped from DePaul's and crept around Audubon Park at night, attacking couples making out in cars." Bob White laughed until tears welled in his eyes.

Then he broke down and sobbed.

"What a cut up," Gary said, handing him a napkin. He put out the joint in the ashtray and slipped it into his pocket. No more medicine for the doctor.

"Marky probably missed his calling as a terrorist," Bob White said, wiping his eyes. "It was a drive-by, right? Do the police know who did it?"

"The fuzz think I had something to do with it, so a detective dragged me down to Parish Prison. It wasn't a complete bummer because I scoped out who ordered the drive-by."

"Who do you think?" The doctor shifted in his seat.

Gary studied Bob White, who had taken off his oval specs, polishing them with the napkin. Should he risk it? He took a deep breath. "He runs a bookstore on Rampart Street that you might remember. Minerva's Owl."

The doctor's mouth fell open. For a while he just stared at the ashtray.

"Well, well, well," said Bob White, straightening up. "Eliphas Labat. How that name keeps popping up when least expected. Marky dragged me to his bookshop a few times. Eli is from here but was a student at Berkeley while I was there, and later he turned up at Esalen. None of us lowly staffers at Esalen trusted Eli. He was always involved in some nefarious cult and for a while represented an outfit that sold lessons in mind control. A real hustler."

"Now he's part of some group called the Mani, and Marky was at odds with them. Said they were dangerous and into black magic. He may have tried to expose them."

"Yes, I'm familiar with them. Mani, if I remember correctly, was a Mesopotamian mystic, and the Mani is an offshoot cult that traces its lineage back to the Manichean Cathars in Southern France. They were part of the dualistic tradition that goes back to Egyptian Gnosticism and claim God may run heaven, but the devil rules the earth. The church branded it the Albigensian heresy, and the Cathars were defeated in the fourteenth century. When was Marky trying to expose this Mani cult?"

"Their run-in may have happened right after the storm," Gary said, "when he came back. The devil sure ruled the city then."

"Give me your phone number," Bob White said, rearranging his prosthetic leg. He wobbled to his feet and, reaching for his crutches, glared at Gary with storm clouds gathering in his eyes. "Look, pal, you might as well go ahead and ask why I'm crippled. That's what you're really thinking, isn't it?"

"Well, I—" Gary was stunned by the sudden accusation.

"It happened three years ago with Marky, in a car accident in Mandeville."

"I'm sorry."

"Like Marky, my phantom limb still haunts me. Damn," said Bob White, checking his watch." I just missed a consultation I had at four o'clock. Police work. I was supposed to meet with a detective at the Eighth District to go over the case of a young man who committed suicide yesterday. I'll have to reschedule, although I don't know when. I'm one of the handful of psychiatrists left in the city, and they call me for everything. This detective sounded overly friendly, and I'll bet he wants to ask another favor of me, too. Since the storm, the police can't keep up."

"Is this about Hunter Finn?"

"Oh, so you saw the news. Finn had been a patient of mine at Veterans' Hospital after he was released from the army. He was already disturbed, but the hurricane did a real number on people's psyches and brought out whatever nastiness lay buried inside."

"Don't tell me it's Lieutenant Panarello you're going to meet."

"How did you know?"

"Don't mention a word to him about Labat."

"Why should I?" the doctor asked, an edge to his voice.

"He's on Marky's case, too. And I don't want the cop to run in there with guns blazing. Labat could wrap the fuzz around his little finger, and then we'd never be able to corner him. I want him to pay for this murder."

"I see what you mean," Bob White said, drifting into thought.

"You know, Hunter and Deckie lived in the apartment right over Labat's bookshop."

"Interesting."

"Hunter and Labat were in tight." Gary wondered if the shrink was even listening to him.

"More interesting." The doctor turned toward the door.

Gary followed closely behind. "What kind of relationship could they have had?"

Bob White pivoted around on his crutches. "The next time we meet, let me tell you what I know about mind control. Let's just say that Eliphas Labat didn't waste his time studying it for nothing. His outfit's slogan was 'Decide, Dominate, Destroy.'"

# Ten

KELLY COULDN'T RESIST A FAT FEMALE—crab, that is—and so on Thursday afternoon he decided to pick up a dozen boiled ones at the first seafood shack to open its doors after the storm. Now the table in Nicole's kitchen was spread with soggy pages of *The Times-Picayune*, and he, Nicole, and Miss Gertie sat around cracking claws and lifting Abita Ambers to salty lips. Kelly still chuckled at the swamp wisdom of the old blue-legged lady he'd met after the storm. And what she said was so true. The crabs were fatter this winter. Only he didn't want to think about what these clawed scavengers had gorged themselves on.

After being airlifted off his rooftop in Lakeview, Kelly had been dumped at the makeshift triage center set up at the airport. There, moaning between luggage carousels, were the scores of dying patients evacuated in helicopters from flooded Memorial Hospital. The scene was like a primitive Civil War hospital dropped into a shopping mall. Some patients were hooked up to impromptu IVs, some strapped barely conscious into wheelchairs, while others had curled into fetal positions on the floor, foreheads glazed with sweat, waiting to die. He and

116

an old Cajun lady with a bandaged head and swollen varicose veins were staring like zombies at a generator-powered TV, mesmerized by the CNN coverage of the nasty brown waters swirling with dead things.

"I tell you for true, cher," she said, turning to him and cackling, "there gonna be some fat crabs this year, yeah."

Even though Kelly was enjoying the storm crabs, he tried to distance himself from the family cat fight at the table. Unfortunately, a week-old copy of *The Times-Picayune* had been spread out with the story of the murder-suicide face up, and they found themselves sucking spicy claws over the haunting faces of Hunter Finn and Deckie Hall. One fist around a beer, Miss Gertie was flicking crab shells out of the way to read aloud whole paragraphs of the story, bifocals sliding to the tip of her nose.

"Momma, just stop it!" Nicole demanded. "We're trying to eat."

"Gary told me that Labat is a devil worshipper who hypnotizes people," Gertie said. "I'll bet you anything he used mind control to make that Hunter boy do what he done."

"How?" Nicole rolled her eyes.

"He could have planted an electrode in his head when he wasn't looking—"

"You're talking crazy," Nicole said, reaching for the pecan cracker they used to open claws. "You sound like those homeless people ranting about how Satan stuck a transistor radio in their brains. People need to take responsibility for their actions and not just blame the devil or the government."

"Gary went on the computer and found out a lot about how the government been using people for years to test mind control and ESP and other monkey business."

"I know for a fact," Kelly said, leaning back and trying to appear impartial, "that the CIA did give LSD to hundreds of unsuspecting soldiers back when they were trying to beat the Ruskies at the mind-control game."

"There," said Gertie, pointing a knife at her daughter. "You see, Miss Smarty Pants. Maybe the CIA was the one fed you that LSD up in New York and that's why you like you are, always contradicting your momma."

"For the life of me," Nicole sputtered, bolting up and throwing down a handful of crabby paper towels, "how could my own mother get mixed up with cannibalism . . . and mind control . . . and drugs . . . and perverts and—"

"Go on, say it. Murder. *Murder!* Cause somebody murdered my son, that's why. And I lost my house and my precious boy and everything I love in this world—"

Nicole winced. "Thanks."

"—and Gary found out in jail who killed him. Labat probably tried to plant a seed in Marky's brain, but Marky wouldn't let him, so he hired some gunmen—"

"Kelly," Nicole said, the color draining from her face. "I'm going to bed. I can't listen to this raving insanity one more second."

After the old lady trudged next door, red-eyed and teary, Kelly rolled up the newspaper bulging with rank crab shells to store in the refrigerator. The freezer would kill the smell until the next garbage trucks lumbered through the Quarter, whenever that might be. In the bedroom Nicole was murmuring on her cell to Auntie Dixie. He could make out "talking crazy" and "selling drugs on the street" and "social worker." When he crept into bed, Nicole whisked the cell into the front room, where she rattled on half the night to that Uptown mummy kept alive by massive transfusions of gin and tap water.

# Higher Ground

THIS MORNING, KELLY'S HEAD POUNDED and a salty crab stink clung to the kitchen. The sink was stacked with plates milky with rancid potato salad, and the garbage was overflowing with beer bottles. Nicole had a point. The old lady was talking out of her head big time, but Nicole herself was acting so frantic that Kelly had only gotten a couple of hours of sleep. In a daze, he stumbled around the kitchen making coffee, the back shutters thrown open to the courtyard.

Usually this was an hour that Kelly cherished: Nicole had already left for work; her mother was zonked out on whatever pills she may be popping these days; and Gary's slave quarter was dead quiet, the midnight Rolling Stones broadcast long over. This was when Kelly, bundled up in his olive cardigan sweater, would sit under frayed banana leaves at the wrought-iron patio table nursing a hot mug of café au lait, birds twittering overhead and garden lizards darting through the first rays of sunlight falling across the crumbling brick wall held up by a dense tangle of ivy. Often a leprechaun smile would crinkle his pug-dog features as he sat there, grateful to be alive in the cool blue light of a new morning.

But standing at the stove, gulping a cup of coffee, he didn't have a good feeling about today. There was something about the way the sky had clouded over and the air had turned a soupy pewter-gray. Sometimes the futility of trying to restore the house in Lakeview alone, while its considerably pissed-off half-owner was suing him for divorce, rose up to smash him over the head with a two-by-four.

What had to be done, as he explained to his wife a million times, was to strip the walls down to the wooden studs and then swab them with bleach to keep the mold from climbing into the attic. Once decay reached the attic, their house would collapse on itself like a jack-o'-lantern a week after Halloween. The mold had gotten a galloping head start during the two

119

months after the storm when National Guardsmen with M-16s crossed over their chests kept residents out of their neighborhoods. Lena didn't understand anything about mold remediation but had to recognize how important the house was to him. No matter what the settlement, of course, the house would be his. Because he deserved it. He really did. After all, she never cottoned to New Orleans and had no intention of ever living here again.

Come on, why would she want the house?

The last Kelly heard, she had gotten a job as a docent at Sundown Plantation in St. Francisville. Her maiden aunt had been the grade-school teacher of the current administrator—or some small-town shenanigans like that—so the old biddy just snapped her fingers and now Lena was dressed in a hoop skirt and bonnet, leading tour groups around the plantation that some great-great-great relative once owned before his legendary fornications led the family to the poor house after the Civil War. Maybe that was where Lena belonged, ensconced in a glass vitrine in the past—his past. The bride and groom from atop their wedding cake had probably floated from the flooded china cabinet to join the other sweet memories of a lost city at the bottom of a lake crawling with fat crabs.

Walking down Dauphine Street to his car—parked way the hell on the other side of Frenchmen Street in the Marigny—Kelly was tempted to turn on his heels to slide back between the sheets and spend the morning snoozing. But if he didn't get a move on, he might miss Jesús at the gas station, and then nothing would get done today.

Last week he had picked out Jesús from the gang of Mexican workers loitering in front of the Shell station at Lee Circle and hired the hardworking guy to help him rip corroded wiring out of the stripped walls. Jesús told him, as best he could in his broken English, that he was working freelance now because the previous week he'd been stiffed by the subcontractor who hired him to lay blue roofing tarps. After a solid week of grunt and sweat, the sleazeball who hired him said, "Hey, amigo, I don't pay you, my boss does," and gave him an address. When Jesús went to that address, he was given the address of another boss, who referred him to yet another boss, who had gone out of business and left the state two months earlier.

There was Jesús now, huddled in a red windbreaker, nursing a Styrofoam cup of coffee. Kelly nosed the SUV into the Shell station, and ten Latinos rushed over to his car window. Kelly waved them away and honked the horn, waving at Jesús, who shot him a lopsided grin and a thumbs-up.

"Hey, Geesus, ready to crawl back on the cross?" Kelly asked, leaning out of the car window. "Need some help hooking up those wiring and air vents we got at Home Depot. Twelve bucks an hour still okay?"

"Sure, boss." A short, barrel-chested young man jumped into the passenger side, the silver insetting in two front teeth flashing in a broad smile. They shook hands. The dark dinner plate of his Indian face looked haggard this morning, and Kelly figured he probably hadn't gotten much sleep either. After all, Jesús lived with his brother and cousin in a single room in the Bywater without hot water renting for three hundred dollars a week. They were from Playa Azul, a small seaside town in Michoacán, although the brother had lived for two years without papers in Atlanta doing carpentry. Jesús and his cousin José Luis, fishermen without their own boat, had answered the brother's call to come do construction after the storm. They hoped to earn enough money to buy a trawler and set themselves up in the swordfish business in Playa Azul, although Jesús couldn't stop ogling huge cars and blond gringas on the streets of New Orleans.

Kelly flicked on the radio, not yet awake enough for

charades with Jesús. His head felt bigger than a breadbox.

"Four American soldiers were killed today," the newscaster intoned, "in a suicide bombing at a crowded intersection in Baghdad. The death toll of American military in Iraq has now reached three thousand."

"America bery estrong." Jesús mimed a machine gun spraying bullets through the windshield.

"Yeah, right."

"*Los méxicanos tocan la guitarra*," Jesús said, strumming air guitar, "*y echan la siesta.*" He dropped his head and snored. Then winked.

"I'll take the guitar and the siesta any day," Kelly said, cutting off the war news on the radio. "Superman is shit."

"*Supermán es una mierda.*" Jesús chortled, clapping his hands. "*Y la migra también,*" he said, slipping his wrists into imaginary handcuffs. "Yesterday Immigration carry my brother Antonio *a la cárcel.*" He looked out through a barred window. Then he pointed to a swollen bruise on his forehead and mimed being hit with a club.

Kelly knew these people had a rough time in this country and admired their sense of adventure and strong work ethic. Americans used to have that risk-all, can-do attitude, then something went soft and they became a bunch of over-insured wusses haggling in court. Now everything was "for your own safety," a canned phrase that made Kelly's blood boil. After the storm, that was what the soldiers at the roadblock had told him when he tried to sneak into Lakeview with the fake Red Cross ID he concocted at Kinko's. "For his own safety" he wasn't allowed to drag out the soggy carpeting and save his house from rotting. He should have told those National Guardsmen what the blue-haired lady in front of him had shouted back at them as she gunned her engine to speed past their roadblock: "So shoot me."

# Higher Ground

Judging by the determined attitude of that old dame, Kelly was sure that if this monster hurricane had hit the city during his parents' or grandparents' time, the town would already be up and running by now. The minute the flood waters receded, they would have pulled out their hammers and just done it. There wouldn't have been any FEMA-this and Road Home Program-that, these double-talking Bring New Orleans Back Plans A, B, C, and D, this shuffling up to the Big House in Washington to ask Master pretty please if he could lend a hand, letting the whole city putrefy until Master could locate his checkbook and his conscience.

Kelly felt himself speeding into furious indignation again, through a motley forest of signs offering "house gutting" and "mold remediation." Cool it and smell the roses, he told himself, slowing down to enter Lakeview. He was building a new life with someone he loved, and his house would be finished in a matter of months. Everything was looking up. He spotted the smashed trailer in front of the wreck of his house and sighed as he pulled past the weeping willow into the driveway.

See, the glass was half full.

Home, sweet home. The very sight set him to coughing.

The front door stood ajar. That was funny, Kelly thought. He never locked it—couldn't even find the key—but he always shut it before he left.

"Hi, honey," he boomed, "I'm home." His work boots crunched along the gravely cement of the foundation, and he could take in the entire three-bedroom house through the skeletal wall joisting. Rolling up his sleeves, he stepped into the kitchen and then did a double take.

All the new stuff was gone.

"What the fuck?" He paced around the kitchen floor, now empty of the coils of copper wiring, plastic tubing, pipes, air vents, and crated central-air units. Just this Wednesday Jesús had helped him lug the equipment in the back of the SUV from Home Depot. It had taken four trips and maxed out Kelly's Visa.

"Geesus," Kelly shouted, "get your wetback ass in here." When Jesús stumbled into the kitchen, his sleepy brown eyes bugged out. "*¿Dónde se fueron los hilos eléctricos y las tuberías?*" he asked with a blank look on his face, miming wires and pipes wiggling away like snakes.

Kelly rushed over, grabbed him by his windbreaker collar, and shook him.

"You fucking beaner thieves," he shouted. "So you and your amigos snuck in here last night and vamoosed my stuff, huh? Where is it, goddamn it? Speak up, spic, or I'm gonna slit your throat." Kelly whipped a utility knife out of his cargo pocket and held the blade against Jesús's throat.

"*Suélteme, pinche pendejo,*" Jesús shouted. "Let go." He kicked Kelly in the shin and jumped back, pulling a switchblade from his back pocket and flicking it open in one smooth gesture.

Kicking warped floor tiles out of the way, the two circled each other like cats, knives held erect at chest level.

Kelly lunged. "Take me to my stuff," he spit out, "or I'm on the cell to Immigration pronto, asshole."

"*No sé nada.*" Jesús jerked back. "*Te robaron unos ladrones.* Stealers," he whimpered. "Stealers come here. Me, nothing."

Eyes hooded with suspicion, Kelly studied the quivering young man. Jesús and his cousin José Luis didn't have a truck, but what Mexican didn't know someone with a goddamn truck? Who else would have known he had a kitchen full of expensive building supplies? But if Jesús had ripped him off last night, would this jerk have jumped into the car this morning? Would he have risked getting caught lifting thousands in building equipment for a lousy hundred bucks in day wages? Why waltz back onto the scene of the crime with a smile on his face? No, Jesús wasn't stupid.

Kelly was.

Lakeview at night was rife with well-organized gangs of locals carting off anything not bolted down. Circling the neighborhood late last night, they must have spied the dark, crumpled FEMA trailer out front and thought, hey, this sucker is rebuilding but isn't here. Then they tried the door. Open.

*Come rip me off,* the whole scene screamed.

Kelly threw his knife clattering to the middle of the floor. He leaned back against the kitchen counter, lifted his head, bit his lower lip hard, and couldn't help but start sobbing. Let her rip. Bombs away. The storm. The flood. The rooftop. The airport. Houston. Lena. Macy's. His rotting house. His busted trailer. His broken city. Marky. Murder. Nicole's momma. Blinger. Iraq. The mess. The ugly, stinking mess he was in. His town was in. His country was in.

In a couple of months, Kelly would turn fifty.

"Oh, man," he groaned, yanking out a snot rag and blowing his nose like a trumpet.

Jesús slipped the switchblade back into his pocket and stood there staring at Kelly, as if for the first time in his life he'd witnessed a gringo act like a real human being. Like a Mexican, that is.

"*Cerveza?*" Kelly asked.

"*Sí.*"

"*Vamos.*" Kelly clapped his hands together. "Let's go."

KELLY AND JESÚS HAD ALREADY started on the first bottle of tequila when they swerved into the only gas station open in Lakeview. A rap song was blaring on the radio—Kelly didn't care what he was listening to at this point—and the engine smoking. Kelly leapt out the door and cupped his hands to his mouth.

"Hey, Hewitt," he bellowed.

Digging a roofing nail out of a tire, Hewitt was seated next to the Pepsi machine listening to a talk radio station turned up loud. He lumbered out to the gas pumps, squinting and waving.

"Kelly, where y'at," he said. "How Miss Gertie making?"

"Somebody just ripped off all my building supplies. Vents, copper wiring, air units, plumbing, everything. Seen any suspicious activity around here?"

Hewitt shook his head. "All I see these days. Suspicious activity."

"Government agencies are squelching free enterprise in this country," boomed the snarling voice on Hewitt's radio. "The good old American pull-yourself-up-by-your-bootstraps system. . . ."

At the same time, the SUV windows were vibrating to the woofer beat of a rap song: "Brotha got a rock that he pull up out his sock / But the nigga round the corner sell it for a quarter."

"What?" Kelly screamed over the cacophony of competing radios.

"Said that's *all* I see."

"Will you turn down that fucking radio?" Kelly's eyes bulged, a vein pulsing at his temple.

"It's my gas station, pal. You turn off that jungle music."

"Look, man, I just lost everything I been working for since the storm."

"Don't tell me what you lost. I'm sleeping in my damn car."

"See a truck with looted building stuff on the bed in the last twenty-four hours?"

"How I'm supposed to know if—"

"Don't bullshit me. You *know*. Probably tell 'em where the picking's good." Kelly could read it in Hewitt's shifty eyes. He was in on the heist.

"Get the hell out—"

Kelly raised his fist. Hewitt stepped back, grabbing a tire jack. Red-faced, the two men stood there screaming at each other while the radio commentator raved about "do-gooder tree huggers protecting cuddly owls" and the rap song crescendoed with electronic squeals celebrating "bizness in the hood."

Jesús leaned over to beep the horn. Then he staggered out of the car toward the men, the bottle of tequila in his outstretched hand.

# Eleven

NICOLE BUTTERED ROLL AFTER ROLL under the leaded crystal window at Arnaud's, waiting for Auntie Dixie to show up. Dixie had insisted that she take Nicole to lunch at the traditional French Quarter restaurant ("Since 1918," the sign said) before they drove to Magazine Street for a 4:30 p.m. appointment with Modene Holiday, the psychiatric social worker. The social worker was booked solid for weeks with storm-troubled clients, but since she and Dixie had worked together once on the Harvest House board, as a favor she made room in her schedule on late Saturday afternoon. Nicole had to do something about her mother. This case was straight out of the paranoid delusions chapter of her college psych textbook. She couldn't listen to any more about mind control and murder or spend any more time snooping around the French Quarter to find out what felonies her mother was committing.

And to top it off, now there was Kelly. He had come home late last night drunk out of his gourd with two Mexicans, raving about what he was going to do to the thieves who stole his building supplies. He laughed in Nicole's face when she suggested calling the police, and whenever she proposed a reasonable solution, started yelling "so shoot me." Kelly and the Mexicans slouched at the table in the courtyard until the wee hours, slurring in unintelligible Spanglish and draining a bottle of tequila.

This morning Kelly had been delirious and told her he was moving to Mexico, of all places. He would sell the house and take whatever money he had left to open some sort of fish restaurant on the beach in Plaza Azul. "Picture it," he told her. Nicole would be his *mujer*, dancing barefoot along the sand to serve beer at the tables of their thatched beach *palapa*. Evidently, he had already gone native and crawled back into bed for an all-day siesta. Nicole wondered how in the world she had become the stable one, Miss Reality Check. That was one role she never imagined herself playing. Usually, she was the distraught one, crying on the shoulders of the comforters gathered around her. Okay, so she had always been needy and now she was needed. If only she could rise to the occasion.

She just hoped nobody else went off their rockers. She was running out of shoulders.

Aunt Dixie strode into the dining room in a fake leopard-skin coat. The heart-shaped smear of crimson outlining her thin lips was the only definition on a pale parchment face. She caught Nicole's eye, marched over to the window table, and plunked down her drink.

"I thought you said one o'clock," Nicole said.

"I been in the bar," Dixie said, taking her seat in a huff. "Didn't think to look for me there?"

"But you specified the dining room."

"Said I couldn't smoke in here. You believe that bunch of baloney? I told the waiter, 'Honey, I been smoking at this table for fifty years, before you was born. So bring me an ashtray.' Then Sal the manager came over—old friend of Abe's—and bought me drinks in the bar, where you can still light up."

Dixie glanced around the empty restaurant. "Never thought I'd live to see the day. Sal said it was because of the tourists they got to cater to now. Think everywhere they go is their own living room."

Nicole didn't want to get into another argument with her aunt about second-hand smoke, not on the afternoon she was planning her mother's intervention.

"So, how's my favorite niece?" Dixie asked, patting Nicole's hand.

"Your only niece is wiped out. I didn't get any sleep on Thursday after the blow out with Momma, when I was up all night talking to you. Then last night Kelly came in plastered."

"I told you about them Irish," Dixie said, shaking her head. "Why don't you go out with a nice Jewish man. Abe's nephew Nathan, very well-to-do in the mattress business, says this time he wants to marry a sexy *shiksa* like his Aunt Dixie. Why don't I invite you two—"

"I don't want to be some mattress king's *shiksa*. I've been in love with Kelly since I was sixteen. Everything else has been a mistake. But after his building supplies were ripped off, he's talking about moving to Mexico."

"That's where Americans go to drink themselves to death," Dixie said, rattling the ice cubes in her gin. "What the hell would he do in that filthy place?"

"He said something about starting a restaurant on the beach and selling swordfish grilled on sticks to—"

"Ain't that pathetic. Who's going to buy fish sticks from him? Mexicans can't even afford Mexican food."

"He's ready to give up on New Orleans. Everybody is."

"Terrific news. Listen up. Bitsie Landry's son Mike is running for mayor in the March primary. He'll be a shoo-in after that nincompoop Roy Blinger. We've got to take the city back from those people. Let Houston keep them, if you know what I mean."

"It's not just African Americans. Plenty of white people can't come home either," Nicole mumbled, hoping not to incite her aunt's tirade about welfare queens and fatherless kids, the one that went off like a car alarm at any mention of local politics. "Maybe Momma would have been better off if she'd stayed in Texas. What's there to come back to?"

Dixie explained that if her mother put up any resistance during the intervention, Modene could have her committed. All she had to do was pick up the phone and call the Coroner's Office, or at least that was what Dixie's in-laws had done to her twenty-five years ago when they confronted her about drying out. After Dixie threw a drink in her husband's face, they sent her to DePaul's, where friends smuggled in gin bottles hidden inside of gladiola arrangements. Nicole didn't want to contradict her aunt—that was always an invitation to trouble—but assumed that these days hospital commitments involved court hearings.

"Your momma gonna move in with me," Dixie croaked, snapping open the menu. "Uptown is doing just fine, thank you. I got a security system and a maid. Langenstein's grocery is five minutes away. What more could anyone want?"

"But she doesn't want to live with you."

"Then Modene will fix her little red wagon."

LATER THAT AFTERNOON, AFTER a lunch of shrimp remoulade, stuffed flounder, and more drinks on the house from Sal the manager, Nicole and Auntie Dixie rushed in high spirits into the office of Modene Holiday, who sat behind her desk and pointed out there might be one tiny snag in the intervention plan.

"Even if we do get a court order, there aren't any mental-health facilities open now in New Orleans," she said, adjusting her lacquered spit curls. "Can you believe that, with all of the unhinged people in this city after the storm? For an empty bed, we might have to send your mother to Houma or Thibodaux."

Then Modene pushed a half-eaten king cake frosted with purple, green, and gold icing to the center of the desk. She said one of her bipolar patients was revving up her annual Carnival mania with a sugar jag and had brought the cake from Gambino's to celebrate the first parades to roll this weekend.

"If I eat any more of this," Modene said, "I won't fit into my Cleopatra costume. Y'all going to the parades tonight?"

Shaking their heads, Nicole and Dixie peered at the garish coffee cake.

Modene Holiday reminded Nicole of one of those wise-cracking older women, the sadder-but-wiser types who steered volatile chorus girls through their troubles in the black-and-white movies she used to watch on cable in New York. Maybe it was the polka-dotted scarf knotted around her neck or the adenoidal voice, but Nicole keep imagining that she was talking to Agnes Moorhead, capable if slightly grating.

"I assume your mother has Medicare," Modene said, taking notes. "Private hospitalization insurance?"

"She dropped that after the storm," Nicole said. "Couldn't afford it. I really don't understand how she makes ends meet. All of Daddy's Shell pension and their Social Security go to paying the insurance, taxes, and note on a house where she can't live. I guess my mother gets the money to pay rent by dealing drugs. I can't believe I just said that, but it's true."

"She won't have any expenses at my house," Dixie said. "She can live high on the hog. Of course, if she prefers a padded cell in Houma to State Street—"

"Will you be present during the intervention?" Nicole asked Modene.

"If you want me to, sure," Modene said. "But that may make her feel like we're ganging up on her."

"Well, we are," Dixie said with a cackle.

"For her own good, of course," Nicole added. "You should be there. Someone from outside of the family needs to point out that the bizarre stuff she's obsessing about is delusional. She must be stoned on something."

"Barbiturates?" asked Modene, glancing at her watch.

"Whatever pills she gets from the drug dealer in the slave quarter. Probably the same ones she tries to sell at the gay bar."

"It's that crowd she runs with," Dixie said. "Nothing but queers and niggers."

Nicole bridled at her aunt's remark. "She just needs a long rest."

"We all do," Modene said, filling out a form. "Since the storm this whole town has turned into an open-air mental hospital. Your mother's case isn't that unusual. Older folks who lost their homes are dropping like flies from stress and depression. One week you hear they've moved from a FEMA apartment into assisted living, and the next week they're gone. People are abusing drugs, snapping left and right, not sleeping for weeks, throwing tantrums in insurance offices, getting into fist fights over parking places, divorcing, drinking too much, and beating up on their kids or wives."

"Has that Kelly ever hit you?" Dixie asked, turning to Nicole.

"Of course not," Nicole said. "He's very loving."

"Her boyfriend wants to move to Mexico and sell fish sticks," Dixie told Modene, as though it were a reportable offense.

"Let me tell you, last month I was in Puerto Vallarta, and after the dysfunction I see in New Orleans now, Mexico was like Switzerland. Everything seemed so clean and efficient, and the people so reliable."

"Look, when can we do this?" Nicole was twisting the handkerchief she'd used to dab her eyes while recounting the long story of her brother's murder.

"Has she threatened to harm herself or another?" Modene asked.

"Not really," Nicole whispered.

"She threatened me plenty," Dixie barked. "Said if I didn't shut my big trap she'd throw me out in the gutter with my gin bottles."

"Okay," said Modene, winking at Nicole. "I can't get to this until after Mardi Gras. I'll have to prepare some preliminary paperwork if we're going to seek a court commitment. Let's see. March 1. Actually," she said, flipping through a calendar, "that's Ash Wednesday, if it's okay?"

"Eleven whole days from now?" Nicole whined. "Why not tomorrow?"

"Think I like coming in on weekends to deal with a bunch of nuts?" Modene's face flushed red, temples pulsing. She bolted up, hands trembling as she stuffed the papers into a folder. "Who do you people think I am, Mother Teresa?"

Nicole and Dixie shot looks at each other.

"I'm sorry." Modene took several deep breaths. "Any stress at the moment makes me act out. I'm living in a FEMA trailer in Kenner. My house on Calhoun Street got four feet. I don't think I can do," she said with a pasted-on smile, "any more than I do do."

"Come live with me and Gertie," Dixie said. "The more, the merrier."

Modene Holiday briskly escorted them through her waiting room. "I'll call you bright and early on Ash Wednesday," she told Nicole, slamming the door behind them.


"WELL!" SAID NICOLE, SEATED AGAIN inside her aunt's Cadillac.

"That Modene was always a little peculiar," Dixie said, sucking on a Kent.

So, thought Nicole, Miss Reality Check went to cry on somebody else's shoulder for a change and that person threw up on her. What ever did that foul-tempered bitch mean by "a bunch of nuts?"

They turned onto Pleasant Street and drove in glum silence approaching St. Charles. The brassy strut of a high school marching band soon rose to meet them. In the distance was a crowd, and a glittering papier-mâché Red Cross boat was sailing under the canopy of live oaks. Everyone was waving their arms and screaming, jumping up and down as if Jesus Christ were passing out cashier's checks.

"Hey," shouted Dixie to a stocking-capped man with a grubby boy on his shoulders clutching a handful of plastic beads, "what parade is this?"

"This one Sparta. Next one be Pegasus. Happy Carnival, y'all," he said, pumping his fist in the air.

"Who wants to see these tacky krewes?" Dixie raised her window and turned the corner, taking Harmony Street back toward the river. "Abe used to ride with Hermes, and I wouldn't miss that parade or ball for anything. This year Blinger tried to cancel Carnival, but we wouldn't let him. That's the only thing this city knows how to do right any more."

When they turned onto Tchoupitoulas, a dimly-lit street of abandoned warehouses running along the river, they found themselves stuck behind the empty floats of a disbanded parade rumbling back to the barn. Their headlights illuminated the float in front of them, one bearing a wobbly caricature of Mayor Blinger dressed as Moses. He was carrying a stone tablet marked FEMA and pointing the way through tinselly red waves. On the rear of the float was a scroll that read *Let My People Go.*

"How in the dickens did we wind up behind this mess?" Dixie lit another Kent.

"Doesn't this just say it all?" Nicole said, starting to tear. It was as if she were part of some funeral cortege for the city, stuck behind the riderless floats of a Carnival parade lumbering through the darkness, undoubtedly following the dump trucks she counted every day as they carted off the soggy possessions of the dead and gone.

These days Nicole couldn't separate herself from an end-of-the-world feeling. It followed her as she peered into the plate glass windows of closed store fronts, empty but with huge NOW OPEN banners strung out front; as she called one disconnected phone number after another; as she drove along the spectral streets of her childhood, following the water lines on the rotting houses; as she stepped out of the shower in the morning and realized she couldn't do a single thing she'd planned during the day because the stores and offices and restaurants weren't there any more, and when she did arrive at those few places where she could go, the bank was out of money and the gas station out of gas and the supermarket out of bread and onions.

At these moments it dawned on Nicole what she'd run out of.

A future.

"I couldn't wait to come home but now don't know what to do." Nicole pointed through the windshield to the corner. "Auntie Dixie, look at that broken traffic light manically blinking *go* and *don't go* at the same time. That's the mixed message I get everywhere in this crazy town: *stay, leave, stay, leave.* I don't know whether to plant a live oak that will take a hundred years to grow or to start packing my suitcase tonight. *Red, green, red, green.* It would be hard enough if the instructions were clear—stay or go, fight or flight. But day after day, getting both signals at once?"

"You can't just make yourself up at some U-Haul office." Dixie took an impatient suck on the Kent, the wrinkles puckering around her ruby lips. "Girl, you from *somewhere*, not like those lost souls spinning around on the freeways with nowhere to go. You don't seem to appreciate what we tried so hard to give you, a place to call home."

"Face it," Nicole said, eyes brimming. "One day I'll come knocking at your door or Momma's, and strangers will be living there. And the love of my life will be off in Mexico . . . I don't know, selling fish sticks. And here I'll be, working some dead-end job, old and alone in a shabby rental with broken pipes and a leaky roof, still waiting for the city to turn itself around and for that flashing red light to finally turn green. And you know something? The only green lights left in this town are like the ones at the end of *The Great Gatsby*, lights from the past."

"I don't give a rat's ass what color the light is, but I'm moving this crate down the road." Dixie blasted her horn at the stalled floats and then sped around them, straight through the intersection with the broken light. "Some of us don't have a choice. We were born here and we'll croak here, no matter what the stupid traffic light says, which we never pay no attention to anyway." She reached over to squeeze Nicole's shoulder. "Where else can you see a Hermes parade?"

"For years I dreamed of coming home for Mardi Gras, but now with Marky dead and Momma like she is and the city half gone. . . ."

"Honey, don't you know the worse you feel, the better Mardi Gras is. We don't celebrate because we don't have any problems, but because we got too many." Dixie threw back her head and laughed. "So this year is going to be a humdinger."

# Twelve

That was creepy, Vinnie Panarello thought.

The photo of a much younger Marky Naquin was lit by a votive candle on top of a bookcase in the darkened hallway to Dr. White's home office. After White had missed his appointment last week, the psychiatrist invited him to drop by this Saturday afternoon, explaining that he was booked solid during the coming week at his Touro Hospital clinic. Vinnie had been buzzed in from the iron fence surrounding the pillared mansion and almost got lost maneuvering the crooked brick pathway through a jungle of overgrown ginger bushes and banana trees. But eventually, toward the back, he stumbled upon the white carriage house the doctor had described. Inside the vestibule, carved tribal masks with bared teeth and protruding tongues leapt out at Vinnie from the blood-red walls. It smelled like church, the air musky with incense. He was just about to jump out of his skin when a toilet flushed.

"Hello," Vinnie called out. "Anybody home?"

A metallic creaking grew louder behind the door, followed by a hollow *thump thump thump*, and then a square blond head peered out.

"Lieutenant Panarello?"

Vinnie followed behind the limping man in the wool djellaba, who pointed to a seat. The room was lined with towering bookcases, and the lone green desk lamp cast menacing shadows behind gyrating, six-armed gods and severe Buddha heads mounted on pedestals. The psychiatrist swung around, sliding into a seat behind the monumental walnut desk. Then he adjusted his prosthetic leg and looked up.

What was this, Vinnie wondered, a voodoo confessional? And what was with this kook's hooded dress?

"I usually hibernate in here on weekends, away from all that," Bob White said, gesturing at the cracks of sunlight peeking between drawn velvet drapes. "I was just going over the notes for my book. Again, sorry I missed our appointment last Saturday at Eighth District. So you're on the Hunter Finn case?"

"Thanks for your time, doc," Vinnie said, studying the icy blue eyes magnified by rimless spectacles. "I heard you treated Finn at Veteran's when he first blew into town. What was the guy like, somebody who could pull a hideous stunt like that?"

"As depersonalized and delusional as you would expect from a soldier who had spent six months as a guard at Abu Ghraib prison in Baghdad."

"That the place where they made them Iraqis wear masks and do weird sex things?" Vinnie had been as fascinated as he was repulsed by the news images of buzz-cut American soldiers leading around naked prisoners by dog collars. In Nam he had gotten drunk with hookers after they massacred a village. Nothing kinky about that.

"Precisely," the doctor said, tapping a pencil eraser on a legal pad. "Finn was deeply disturbed by what he saw and the sadistic things he was told to do. That's why he was given a psychiatric discharge."

"Explains a whole lot, don't it?"

"Finn was good at following orders and gravitated toward strong authority figures. He adapted well to the jailer role," Dr. White said between clenched teeth, "as many people obviously do."

"So who ordered him to choke his girlfriend and chop up her body?"

"Voices." The doctor looked intently into Vinnie's eyes.

"In his head?" Vinnie averted the doctor's stare.

"When I was treating him before the storm, he suffered from acute aural hallucinations."

"His voices were pretty damn street smart. I mean, no corpse, no case. Obviously, his first thought was to cook down the body and then get rid of it, piece by piece, but then he panicked. And committed suicide."

"Lieutenant, you didn't come here to discuss Hunter Finn, did you?" Bob White steepled his fingers, staring at Vinnie. "You haven't taken a single note."

"Hey, you got ESP."

"So I've been told."

"Say, doc, what's up with this post-traumatic stress disorder, or whatever you call it?" Vinnie was fishing for a way to fit in his own little problem: negligent homicide.

"When the nervous system is under severe, life-threatening stress, it goes into survival mode fueled by adrenaline. When the threat has subsided, the numbing adrenaline disappears, and the system re-experiences the trauma, finally feeling the pain."

"So first you gotta go through something bad," Vinnie said, "then it gets to you." Yep, that fit him to a T. "So that's what Finn had, from the storm?"

"Yes," the doctor said. "And no."

"Oh."

"Although perhaps it's what you have," the doctor said, peering again into Vinnie's eyes.

"Boy, you smart as a whip. You got it, without me saying a word. Look, you ever heard about the shooting that happened in the Walmart parking lot after the storm?"

Vinnie leaned forward, elbows on knees, and recounted the whole incident, blow-by-blow: the lack of sleep, the heat, the call to the parking lot, the milling crowds, the gunshots, the teenagers running away, the slain deaf man and his thirsty dogs. He hammed it up as much as possible, the anguish about his own family, the looted Ding Dongs and instant coffee that kept him going, the corpses, the stench, the guy who kept racing toward him with a shiny metal thing in his hand. Had the gun found in the dumpster belonged to him or his cousin, did the teenagers toss it there, or did another cop plant it? Would the prosecution prove a police cover-up that would portray Vinnie as a liar? Could Vinnie plead temporary insanity?

"But you'd lose your job on the force," the doctor said, his fingers tented, thumbs on chin.

"I'm planning on an early retirement."

"And now, are you bothered by any recurring dreams?"

"Nightmares," the lieutenant said, "whenever I get to sleep, which isn't often."

"Appetite?" The doctor was taking notes.

"This sure as hell ain't Atkins," Vinnie said, pulling at his loose belt.

"Libido?"

"What?"

"Do you feel like fucking?"

Vinnie crossed his legs, hearing the question wrong, way wrong. Then it sank in. "Hey, after twenty years of marriage," he said, chuckling, "my wife and I finally agree on something. Now we both got a headache when it comes to that."

"Do you think life is worth living?" the doctor asked.

"Doc, let me tell you something. It's all about my kids at this point. To see them get through school, go to college, get married, be happy. If it weren't for them, I don't—don't know how. . . . You got any kids?"

"An older son."

"Doing good?"

"He's living in a Buddhist monastery in Thailand."

"Geez." Vinnie never had been able to figure out rich people. They sure didn't enjoy what they had.

"Since the grand jury has indicted you, you want me to testify on behalf of your temporary insanity plea when the case comes to trial," the doctor said, scribbling notes. "And to write a report on your post-traumatic stress disorder to justify an early retirement?" He put down the pencil, smiling.

"You hit the nail on the head."

"I'll have to speak with you in more detail over time. You have health insurance with the force, so there shouldn't be any financial issues. I want you to write down your recurring dreams. And to recreate your thoughts on paper the day of the shooting at the parking lot."

"You mean like a perm?" Vinnie had written a few poems years ago and had even started going to open-mike readings during an off-duty investigation in the Quarter. The poets called him "Lieutenant Girlfriend" because he first showed up in fruity undercover clothes carrying a book of poems by Oscar Wilde.

"Yes. Stream-of-consciousness. I need to be able to recreate your aberrant thoughts at the moment of the shooting for the jury."

"Anything else?"

"Yes," said Dr. Robert White, steadying his fingertips on the desk and then rising. "I want you to arrest Eliphas Labat for the murder of Marc Rousell Naquin."

Here we go, Vinnie thought. The tit for the tat.

"I saw Naquin's picture in the hall when I came in. You two was friends?"

The doctor glanced down at the shoe on his prosthetic leg. "Let's just say he's my phantom limb. I still feel him."

"So, who is this Labat," Vinnie asked, "and how do you know he killed Naquin?"

"Labat runs Minerva's Owl Bookstore on Rampart Street."

"That's right," Vinnie said, slapping his forehead. "That weird bearded guy." He shuddered, recalling the piercing look Labat gave him at the St. Jude altar. "Finn and that Deckie dame lived upstairs. But, wait a sec, who tipped you off he had something to do with Naquin?"

"I can't say."

"So, you think he's a person of interest in—"

"I don't think anything. I'm telling you he ordered that drive-by shooting. But whatever you do, don't involve me."

"But Dr. White, I need proof before I—"

"Then get it, Lieutenant Panarello, soon to be a former lieutenant, happily retired from the New Orleans Police Department, free as a lark."

"I see. You really want me to get this guy." Vinnie glanced up. On the wall behind the doctor's desk hung a huge faded tapestry, barely visible in the dusky office. It portrayed a bearded head served on a platter, eyeballs bulging out of the skull, held aloft by a dancing girl.

Vinnie squinted up at the tapestry. "That's one gory piece of art you got there, doc."

"It's St. John the Baptist and Salomé. Fourteenth century, Carcasonne, France."

"Must have cost a fortune," Vinnie said, backing toward the door.

I get it, he thought. The doctor will testify to get me off the murder rap, but in exchange, he is assigning me this task to perform, like in a fairy tale. A golden fleece. A sword buried in stone. A dragon to slay.

Bring him the head of Eliphas Labat.

# Thirteen

"WHAT'S IN THIS ONE?" GERTIE asked, prying open the flap of a Cutty Sark box.

"More books," Gary moaned, slumping into a lawn chair in Miss Gertie's parlor. He had no idea what a big job it would be to clean out Marky's room over the dry cleaner's on Barracks Street. "All I've found are books and more books. And bag after bag stuffed with papers. Thing is, it's real hard to read Marky's spidery handwriting."

"But he always got gold stars in penmanship." Gertie slipped a few books from the box and held them up to the light.

Gary realized how attached Marky's mother still was to the little boy he had once been and how little she knew about the man he'd become. Maybe going through his things would help her to put him in perspective. They had no choice now but to dump these boxes in her parlor and then stack them along the walls, next to the crates of belongings salvaged from her flooded house. The elderly dry cleaner who owned the building had contacted Gertie to ask that she clean out Marky's room before March 1. Either that or pay another month's rent. So Gary volunteered to haul the stuff over in his ancient Chevy van.

Gertie plowed through the box of books, reading off titles. "*A History of the Knights Templar, Violence and the Brain,* and hey, listen to this one, *Secret Agenda: The United States Government, Nazi Scientists, and Project Paperclip, 1945 to 1990.* I bet this explains everything." She held the book at arm's length, squinting at the type, then passed the dusty book to Gary.

"Here's some more," she said, handing him *Mind Wars* and *The Mind Manipulators.*

"Look," Gary said, holding up the cover of *The Mind Manipulators.* He pointed to a hand-drawn box inked around the first four letters of the word "Manipulators." "Get it? It says 'Mani,' the name of the cult that Labat belongs to, the one Marky accused of practicing black magic. Bob White says it goes back to fourteenth-century France." Gary paged through the book, eyes bugging out. Every time the words "manipulation," "manipulate," or "manipulator" appeared— on almost every page—Marky had drawn a black box around the first four letters.

"This is some twisted stuff," he said, engrossed in the book.

"I'm all turned around," she said. "Mind control? Fourteenth-century France? How does that fit in with my poor baby?"

"Your poor baby was onto something." He picked up another book, reading while she shoved the boxes into a corner.

"What else you find in that room?" Gertie asked. "Nicole went up there once, before the storm. Said the place smelled like a dirty clothes hamper and the walls was covered with Marky's writings. Why would he write on the walls? I feel sorry for that landlord and hope he don't charge me no damages."

"He told me he wrote on the walls," Gary said, not looking up from the book, "because it was like an Egyptian tomb."

"A tomb?"

"The walls of the vaults where they buried the Pharaohs were covered with a road map to the underworld from the *Egyptian Book of the Dead*. Marky was convinced that at the moment of his death he'd be able to work great magic."

Gertie sighed. "What's that book you reading say?"

"Listen to this, from a declassified CIA memo from May 5, 1955."

"Marky was just a baby then." She stared down into her empty hands.

"Post-hypnotic suggestions reiterated during several sessions," he read, "have been known to endure for years. A skilled operator with a good subject can not only find out completely about a subject's past, he can cause the subject to re-enact a recruitment, training, briefing, etc. Perhaps less obvious is the possibility of using regression to build a new identity, and in some degree a changed personality."

"So those mind-control goons can turn people into zombies, right?"

"It goes on to say—this gets really freaky—that through hypnosis, they can create multiple personalities in the same person. They implant code words or phrases through hypnotic suggestion, which they use as signals to activate different personalities, and can even get someone to do stuff he's opposed to. And that he has no memory of."

"Sounds like *The Manchurian Candidate* with Frank Sinatra," she said.

"Exactly like that. Remember in the movie when poor hypnotized Laurence Harvey plays solitaire and the Queen of Diamonds comes up. It puts him in such a trance that he's powerless not to obey. His 'linkage' is the Red Queen card, the trigger that the Russians planted in his mind to make him kill."

Gary wondered what Labat's conditioned link could be. One enigmatic expression he'd heard over and over from Marky was "as above, so below." Hadn't that been scrawled on the putrid refrigerator ditched in front of the house on the night of the drive-by? That refrigerator had been parked there for weeks, but Gary didn't notice the graffiti until the night of the murder. Did one of Labat's minions write it there to identify the Naquin place for the thugs who killed Marky? And hadn't Nicole told him that Hunter Finn repeated the phrase to her in the cemetery, just a few days before he murdered his girlfriend?

Could it be a hypnotic signal to kill?

"Don't you get it?" Gary jumped up and began pacing the room. "I saw it all the time in California. You have these spaced-out young people floating around the country, waiting for someone to tell them what to do, who to be, and why. Then you have these older people with some sect or cult or religion or drug or other form of hypnotic control. The Mani, the manipulators! The Mani can tear a person down and recreate him from the bottom up, separate him into different personalities to do their bidding, even to kill or commit suicide. Like the Manson family, or Jim Jones with the People's Temple."

"You saying Labat hypnotized Hunter to murder his girlfriend and then the boy killed himself when he realized what he did?" She faced Gary, wringing her hands.

"Just like Laurence Harvey did at the end of *The Manchurian Candidate*, after Frank Sinatra shows him how the Russians stole his soul."

"And Marky knew what kind of lowdown stuff was happening and was gonna turn Labat in. So he had Marky shot?"

He stopped pacing and nodded.

"I'm gonna go punch that Labat in the mouth."

"Wait a sec. Let's think this through. Labat and Marky were probably drawn together because of the Gnostic thing. They were both into this Manichean mysticism, God above, the devil below. That's the only real clue we have to Labat's world. Marky probably bought half of these books at Minerva's Owl."

"Marky was always real religious. When he was twelve he told me he wanted to be a priest. But my husband said over his dead body, and I gave in. That was our big mistake. But Marky was always making them little altars and saying Mass over dead birds."

"I don't know how religious they were, but Labat had no lack of spaced-out subjects to work on. Every time I walked past Minerva's Owl, all these young guys were sitting around inside throwing the Tarot or reading books. So Finn came back from Iraq broken in pieces—Bob White said he had a psychiatric discharge—and was a holdout here in the Quarter after the storm then moved above Labat's store. Then somehow Labat hypnotized him into a killer. But why would he want him to cut off his girlfriend's head?"

"Yeah, who wants a head?" she said. "Does Labat live in one of those apartments above his shop?"

"That building is owned by Duffy Bordelon, a rich guy running for mayor. Sweet Pea claims he came on to him one night. I bet Labat lives somewhere else. You have a phone book?"

"Sure." Gertie yanked a phone book from under a suitcase balanced on a stack of boxes, its wheels in the air. "This place may be a mess, but I know where everything is."

"Let's see." He cracked open the white pages. "Labarre, Labarriere . . . no wait, Labat, E. M. Here it is. He lives on Leda Court. It says Apartment C."

"That street is just a block long, over by the Fair Grounds. The only apartment building there must be the old Pelican Club, a big mansion where the baseball team used to stay. It's down Esplanade toward City Park, the last street on the right before St. Louis Cemetery Number Three."

"I'm going to snoop around," he said, fishing in his pocket for the van keys.

"You be careful with that man."

"Labat is like Santa Claus, just a bearded old fool unless you believe in him."

THE DAMP CHILL OF LATE AFTERNOON had turned into a cold, blustery night, and walking to his van, Gary zipped up his denim jacket and wound the Hindu scarf twice around his neck.

A full moon winked at him through the overhead trellis of branches on Esplanade Avenue, and soon Gary's van was approaching the cemetery. The street lights were finally on in this neighborhood, although most of the houses remained dark and boarded up. The area had flooded only a couple of feet, and here the nineteenth-century shotguns were raised above the ground on brick pillars. Gary figured the water must have come up only to the porches, but the stink of mold and mildew after months of abandonment didn't entice residents home, particularly renters. Along the sidewalks, tenants' furniture and household items were tossed into heaps. He had never been back to his flooded shotgun in the Bywater and heard the landlord dumped his soggy belongings on the street. Block after block, pestilent refrigerators stood guard along the curb, white boxes gleaming in the moonlight like the rows of little white houses at the cemetery.

He turned onto Leda Court. In the middle of the block

was a rusty spiked fence, behind which loomed a moldering Mediterranean-style mansion flanked by arched doors that gave onto a wide second-floor veranda. He climbed out of the van and peeked through the gate across a brown expanse of dead grass. The amber house was half hidden by a tangle of live oak branches.

Crickets chirped. Gravel crunched under Gary's high tops.

He glanced over his shoulder. Another car down the block was parked across the street, engine idling, the windows fogged by a heater. Then the window rolled down.

And the unmistakable schnozzola of Vinnie Panarello poked out.

What possible motive could the cop have for staking out Labat's house? He knew nothing about Labat's connection with Marky, did he?

Or was the lieutenant now following Gary?

He turned his back, wondering if the cop had recognized him in the dark. Was Panarello getting out of his car and walking toward him? On the gate hung a lopsided "For Rent" sign. An orange tag identified a corroded doorbell as "Manager." Impulsively, he rang it. The gate buzzed, and with an ominous creak he pushed it open, then stepped inside. It swung shut with a clank behind him.

He walked onto the grounds, out of the cop's line of vision.

Snarling, a Doberman pinscher leapt out of a shadow, latching onto his jean cuff with razor-sharp choppers inside of a mouth that looked like raw hamburger. Another Doberman growled at his heels, shattering the night with staccato bursts of a throaty bark.

A light flashed on the veranda. A man emerged from a doorway, clapped his hands three times, and the dog let go of

Gary's leg. Whimpering, the two Dobermans sprinted with bowed heads toward a robed figure descending the steps.

"I'm here about the apartment," Gary shouted. "Are you the manager?"

"Yes." Suddenly Gary was facing Labat, the dog-headed Egyptian amulet gleaming on his chest. The Dobermans panted at the bearded man's side, flexing to lunge, restrained by an invisible chain. The magnetic gaze took in Gary, sapphire eyes boring into his forehead.

Labat smiled. "I've seen you before."

"Maybe in the Quarter." Gary felt paralyzed, barely able to speak.

"Or in the pyramid," Labat said, "or at the center of a full circle."

"As above, so below." The words came rushing out of Gary's mouth, he wasn't sure how or why.

"Come in," Labat said. "I've been expecting you."

Gary held his breath as he followed Labat up the steps. He kept his distance from the growling Dobermans and tried not to make any sudden moves. The rooms in the Pelican Club were cavernous and sparsely furnished, as if used as a staging area for something. One dog stationed on either side of him, the bearded man sat enthroned under a stained-glass lamp in an elaborately carved Queen Anne chair, chain-smoking Chesterfields and smiling benevolently. Labat told Gary that when two souls from the Mani met, there was an instant recognition between them, a lightning bolt between their eyes.

Gary nodded, playing along as a Gnostic adept, rattling off the top of his head any details he could remember from Marky's books. Muscles rippling, the Dobermans fixed him in a menacing stare, and even after Labat sent them back outside, Gary still felt overpowered in the bearded man's presence.

"When Jeanne d'Arc crossed paths with Gilles de Rais in the fourteenth-century court at Orleáns, they instantly recognized each other," Labat explained. "She was a transvestite who wore men's clothing and he was a sodomist accused of murdering babies. What he was, of course, was an abortionist. They were both persecuted as heretics and burned as witches. That's the sad story of our religion."

In the Mani sect, Labat explained, the only mortal sin was procreation, to ensnare angel spirits in the flesh. Apart from this, sexuality was encouraged until the initiate was given the sacrament of *consolamentum*, after which total asceticism was expected. Only Labat, with his angel soul, could perform the highly secretive initiations or this deathbed sacrament. Until that final sacrament, he said with a wink, "anything goes. Happy Carnival."

Above Labat's throne was a gold-framed painting of what Gary recognized as Salomé bearing the head of St. John the Baptist on a platter. Gary pictured Deckie Hall's head as it must have looked, pop-eyed in the freezer. Fidgeting, he picked up the leather cigarette case on the bronze Indian table between them, feeling the crinkly texture.

"I ordered that from the Golden Dawn Bookshop in London," Labat said, "where we get most of our stock. It's made of human skin."

Gary put it down.

Labat quoted Aleister Crowley and spoke of the Cathar temple he had founded here in the new Orleáns, where he'd been born in a hospital named Hôtel Dieu, or God's Hotel. Every syllable he uttered seemed pregnant with esoteric meaning. Gary felt mesmerized by his voice and erudition and wondered if Labat were trying to hypnotize him. Or seduce him. Of course, Gary mentioned nothing about Marky Naquin or Hunter Finn. He kept one observant corner of his mind clear and detached, and let the rest of himself fall under Labat's spell. He had the odd sensation that he was watching himself listen to Labat. In the lamplight, the bearded man's features appeared carved out of ivory, and Gary tried hard to imagine this lofty hierophant conspiring with thugs in long white T-shirts to commit murder.

He felt woozy and needed air.

The spell was broken when a withered old lady in dark glasses clanked in on a walker, sweeping the floor in front of her with a white cane. Labat introduced her and, with great ceremony, excused himself. He now had to prepare her for bed. Gary was astounded: Labat the devil worshipper and mind-control expert lived with his blind mother.

Gary creaked open the front gate, scanning the street for the cop's car. Panarello was gone, and it was almost 1 a.m. Exhausted, he slept for twelve hours. In his dream, Labat's dog-headed amulet swayed back and forth, back and forth, and then the Dobermans, transformed into gigantic scorpions, lunged at his throat. Panarello burst through the door, gun in hand, and finally carted them all off to the dog pound.

Gary awoke with his jaw clenched, braced for attack.

# Fourteen

"WE'RE JUST TWENTY-FIVE MINUTES from Canal Street," Gertie sang in mezzo-soprano. "Let's go see the parade."

She'd been rushing from room to room of Nicole's shotgun, belting out that ditty for a solid hour, and Nicole's patience was wearing thin. What in the world was her mother on now, cocaine? At first she and Kelly greeted her mother's outbursts of song with polite applause, but then they locked themselves in the bathroom or hid in the courtyard. Nicole's grandfather, whose swing band the Tip Tops played the Blue Room at the Roosevelt Hotel during the forties, had written this and other songs, and as a girl Gertie sang them on the radio. When Gertie was most stressed out, Nicole noticed, she reverted to little Shirley Temple on the Good Ship Lollipop. No wonder her mother wound up getting drunk in gay bars. She wasn't the only one around who wanted to turn everything into a musical comedy.

"I'm so excited," Gertie said, putting on her Goodwill coat and tying a rayon scarf under her chin. "I haven't been to a parade downtown in years. It's getting cold out there, so bundle up."

# Higher Ground

Not only was Nicole humoring her mother along until the intervention on Ash Wednesday, but she was trying to dig Kelly out of his black hole. And this was after a long day counting dump trucks. She was learning that the only way to help people was simply to be there and listen. And not try to fix things. So she assured her mother that she'd be delighted to read Marky's book about Nazi experiments with mind control—the very idea made her blood freeze—and she accompanied Kelly to root around at filthy building scavengers to search for his looted supplies. Often, between indulging their twin obsessions with mind control and copper wiring, she thought back to those halcyon days when her only worry was her doctor husband peeking at other women's pussies all day.

Gertie had made a bagful of ham sandwiches to bring to the parade, just as she had every Mardi Gras when she took little Nicole and Marky to Canal Street in their princess and clown costumes. Kelly had cranked up some Carnival music on the boom box and was well into his third cocktail. As Nicole put on a windbreaker and draped a few purple, green, and gold beads around her neck, even she was stepping a bit lighter, getting in the spirit. If anyone could have promised her last year that she'd now be going to a Carnival parade with her high-school sweetheart, she would have signed over her whole 401(k).

> Party Mardi Gras mambo, mambo, mambo
> Mardi Gras mambo, ooh
> Down in New Orleans.

"Okay, do we have everything?" asked Nicole, the new troop leader. "Coats, hats, scarves?"

"Yeah," screamed Kelly and Gertie, buttoning up.

"Ham sammiches?" Nicole giggled at her attempt to recapture the local accent.

Gertie held up a greasy brown bag.

"Go-cups?"

Kelly lifted his hip flask, along with three plastic cups.

"A sack for throws?"

Gertie waved a handful of bags from Tony's Superette.

"Everybody been to the rest room?"

"Oooh, I gotta go," Gertie squealed, ducking into the bathroom.

Kelly reached over and kissed Nicole on the lips, cupping his free hand around her breast.

"I love you, babe," he said, eyes meeting hers. "Couldn't live without you."

Nicole bit her lip. "I really need to hear you say that." Settling into his arms, she imagined she was sixteen again and had never left them. The first love, she realized, gets it right, before the heart breaks into jagged shards of glass.

He chucked her under the chin. "At least the storm blew one good thing into my life."

"If ever I cease to love," she breathed in a teary soprano into Kelly's ear, "if ever I cease to love. . . ."

"May the fish get legs and the cows lay eggs," he sang back, picking up the lyrics of the familiar Rex anthem dating back to the first Mardi Gras, "if ever I cease to love. If ever I cease to love. . . ."

Her neck tingled as he sang into her hair.

He took a deep breath. "You're the only woman who has ever—"

"Nicole," Gertie shouted from the bathroom, "you out of terlit paper."

"I'm coming, Momma."

# Higher Ground

THEY WERE SUPPOSED TO MEET DIXIE at the side entrance to the Louisiana Club on Common Street, after she had finished hobnobbing with the past kings and queens of Hermes at the champagne gala pre-party. But by the time they made it around the parade barriers lining Canal Street, Dixie was already huddled on the corner in her mink, gnarled hands set at their default position: a Kent between two fingers in one mitt, fingers clutching a go-cup in the other.

"We're just twenty-five minutes from Canal Street," Gertie sang operatically as she approached her sister. "Let's go see the parade."

Dixie winced, stamping out her cigarette with the pointy toe of a strappy high heel.

"Remember that song?" Gertie asked, hugging her sister.

"How could I forget it? That's all I listened to in the Home for Wayward Girls, my cute little sister on the radio. Surprised I didn't abort right then and there."

"Okay, you two," Nicole said, high-pitched as a referee whistle. "Let's put on a happy face. It's Carnival."

"Yeah," Dixie croaked, gesturing at the crowds. "Get a load of this." Peanut, cotton-candy, and balloon vendors were wheeling up and down St. Charles Avenue, hawking their wares from shopping carts. Squealing kids were perched on top of viewing ladders behind the metal barricades, and the smell of grilled sausage and smoked turkey wafted from food trucks stationed in the alleys. Couples were kissing, and strangers joked with each other as if they were at a family reunion.

"New Orleans is back," Dixie proclaimed, holding up her go-cup in a toast. "Y'all believe this street was a stinking sewer full of looters just six months ago?"

"Back in spirit, if not in the flesh," Kelly said, joining the toast. "Personally, Miss Dixie, I can't wait to get the hell out of here."

Nicole was determined not to let the conversation veer toward either building materials or murder and to keep her mother and aunt separated, like two squabbling toddlers. This was her Mardi Gras, the first one she'd had in twenty-eight years, and she wasn't about to let anyone spoil it. Like most of the people around her—displaced, depressed, and unhinged—she intended to celebrate with a vengeance, come hell or high water. Okay, so she no longer had a house with a two-car garage. But this was home, standing at the corner of St. Charles and Common with her family and the love of her life, waiting for a parade.

"Hey, splash a little more bourbon in my Coke," she told Kelly, resolved to do whatever it took. "Happy Carnival," she said, pecking him on the boozy lips.

Soon krewe captains in velvet Renaissance costumes came prancing by on horseback, pressing plastic Hermes doubloons into outstretched hands waving from the curb. Then came the high-stepping marching bands from local high schools, with a jazzy syncopation of brassy horns, clarinets, and kettledrums that had people jigging on the curb. The whole street exploded into shouts and whistles as the floats swayed by. The papier-mâché confections were sculpted into the most fanciful forms, whole miniature worlds contained within scalloped swirls. Alongside of the floats, men with rags tied around their heads carried bobbing kerosene flambeaux balanced on their hips. Twirling the flambeaux, they strutted down the street after stooping to pick up quarter tips that clinked onto the pavement.

Gertie and Dixie swooned with *oohs* and *aahs* as glittering Lotus Eater, Cyclops, and Siren figures passed over their heads like dreams. The theme was the Voyage of Ulysses, and once again the street was filled with water, but this time the mythical waves were redeemed by the imagination and sprinkled with fairy dust. Kelly jumped to the left and the right, snaring handfuls of beads that he layered around the ladies's necks like leis. Dancing in the street, Nicole felt like a bejeweled princess and kept stealing peeks at her storybook prince. This was the moment she'd been waiting for ever since she moved back to New Orleans. Although she knew she could never make it last, she reached out, grabbed it like a throw, and held it close.

"Miss Gertie," screamed a short, cinnamon-colored woman dressed in a gold lamé sheath, wrapping her elbow-gloved arms around the old lady and squeezing. "Guess who?" She sashayed in a circle, fluttering her fingertips through the air and singing, "I'm in the middle of a chain reaction."

"Sweet Pea!"

"Better not miss my number at the drag contest on Mardi Gras, hear?" Sweet Pea slow-eyed Kelly. "Oh, Mr. Booty Call, see you still around. What I tell you, girl? It work, or what?" Sweet Pea high-fived Nicole. "Y'all, this is my escort for the evening. Oscar, this is. . . ."

Sweet Pea hesitated. A cloud crossed his mascaraed eyes and his jaw tightened. But he held his head high and continued the introduction, his voice dropping to a whisper. "Oscar, this Miss Gertie, Marky Naquin's mama. Miss Gertie, this here is Oscar Batiste, Latrome's uncle. Guess the good Lord want you two to know each other."

"You the lady whose son . . . ?" asked a dark, balding man in a cracking voice, a diamond stud gleaming on his ear lobe.

"That your nephew who . . . ?" Gertie asked, her face crumbling.

Nicole's soaring heart plummeted, and she grabbed Kelly's hand. Here she was covered with Carnival beads, blubbering like a bourbon-besotted baby in the middle of St. Charles Avenue. Gertie and Oscar embraced as if, for a moment, they could reclaim the dead in each other's arms, flesh of their flesh, love of their love.

"I'm Miss Nida Mann," Sweet Pea said, fingering Dixie's mink.

"You need one, too, huh?" Dixie stared straight ahead.

"Looove your coat."

"Tell that guy bawling with my sister to buy you one." Dixie pushed up the collar around her throat. "If he don't, drop him like a hot potato."

"Oooh, I likes you."

The blaring horns of a marching band were approaching the corner, blasting "It's Carnival Time." Then before Nicole knew it, another parade was upon them. She dried her eyes and, plastic beads rattling, moved back to the curb while Gertie and Oscar spoke mouth to ear, huddled at the edge of a surge of people.

"Wait till y'all see this one," Dixie said, holding out her go-cup for Kelly to fill with bourbon. "It's a new bunch that come out of the old-line krewes called Le Krewe d'État. They don't have a king but a dictator dressed like a skeleton."

The floats wheeled past like the stations of everyone's cross. The theme was the Hurricane Olympics, and Kelly roared at the float called Looter Shooting, bearing the slogan "U Loot, We Shoot." The next was Insurance-Adjuster Wrestling, in which a house under water bore the sign "Not Covered," followed by the Refugee Relay Race, a cloverleaf of cars spinning between Baton Rouge, Houston, and Atlanta. Nicole, who had cleaned out her mother's Frigidaire in Lakeview two months after the storm, almost lost her cookies at Refrigerator Hurling, a float on which an athlete heaved a fridge oozing with maggots, an arc of vomit gushing from his mouth.

At the end of the parade loomed a gigantic papier-mâché skull crowned with a motley jester's cap, grinning.

And the crowd went wild.

KELLY SLIPPED TWO PINK BALLOONS inside his brownie blouse, wondering if they were too small. "Think my tits need more air?"

"They're a lot bigger than mine." Nicole zipped up her brownie skirt and slipped into a pair of saddle oxfords. "Don't you have any other shoes?"

"What's wrong with these?" Kelly hiked up the brown skirt, staring down past his knobby knees at running shoes crusted with Lakeview muck. Nicole had already talked him into dressing up like an eight-year-old girl, complete with yellow pigtails. What did she want him to do now, squeeze into a pair of Mary Janes?

Kelly flipped the pigtails over his shoulder, took another slug from his Jack and Coke, and turned up the boom box. "You will see the Zulu king," Professor Longhair sang, "down on Rampart and Dumaine." He hadn't been sober for a minute during the past four days, ever since the parades on Friday.

This morning they were trying to get their own merry krewe on the road. Nicole had spent the entire weekend haunting thrift shops, searching for a cheap, last-minute costume inspiration. She finally came across a ratty wad of adult-sized brownie uniforms, probably leftover from some scout-themed truck parade years ago. Kelly was astounded by her Santa's-elf energy. While he worked on a new painting—the canvases from his lizard series filled a whole corner of the bedroom—she mended, washed, and ironed the four uniforms, and then concocted pompoms out of shredded blue roofing tarps and knotted wigs out of skeins of yellow yarn. Their theme, Nicole warned, was top secret, to be revealed only at the last moment.

"Where's your momma?" Kelly asked.

"Putting on her costume next door. She's been in a tizzy all weekend talking to her new friend Oscar about who killed Marky and Latrome." Nicole dangled a large red cardboard *F* around Kelly's neck. "Probably to shut her up, he invited her to audition for the choir at Our Lady of Guadalupe, where he's the music director."

"What's this *F* for?"

"You'll see." She then hung a red cardboard *E* around her own neck.

"Fe Fi Fo Fum?" Kelly asked.

"Not even warm. Listen," Nicole said, handing Kelly a pair of roofing-tarp pompoms, "Gary is really wigged out after his run in with Labat. Please don't mention anything about cults or mind control. Promise?"

"Cross my heart."

Then Nicole banged on the wall of the shotgun double, shouting, "Momma, meet us in the courtyard. *Now.*"

Once assembled outside, Kelly thought that Gary and Gertie both had overdone the rouged apple cheeks, although Gary managed to look the cutest in a pair of yellow knee socks that matched the yarn wig.

"Hey," said Kelly, tugging on Gary's pigtails, "you do look wigged out."

Nicole cut her eye at him and then hung a red cardboard *M* around Gertie's neck and an *A* around Gary's, sticking roofing-tarp pompoms in their hands. Then she made them line up.

"What are we, FEMA?" Gertie asked, studying the letters. "Thought we was supposed to be brownies."

"We're both. Okay, let's rehearse. Stand in a line spelling out F-E-M-A, wave the pompoms over your head like this— *sis, bom, bah*—and cheer: *Heckuva a job, heckuva a job! Brownie! Brownie!*"

"So we Heckuva-Job Brownies," Gertie said, waving her pompoms. "That's a riot. You could work for the funny papers, Nicole."

"It hit me the minute I saw the brownie costumes at

the Salvation Army," Nicole said, beaming. "'You're doing a heckuva job, Brownie.' I mean, who could forget what the President said to that idiot Michael Brown, the FEMA director who worried about his dinner reservations in Baton Rouge while everybody here was drowning."

"I want knee socks like hers," Kelly whined, sticking out his tongue at Gary. "The little hussy."

Kelly and Gary bumped hips, then threw their arms around each other's shoulders.

"The *F* and the *A* aren't supposed to touch," Nicole said, separating them. "Now let's file down the alley—in order—and burst out on the street doing our cheer. Ready?"

THIS WAS THE BEST MARDI GRAS ever, Kelly decided. Everywhere they wandered in the Quarter, the Heckuva-Job Brownies stole the show. As soon as they grouped, raised the pompoms, and went into their cheer, flashbulbs popped and other maskers gathered round. The weather was mild and sunny, and for once the streets weren't jammed with humorless gawkers from Idaho in street clothes. The rest of the country still thought New Orleans was uninhabitable, yet here they were, locals everywhere in feathers and face paint and G-strings and velvet, running into family and old friends for the first time since the storm, skipping directly from *how'd you do?* to *what you wanna drink?* Many maskers shared the same satirical bent as they did, and the Heckuva-Job Brownies ran across packing-crate refrigerators studded with jelly-bean maggots, tipsy Red Cross nurses carrying enema bottles filled with booze, minstrelly Roy Blingers in blackface, dowdy drag-queen governors, and hideous rubber masks of the President shooting everyone the bird.

Waiting in line for a beer, Kelly was intrigued by the

homemade headdress in front of him fashioned out of rubber snakes woven through plumes of dead grass.

"What you supposed to be?" Kelly asked.

The guy turned around. "Lakeview."

"That's where I'm from. Lemme buy you a beer, Lakeview."

With a drunken grin plastered on his face, Kelly felt halfway home. He swore that he would finish rebuilding his house, even if he had to buy second-hand materials from scavengers. Within a month, he vowed, he and Nicole would be living there. The first thing he would do tomorrow would be to post the biggest sign in the world in front of the house: U-LOOT, WE SHOOT.

The Heckuva-Job Brownies arrived in front of the Aftermath Lounge just in time to catch Sweet Pea mounting the contest platform. Oscar Batiste, dressed in black leather chaps and a harness, was guiding Sweet Pea up the steps, wobbly in his towering afro, floor-length red feather cape, and six-inch platform heels.

"Take your hands off your dicks and put them together," announced the drag-diva emcee, "for Miss Nida Mann! Before this bitch falls down and we needa doctor."

Sweet Pea approached the audience, grabbed the emcee's mike, and said, "I dedicate this song to the memory of Latrome and Marky and everyone else been murdered in this damn town since the storm."

The crowd went silent.

Then he snapped his fingers over his head, arched his back, struck a haughty profile, and froze.

"Diana," Gary screamed, jumping up and down, pigtails flapping.

Kelly and Nicole were the first to start dancing as the Motown beat pumped from the speakers. Sweet Pea vogued to the edge of the stage, pointing an index finger to the sky. "You took a mystery and made me want it," he mouthed, fluttering his fingertips. The Heckuva-Job Brownies slid their arms around each other's waists and step-kicked in a line dance, snaking through the crowd while Sweet Pea strutted across the stage lip-syncing, feather cape and auburn afro shimmering in the sunlight. Kelly couldn't remember when he'd had so much fun as he plopped a wet kiss on Nicole's lips, goosed Gary, and squeezed Gertie close.

> You gotta plan, your future is on the run
> Shine a light for the whole world over
> You never find your love if you hide away
> Crying, dying, all you gotta do is
>
> Get in the middle of a chain reaction
> You get a medal when you're lost in action . . .
> We talk about love, love, love
> We talk about looove . . .

After Sweet Pea stumbled off the stage to thunderous applause, they gathered around the sweaty star, fanning himself. They were discussing taking Sweet Pea into the Aftermath for a congratulatory drink when the biggest, darkest mountain of queen flesh that Kelly had ever seen, dressed from head to toe in pink sequins, sidled up behind them and tapped Sweet Pea on the shoulder with a crimson talon.

"You ain't seen nothing yet, bitch," sneered the Everest of pink sequins, rattling the plastic bangles on his arm in Sweet Pea's face.

"Why it be LaTusha," Sweet Pea simpered, "star of rage and scream. You got so fat I thought you was a float."

"Hi, Big Mama," Gary said. "It's Gary Cherry, remember? From Parish Prison."

Big Mama reached over and pecked Gary on the cheek. "I been looking all over creation for you. Wait till I finish my show. I got something to tell you—about that shooting on Dauphine, hear? But child," he said, stepping back and screwing up his face, "where you get that tacky yellow wig? Who you supposed to be, Heidi?"

# Fifteen

THE F, THE E, AND THE M OF the Heckuva-Job Brownies decided to go home, use the bathroom, and collapse. Gary lingered at the edge of the stage, dressed in his brownie uniform, knee socks, and yellow pigtails. A pall had fallen over him. He wondered if, in spite of himself, Labat had managed to hypnotize him on Friday with that sapphire stare. Even awake, the dog-headed Egyptian amulet kept swinging before his eyes, and often out of the corner of his vision he would catch glimpses of Dobermans pouncing.

Big Mama's resplendent pink sequins gleamed in the sun as the mammoth figure twirled a satin rose umbrella and lip-synced to the heavens that "It's Raining Men (Hallelujah)." Gary moved to the back of the crowd after Big Mama stumbled down the steps, costume in disarray. The bald queen Gary remembered from jail, still with a tank top tied into a *tignon* around his head, escorted the winded performer in a triumphant walk through the cheering audience. With a smile, Gary recognized the terrycloth bag that Tank Top carried, a square sack that the queens made out of jail towels fastened together with twisties, where they stored their toiletries. Gary suspected that this prison tote was now filled with glue, pins, and a stapler to keep Big Mama's costume together.

When he finally approached Big Mama in front of the Laughing Buddha, Tank Top was kneeling, pinning up the frayed hem of the gown already blackened by Mardi Gras street sludge.

"That was far out," Gary said, applauding.

"Lord, my feets killing me in these heels. Soon as she finish down there on her knees, where the bitch feel right at home," Big Mama growled, "I'm gonna go sit down."

"How long you been out on the street?" Gary asked.

"Over a week now, and I couldn't find you nowhere. That kid done the shooting on Dauphine, he come around plenty for his entertaining, believe you me. Two my girls slapped each other silly over his fine ass. I asked, and he told me sure enough, it was this creepy dude standing out front the Nervous Owl on Rampart paid him to do that drive-by."

"A pudgy guy with a beard and blue eyes, right?"

"Didn't say nothing 'bout that. Say the dude crippled."

"Crippled?"

"Yeah, a crippled dude with a funny leg."

Gary's mind raced.

"Heidi," Big Mama said, "you got a dollar? After all that hollering up there, I needs a cold drink."

THAT NIGHT WAS MOONLESS AND exhausted, yet beyond Gary's courtyard wall, laughter still echoed down the trash-strewn streets outside. After dark on Mardi Gras, people lost the lightheaded revelry that kept them bobbing along like balloons throughout the day. And then they got down and dirty. Costumes wound up in tatters, voices hoarsened, and fist fights broke out. Jealous couples stomped off in opposite directions, screaming accusations: she with the car keys, he with the booze. Drunken tourists, who didn't know when to go back to the hotel, staggered around looking for one last piece of ass, finding regrettable pickups among fantasy's leftovers.

Actually, this now-or-never moment was Gary's favorite part of the day. But tonight he wasn't rolling around on the floor of some stranger's condo tugging a ripped leotard over a pair of hairy thighs or clasped in an embrace in the Aftermath Lounge, exchanging sloppy kisses with someone whose smeary clown-white was rubbing off on his own face. After Big Mama's report from the queens' tank, Gary found himself home alone, a man obsessed.

*A crippled dude with a funny leg.*

Who else could the murderer be?

He suspected that the shrink had blabbed to the cop what he said about Labat, and that was why Panarello was staked out in front of the bookseller's house. And why wouldn't White have tried to set up Labat? It was the perfect way to pin the murder on someone else. But could Big Mama's stud in baggy orange be trusted? Come on, why would a gangsta from the projects, already behind bars on another rap, some kid who didn't expect to live past twenty, make up out of the clear blue that particular detail: *a crippled dude with a funny leg*?

What a way to spend Mardi Gras night, bleary-eyed on the Internet.

The Brownie costume lay crumpled at his feet, topped by a tangle of yellow yarn and the scarlet letter. The *A* must be for asshole, because that was what he'd been. Why hadn't he suspected White before? True, Labat was delusional and *manipulative*—that word kept coming up—and was probably involved to the hilt with Hunter and his gristly crime. But apart from dust-ups with Marky over interpretations of a hermetic doctrine from fourteenth-century France, if you please, what reason did Labat have to put out a contract on him? For all of his regal pretensions, Labat was a second-hand bookseller who lived with his blind mother in some run-down rooms next to the race track. Where would he get the bread, even if he did have a plausible motive? And for the life of him, Gary still couldn't imagine that old white queen doing business with crack-head killers for hire. But why in front of Labat's store?

What did the crippled shrink have to do with the bearded cult leader?

The truth was buried on page ten of White's Internet entries. A lot came up when he Googled "Robert White, MD, New Orleans," more than he'd expected: books, articles, and conferences, including the Jung Center events schedule. The listing that blew Gary's mind was that in 1973, when he had been a student at Berkeley, White participated in a controversial psychological experiment in which paid volunteers were locked up in a makeshift prison, one group taking on the role of prisoners and the other guards. The student guards turned sadistic, humiliated and tortured their jailbird classmates, and one guard beat a prisoner to a bloody pulp for organizing an uprising. From the descriptions, it sounded like what went on at the Abu Ghraib prison in Baghdad. This experiment had to be canceled midway, and a few years back a book was published about it, *The Torturer Inside: What Turns Good People Evil.* As the book came up indexed on the screen, the name of the tortured prisoner was Robert White.

And the name of the sadistic guard was Eliphas Labat.

Both, it was noted, were originally from New Orleans, Louisiana.

Police sirens blared in the distance, and Gary jumped up from his desk to close the second-floor shutters. The clock read twenty to midnight, and it was still Mardi Gras. Just before he was about to nod off, he plugged the name "Dr. Robert

White" into *The Times-Picayune* website. Again, conferences, speeches, the Jung Center, society parties. But one old listing led to an article about a car accident in Mandeville three years ago. Marc Naquin had been driving, just signed out of the state mental hospital by Dr. White. According to the article, an argument ensued, in the middle of which the car skidded into a tree, flipped over, and "frightened and confused, Naquin abandoned the car, leaving White pinned inside." Hours later, when the car was discovered, White was pulled out of the wreckage, one leg mangled.

As Gary scrolled through the article, he thought holy shit, after White drove across the lake to sign his former lover out of the loony bin in Mandeville, Marky paid him back by crashing his car and then running away, leaving White trapped inside.

The shrink had every reason both to kill Marky as well as to set up Labat as the murderer. As much as the man repelled Gary—he could still feel the crinkle of that human-skin cigarette case—he had to talk with Labat tomorrow. The police were galloping in the wrong direction, and the big question was, why couldn't Panarello figure this out? Unless his Internet was down.

Or for some reason he didn't want to know.


"Remember you are dust," the priest intoned, smudging an ashen cross onto Kelly's throbbing forehead, "and to dust you will return."

Kelly had accompanied Nicole and her mother to the early-morning Ash Wednesday Mass at St. Louis Cathedral, although he hadn't been to church in years. Under a slate-gray sky, they zipped up their jackets against the nippy chill as they trudged home past heaps of crushed go-cups, broken beads crunching underfoot. Yet this morning the streets seemed surprisingly clean, considering the mountains of garbage he and Nicole had waded through last night, when they dashed out at midnight to catch the traditional parade of garbage trucks rumbling down Bourbon Street to put an end to Mardi Gras.

"Carnival is over," the police chief had proclaimed, riding the horse that led this final procession. "Y'all go home."

This was a city that took its Mardi Gras trash seriously, measuring the success of Carnival by the number of tons collected from the streets. At the moment trash had become an intensely personal subject for people like Kelly, since most residents had just finished throwing out everything they owned, destroyed in the flood. Last night, kicking through a pile of ratty feathers and muddy velour—the remains of somebody's glorious incarnation—Kelly had been reminded that the Latin word "carnival" meant *goodbye to the flesh*.

This morning the deeper melancholy of Mardi Gras wasn't lost on anyone, least of all a Lenten spirit like Nicole. Her face was wan and pinched, Kelly was hung over, and Miss Gertie limped along, complaining about arthritis and damp weather. Together they looked the perfect picture of penitence as they plodded home, ashen crosses smeared on their foreheads.

That was when Kelly got the call.

"My lawyer," he mouthed, cell phone glued to his ear. Nicole and her mother walked ahead.

"Yeah, right," he barked. "What are the terms? . . . Okay . . . Gotcha . . . Wants the goddamn house? But she hates New Orleans. No, I won't sign . . . She promised me an amicable divorce. You tell that sleazy lawyer of hers . . . Yeah, just to get my goat. Meanwhile, I'll try to reason with her."

Kelly stormed into Miss Gertie's parlor, bellowing for Nicole. Yapping, Schnitzel charged at the door, dragging his creaky wheels.

"Get that crippled mutt off me. There you are," he said

to Nicole, punching buttons on his cell. He held up a hand. "Lena, call me," he barked into the receiver. "She must have left for work already. I'm on my way to St. Francisville."

"I was next door on the phone," Nicole said. "What happened?"

"Lena wants the house."

"Let her have it. You can't afford to fix—"

"Over my dead body. That's all I have in the world."

"Sweetheart," she said, "give it time. After my divorce, I really didn't care—"

"I'll sit her down and rationally explain how she's acting like a bitter bitch."

"How was your Mardi Gras?" A forehead smudged with ashes appeared around the opened shutter, followed by a face framed with spit curls. "Hope I'm not too early."

"Oh, hello," Nicole said, in the coldest tone he had ever heard her use. "Kelly, this is Modene Holiday, the social worker."

"I'm outta here." He raced past the startled woman and onto the sidewalk.

"Momma," Nicole shouted toward the kitchen. "We have company."

"Dixie here already?" Gertie called back. "Why in the world does she want to come over on a morning like this?"

# Sixteen

Vinnie Panarello was tired of dicking around.

He had sat for three days straight in his car in front of Labat's house.

Nothing.

On Friday evening, he caught a glimpse of that Gary Cherry clown, who must be in this thing up to his neck, and a stream of rough-looking men visited the place, as if Labat were running a whorehouse or dealing. On Sunday morning, Labat left the house with a feeble old lady in dark glasses, but they drove only as far as Our Lady of the Rosary on Esplanade, just in time for the nine o'clock Mass.

How sweet, Vinnie thought. A murderer who takes old ladies to church.

This morning, after getting his ashes at Our Lady of Guadalupe, Vinnie noticed that Minerva's Owl was open. Again he had visited the St. Jude shrine—these miracles take time and lots of candle wax. Last week he brought his report on the parking lot shooting to Dr. White, and the doctor seemed satisfied that he could swing a temporary insanity plea. Thing was, after that kangaroo court of a grand jury indicted Vinnie, the actual trial could be any day. Without White's testimony, his goose was cooked.

The shrink hadn't filled him in any more on why Labat ordered the drive-by to kill Naquin. All he would say was that the two disagreed about some religious mumbo-jumbo, a motive that would never wash in court. Vinnie had to admit that White seemed to have a screw loose when it came to the subject of Marky Naquin. Couldn't stop talking about him and then *bam*, this furious look would flash in his eyes and he'd clam up. On one level the doctor seemed so rational and could really yackety-yak that double-talk. Yet when the doctor spoke, the big words sounded as crinkly and hollow as bubble wrap layered around something darker. Something scarier. Something Vinnie didn't want to know about.

Now was the time to strike, when the city was empty and quiet, and even the judges and bail bondsmen were nursing hangovers.

"Morning," Vinnie grunted, a bell tinkling on the bookshop door.

Labat looked up. He was seated behind the counter poring over a thick book from behind owlish horn-rimmed glasses. The gray cross on his forehead put Vinnie at ease. Maybe he could talk to a guy who had gone for his ashes like any other decent person.

Yet there was that icy stare again, the one that had sliced through Vinnie like a laser at the St. Jude altar. Vinnie fumbled in an overcoat pocket and took out his shades.

There, that was better.

"Can I help you?" Labat asked.

"Yeah," Vinnie said, peering at a row of titles over the rims of his sunglasses. "I'm looking for a good book . . . on Gawd."

Labat closed his tome. "Any particular god?"

"Vengeance is Mine," Vinnie quoted. "That Gawd, the one that brings evildoers to justice."

"Yahweh," Labat said. "God of wrath and thunder, tribal and unremorseful, thirsting for the blood of one more sacrificed lamb."

"Yeah," Vinnie said. "That one."

"You've come to the wrong shop, officer."

Vinnie swallowed. This wasn't starting well.

"I've seen you at the Our Lady of Guadalupe, praying to St. Jude," Labat said. "You're troubled, aren't you, Officer . . . ?"

"Panarello. Vincent Panarello, Eighth District." Vinnie whipped off the sunglasses. "Homicide."

"We met briefly when Deckie Hall's corpse was discovered." Labat pointed at the ceiling. "Above."

"Okay, Mr. Labat. Let's cut to the chase." Vinnie approached the counter, flipped open his notebook, and puffed out his chest. "When was the last time you saw Marky Naquin?"

"I know he was murdered a month ago," Labat said, "yet I really hadn't seen Marc Naquin much since the storm."

"What was your relationship with the deceased?"

"He'd been a frequent customer and often came to our spiritual discussions. Every Thursday evening we open the bookshop to the community and discuss subjects of esoteric spirituality. During a period, he attended—"

"You two get along?"

"Don't get me wrong. Marc was on The Path. But we diverged in our interpretation of Mani doctrine. He called our group the Left-Handed Path and spread some vicious rumors about us. Of course, nobody took them seriously, considering the source."

"The Left-Handed Path, huh?" Vinnie scribbled in his

notebook. "Where was you on the night of Saturday, January 28, at nine in the evening?"

"At home with my mother."

"Anyone else?"

"Hunter Finn."

"Let me get this straight. You was with Hunter Finn—six days before he chopped up his girlfriend—and your . . . mother on the night Naquin was murdered?"

"Yes, Hunter and Deckie had just moved upstairs a few weeks before. They seemed like a perfectly happy couple."

"What did you and Finn do together?" A snaky smile quivered on Vinnie's lips.

"Discussed spirituality."

Vinnie rolled his eyes. "When was the last time you seen Gary Cherry?"

"I'm not sure I know him. So many people pass through this store."

"Lemme remind you. Cherry went to your house last week." There, Vinnie had caught him in one lie. Everything else was probably a whopper, too. "On Friday, February 24, at 7:32 in the evening."

"Officer, you know things about me I don't even know."

The lieutenant studied the graying beard and greasy locks that framed Labat's puffy face. A pimple was forming at the end of his nose.

"Another thing you don't know," Vinnie said, "is you're under arrest for the murder of Marky Naquin."

"That's preposterous." Labat leapt up from behind the counter. "Everybody knows Marc was murdered with a young Negro in a drive-by shooting. Drugs, I'm sure."

"This ain't no crack case. Naquin and that Batiste kid were both clean. But somebody arranged that drive-by, and reliable sources tell me it was you."

The bell on the bookshop door tinkled. Eyes widening, Labat met the customer with a fierce stare.

Vinnie swung around.

It was Gary Cherry.

"Well, well," Vinnie said, savoring the coincidence. "We was just talking about you."

Gary blanched, looking back and forth between Labat and the cop.

"This the guy you visited Friday night?" The lieutenant jerked his thumb at Labat.

Gary nodded.

"Is this man your police decoy?" Labat demanded of the lieutenant, inflating with indignity. "What do you mean by sending this imposter into my home? I had nothing to do with Marc Naquin's murder."

So Labat assumed Cherry was working undercover for him and felt surrounded. Couldn't have worked out better, Vinnie decided. He wasn't about to pass up this golden opportunity to nail the case, even if he had to play Yahweh and demand the sacrifice of this bearded old goat.

"Okay," the cop said with a slow smile. "We'll sort this out at Tulane and Broad." He yanked out a pair of handcuffs. "Nice work, Cherry. Now make yourself scarce, if you know what's good for you."

"*Nice work.* Man, what are you talking about? Who do you think I am, a snitch like J.J.?" Gary followed them out of the door, protesting. "This is a huge mistake. Look it up for yourself on the Internet. You're pulling in the wrong guy."

KELLY CRACKED OPEN THE MASSIVE front door and slipped into the entrance hall at Sundown Plantation, just as the third tour of the day was getting underway. He crept to the back of a group of ten people, behind a lady in a lime track suit with her hands on the shoulders of two towheaded boys. Under a mahogany banister that swirled up to the second floor, French wallpaper depicted the scene of a maiden receiving a soldier in breastplate and helmet.

"This wallpaper, designed by René St. Clair in 1828 for the Ludlams, depicts adventures from the 'Song of Roland.'" Lena's syrupy drawl echoed in the vaulted vestibule, and done up in a hoop skirt and ruffled blouse, with a straw bonnet tied under her chin, she looked like a Mardi Gras masker from yesterday. Her stiff bearing belied a defeated stoop of the shoulders, and the marionette lines around her mouth reminded Kelly of a talking doll.

Kelly was still panting from the daredevil race up to St. Francisville. He had forked over the ten-dollar entrance fee and sprinted up the gravel walkway under a stately colonnade of live oaks leading to the front gallery. He was hoping to catch Lena between tours but a docent stationed under the white columns whispered that one had just begun and requested he enter quietly. He was holding his breath all right, but not out of respect for the 250-year-old plantation or its prissy restoration.

Kelly was holding his breath so he wouldn't scream.

"In antebellum days," Lena recited, pointing at the staircase, "the ivory inset in the newel post in the banister meant the home was debt-free."

At that moment their eyes met. Her features froze, and ashes still smeared across his forehead, Kelly's face turned crimson.

She quickly recovered her composure. "Now if y'all would step into the library, to your right," she said, leading the reverent group into a carpeted room draped with red damask and smothered in a sepia hush.

"Above the Carrara marble mantel hangs an oil portrait of Hiram Ludlam, painted in 1857. At this time," she said, locking eyes with Kelly at the rear of the group, "the Ludlams had no idea that their luxurious way of life was about to disappear with a sudden disaster, the War Between the States. The distinguished Colonel Ludlam, I might add, was my great-great grand-uncle."

Kelly stifled a guffaw. Leave it to Lena to brag about being related to that old philanderer.

A sheen of perspiration glazed his wife's face, but she soldiered on.

"Here to the right of the portrait, framed in gilded filigree, is his beloved wife Elaine Ludlam, after whom my grandmother was named." Lena stared straight at Kelly, and he could feel the accusatory sting of her eyes. "Colonel Ludlam worshipped the ground she walked on and provided for her comfort long after his death, as gentlemen did at that time for the mother of their children."

Kelly's hand shot up at the same moment he opened his mouth. "Didn't Ludlam keep a mulatto mistress in the French Quarter? There's a whole other branch of the Ludlams in New Orleans who trace themselves back to him. Black folks." Once Lena had showed him a newspaper clipping about mixed families in the city with Ludlam roots.

"If so," she said, signs of exasperation straining her features, "both families were generously provided for. Of course, each lady would have been deeded the house in which she raised her children. That goes without saying among civilized people."

"That's because neither of those dames," he said, voice rising, "were greedy and vindictive like women are today."

The tour participants glanced at each other, conferring in murmurs.

"Ladies like Elaine Ludlam," she said, "didn't have to deal with deceitful men who led their wives on while they snuck around—"

"Look, you fucking bitch. You can't have the goddamn house you abandoned and I've been working my balls off to save."

The lady in the lime track suit leaned over to cover her sons' ears. The tourists turned to huddle in a circle. Clearly this wasn't the question-and-answer interlude advertised in the brochure.

"You asshole, how dare you barge in here in front of—"

"How dare you sic that slime bucket lawyer on me?"

Lena fished a walkie-talkie out of a pocket in her voluminous hoop skirt. "Security," she shouted.

"Me and my wife want our money back," said an elderly man in a powder-blue leisure suit. "We could of heard this kind of stuff on the TV."

Track Suit hurried her two boys into the vestibule, where they broke into a gallop, whooping like wild Indians.

"Boys, please don't touch that wallpaper." Lena rushed after them. "It's from the olden days and can *nevuh* be replaced."

# Seventeen

"MOMMA, WE'RE AFRAID FOR YOU."

Arms folded, Gertie sat at her kitchen table, where she'd placed a fresh pot of coffee with chicory and four cups. Only Modene Holiday was sipping hers. Dixie was dragging on a Kent, and Nicole felt so nervous that coffee was the last thing she needed.

"Ms. Naquin," Modene asked, "what medications are you currently taking?"

"Just pills for this arthur-ritis," Gertie said, rubbing her knees, "that's killing me today. Must have been all that dancing. We had us a good time," she said, eyes narrowing into slits to glare at her daughter, "yesterday."

Nicole burned with shame for what she was doing, but it needed to be done. She had been on the verge of calling off the intervention, but then Modene phoned, gushing with concern, and Dixie was already on her way. If her mother continued on this path, she'd wind up dead or in jail.

"May I see the medicine bottle?" Modene asked, holding out her hand.

Gertie shook her head, shooting her a defiant stare.

"I know Gary has been giving you barbiturates," Nicole said.

"A dependence on barbiturates," Modene said, taking notes, "can cause an onset of the paranoid delusions we've been talking about."

Gertie sat there looking like a scolded child.

"Momma, I didn't want to bring this up." Nicole took a deep breath, and then decided it was for the best. "I talked to the bartender at the Aftermath Lounge. Don't you understand? You could be arrested and thrown in jail on a felony."

"My own sister," Dixie said, shaking her head, "a dope pusher getting booted out of queer bars in the Quarter. And who was that colored hooker come up and hug you at the Hermes parade? What would Papa say?"

"And another thing," Nicole said, "your mind—"

"Would you just shut up." Gertie jumped from her chair, moving away from the table. "What if I brought in some stranger and sat y'all down and told you everything I don't like about *you*. You, my daughter, whoring around with married men, first with Buster and now that Kelly Cannon. And you," she said, turning to Dixie, "my chain-smoking drunk of a sister, who gold dug her way Uptown and now thinks she so much better than everyone else."

"It's because we love you," Nicole said. How could she convince her mother of that?

"Then don't love me." Gertie backed against the edge of the tombstone on top of the utility cart, rocking the urn of ashes. "I don't want your love if it makes me feel awful about myself. Just leave me alone."

"We tired of fooling with you, girl," Dixie said. "You got two choices: come live with me or the loony bin."

"What's the difference? She just wants me to be her maid," Gertie told Modene.

"Well," Dixie said, "at least you'd be of use."

"See," Gertie said.

"Hell, I already got me a maid."

"You just jealous cause your nature was cut out after the bastard you had from that bad man you met at the parade. He left you with some sort of rot inside so you couldn't have no more kids of your own." Gertie turned to Nicole and Modene. "She was always jealous of me and my babies."

"Okay," Modene said with a tight smile, "now we're venturing into territory—"

A sharp rapping rattled a pane of the French doors, and then Gary stuck his head inside.

"Sorry, Miss Gertie, didn't know you had company."

Nicole rose, arms folded. "We're having a family meeting."

"Have to tell you Labat just got popped," Gary said, breathless. "Panarello brought him in for Marky's murder."

"Hallelujah!" Gertie raised her arms to heaven. "See what I been telling you. See which way the mop flop?" Gertie raced into Gary's arms, eyes watering. "They think I'm crazy. Want to send me to an insane asylum."

Nicole sat with her mouth open, and Modene cocked an eyebrow.

"How did you find out?" Gertie asked Gary, her arm around his waist.

"I walked into Minerva's Owl, and there was the cop, taking out his handcuffs."

"Thank you, Jesus," Gertie said, crossing herself. "Justice is done."

"No, it isn't," Gary said. "I have to tell you what I found out last night—"

"That don't change the fact you coming to live with me," Dixie said, throwing car keys into her purse. "Go pack your grip. Either that or a padded cell in Houma. Take your pick. Modene, honey, you got that paper to set up the lunacy hearing?"

"We don't call it that anymore," Modene said, digging into an accordion file, "and a court commitment might be trickier than you think."

"Gary," Gertie said, "go call that nice doctor who was friends with Marky, the one you met over by Napoleon's. Me and him had a long talk. He can vouch I'm not a lunatic."

"Who's this physician?" Modene asked.

"Bob White," Gary said.

"Dr. Robert White?" Modene closed the file. "He's one of the leading psychiatrists in the city. If Ms. Naquin is under treatment by Dr. White, and he hasn't determined any need for hospitalization, there's nothing I can do. May I consult with him?"

"Momma, you didn't tell me you were seeing a therapist." Who could this doctor possibly be? Nicole wondered. Was he the one who had gotten Gary worked up about Labat and mind control? She could barely think straight. Yesterday she felt so close to her brownie troop. Now they were sitting around with crosses smudged on their foreheads, attacking each other.

"Gary, go call that doctor. His number is on the pad by the phone in my bedroom. That's where I keep it," Gertie said, turning to her daughter, "in case I start foaming at the mouth in the middle of the night."

"But what I need to tell you," Gary insisted, "is that he's the one who—"

"Sugar, please."


GARY FELT LIKE CLAPPING.

Not even in a Joan Crawford movie had he ever witnessed such a dramatic exit as when Dixie stormed out of the intervention in a huff, trailing a cloud of smoke and invective. In the course of her hasty departure, she told him he was a big dope fiend who was the worst thing that ever happened to her sister, including the hurricane. Then she turned on Gertie, calling her a hopeless nut case headed for the skids, where she'd wind up like her pathetic son, and soon after took on Nicole, berating her as a spineless milksop who let everyone walk over her, including that drunk Mick with the big *putz*. Dixie saved her final fury for Modene, excoriating her as a phony ding-a-ling with a ridiculous hairdo who didn't know whether to shit or wind her watch.

"And if you change your fool mind," she told Gertie before slamming the door behind her, "that bed in *your* room on State Street is made up with new sheets from Neiman Marcus."

"Talk about acting out." Modene waved a hand in front of her face.

"See why I don't want to go live with her," Gertie said.

After Dixie's departure they sat exhausted around the table, making small talk until Dr. White's arrival. He had insisted on canceling appointments and rushing right over, even though Gary repeated that the situation was now under control. All he had to do, Gary told him, was to reassure the social worker on the phone that Miss Gertie posed no threat to herself or others. But Bob White said that he'd always wanted to meet Marky's mother. This was the perfect opportunity, if he could be of some service.

"The psych ward in Houma?" he'd asked, laughing. "Whose idea was that?"

Gary dreaded coming face-to-face with the crippled man. And was not surprised that the doctor didn't ask for the address. Obviously, he could give directions to where Marky's mother lived, even to thugs high on crack.

As soon as Bob White swung in on metal crutches,

Schnitzel leapt from his basket by the stove, yipping. His chariot wheels squeaked to a halt in the middle of the kitchen floor, where the dachshund and the doctor paused to study each other's creaking metal contraptions. The doctor's brow furrowed, and the dog let out one confused *yip* and then rolled back to his bed.

"That's Schnitzel," Miss Gertie said. "Marky gave him to me ten years ago."

"I've never seen wheels like that on a dog." Bob White lowered himself into a chair with a pained expression. "And I can only imagine what I look like to him." Then he crossed his prosthetic leg under the kitchen table. "Hey there," he said, catching Gary's eye with a broad grin. "You're Marky's friend I met at the Napoleon House. Gary, right?"

Gary nodded. Stonefaced, he glowered from a stool in the corner, watching Modene Holiday suck up to the famous shrink. She was already on her third cup of coffee.

"I don't know if you recall," she said, twirling her chunky terra-cotta necklace, "but I'm a member of the Jung Center. That show you curated, 'In the Shadow of the Shadow,' was so poignant. After the opening I went home and almost had a nervous breakdown."

Gary shrank into himself. This was the second time this week he'd sat facing the man he thought to be Marky's murderer, and his nerves were frayed. Now here was Bob White, sitting across from Miss Gertie at her kitchen table, telling her how close he felt to her son. Gary tried to picture this nerdy pillar of Uptown society conspiring with gangstas in front of Labat's shop on Rampart Street.

"We were like brothers," Bob White said. "You know, the good and bad one, the sane and crazy one." His eyes narrowed behind the oval glasses. "And as you know, for some reason, we always love the bad, crazy brother more, don't we?"

Miss Gertie was beginning to tear, staring with such tenderness into White's eyes. Obviously chagrined, Nicole had fallen silent, and Modene was hanging onto White's every word.

"Wow! Like the Shadow." Modene was excited, whether by the coffee, the renowned doctor, or being privy to his personal life. "So Marky Naquin was your Shadow. But in an act of integration, you accepted and loved him, rather than fearing and fighting him, as Jung says we often do with the negative projections of our psyches. What an inspiring story."

Gary winced. Yeah, he thought, so loving and accepting that after Marky used you, betrayed you, slept with your wife, hit you up for money constantly, then left you for dead, maimed forever, you had him murdered. And then you pinned the rap on the sadistic jailer who tortured you at Berkeley. A dish best served cold. Un-fucking-believable.

So much for the fair, unblemished son, the victim, the helper and healer.

*What Turns Good People Evil.* Indeed.

"What's that?" Bob White asked, pointing at the rusty utility cart.

"Oh, that came out of my flooded kitchen in Lakeview," Gertie said.

"No, on top of that?" asked the doctor, still pointing.

"The marble tablet," Nicole said with a sigh, "that the storm blew off our tomb."

"And the vase on top?"

The kitchen went silent.

"Here," Gertie said, rising. Puffy-eyed, she handed the urn to the doctor, smiling. "Your brother's ashes."

"Marky?" Bob White fumbled, dropping the urn onto the kitchen floor, where it popped open and clattered toward the French doors, leaving a trail of crunchy charcoal.

Everyone stared at each other, stricken. Next to the stove, the gas water heater rumbled on in a soft blue explosion. Fury flashed in Bob White's blue eyes, as if they also had caught fire. He pounded the table until the coffee cups rattled in their saucers, then grabbed his prosthetic leg, weeping. Nicole and Modene fell to their knees, using coffee spoons to scoop Marky's ashes back into the urn with shaking hands.

"I'm so sorry," Bob White repeated between sobs. "You have no idea how sorry I am about this."

Gary sat horrified. This was as close to a confession as he could imagine. Yet it wasn't. At Parish Prison, the lieutenant was grilling Labat this very minute, and Gary bet that the bookseller wasn't spilling half as much as the doctor just did: the murder victim's ashes all over his mother's kitchen floor.

The French doors swung open and Kelly poked his head in, the ashen cross now just a dingy spot on his forehead.

"I'm back from St. Francisville. Hey, what's this?" he asked, glancing from face to face. "A funeral?"

# III

# Climbing

# Eighteen

CLAPS OF THUNDER RUMBLED LIKE cannon blasts on the horizon, and then rain pattered on top of the rusty air conditioner in the sole window of a cramped, putty-colored interrogation room that smelled like burned rubber. Lieutenant Panarello turned from a view of the shuttered barbecue joints and pawnshops at the once lively intersection of Tulane and Broad and went back to his notes. Labat lit another Chesterfield, his arctic glare fixed on the policemen. Vinnie had never questioned a hypnotist before and every few minutes found a reason to look away.

"Okay, Mr. Labat," Vinnie said, "let's go over this one more time."

"We can go over it as many times as you like, officer," Labat said. "The truth never changes, only our perception of it does."

That was just the trouble. Most people telling the truth betrayed certain uncertainties, slipping occasional variations into a fairly consistent story. *The car that hit me was green*, they'd say, *sea-green, no, make that apple-green, now that I think of it*. But Labat's story was scripted, air tight, with not a single detail out of place.

Since Labat's arrest yesterday, the lieutenant had only

seventy-two hours to worm an incriminating story out of him before he needed to be formally charged before a judge. Or let go. And if Labat didn't go to jail, Vinnie suspected that without the psychiatrist's testimony, he probably would. As of yesterday, the lieutenant had only a month to work with his lawyer and Dr. White to prepare the temporary insanity defense at his own murder trial. If they put Vinnie on the stand this minute, he'd be acquitted in a heartbeat. He wasn't sleeping or eating, and this post-traumatic shock absorber or whatever the hell they called it was getting to him.

No, Labat was no angel, whatever he claimed about his "spirituality," and Vinnie read him as a world-class con man, one who was not after dough but power. Power over other people. His checkered past was fascinating. He graduated *magna cum laude* from the University of California at Berkeley in psychology and religion, and then did a short stint in Viet Nam. Vinnie was glad he never had to creep through the jungle with this weirdo. Labat had then been involved in some fly-by-night outfit in San José that sold lessons in mind control, in a Native American church in Nevada that ordained its ministers by mail, and in a New Age bookstore in Venice Beach, California, where he became the resident psychic for one of Lee Marvin's ex-wives.

The background check went on and on, with no criminal charges appearing until Labat was arrested for molesting teenage boys while working as a counselor at a boot camp for emotionally-disturbed delinquents in New Mexico. Those charges were eventually dropped. That must have been when he hightailed it back to New Orleans to live with his mama, the last surviving child of an old blue-blood family that once owned a long-disappeared sugar plantation in St. John the Baptist Parish, where the Labat name was still one to be reckoned with.

And here was Vinnie, who had never left his hometown and barely finished two years at Tulane night school, trying to outwit such a smooth-talking snake charmer. This was quite a dragon the doctor was asking him to slay. Keep it real, he thought.

"Ever had sex with Naquin?" he asked, leaning forward to meet Labat's gaze. Vinnie could tell he was a big fruit the minute he laid eyes on him at St. Jude.

"No."

"Ever bought, sold, or did drugs with Naquin?"

"No."

"Ever took money from him?"

"Only for the books he purchased."

"Ever got in a fight with him?"

"As I've explained so carefully, he accused me of heresy."

"From what religion?"

"It's not a religion as such, but a Catholic spiritual doctrine that descends from the Knights Templar, just as the Masons do, erroneously, I might add."

"You a Mason?" Vinnie tried to picture Labat with a fringed fez riding in one of those go-carts in the Shriner's parade.

Labat closed his eyes, as if drawing on some inner strength. "Of course not."

"Those guys I seen go in your house last weekend," Vinnie asked, "they sex pickups?"

Labat's eyes remained closed. "Absolutely not."

"Give me their names and addresses."

Labat's eyes opened, incandescently blue.

Vinnie's cell vibrated in his pocket. "This the call I'm waiting on, from the officers searching your house."

"Ask them about my mother," Labat said. "Remind her to feed the dogs."

Vinnie stepped into the corridor and returned two minutes later, face blazing. He whipped out the handcuffs, yanked Labat's arms behind the chair and cuffed him, sweeping the Chesterfields and ashtray onto the floor with a clatter. The cop twisted Labat's head at a sharp angle until his face was inches from his own.

And then the lieutenant spit.

Right in his face.

Labat jerked away, but Vinnie grabbed him by the scalp and bent his head back until the bulging blue eyes were looking directly into the narrowing slit of the cop's stare.

"Your mama's fine," Vinnie whispered with a sneer, showing a jagged row of yellowed teeth, "but wants to know how to cook them?"

"Cook what?"

"The three human skulls the officers found in your bedroom closet."

"Those old things? Oh, for heaven's sake. They're from the Anatomy Department of the Tulane Medical School. I acquired them years ago from their excess inventory. My mother knows nothing—"

"Mean to tell me they ain't got nothing to do with that dame who got beheaded right above your shop? I thought you was a kook, buster, but not a monster. You give butcher lessons to Hunter Finn? Bet you had him wrapped around your little finger, didn't you?"

Vinnie grabbed his cell, speed-dialing with his thumb.

"Hey, Dr. White? Boy, I'm really gonna need your help on this one."

GARY COULDN'T BELIEVE WHAT HE was about to do.

Rap with the fuzz, of all people. It made him feel as

lowdown as that despicable snitch J.J. But after what he saw in the paper today, he had nowhere else to turn. It was all in Panarello's hands now.

Gary had made an appointment to meet the lieutenant at the front door of the Eighth District on the corner of Royal and Conti. The white columns of what used to be a stately old bank looked more like a courthouse in small-town Mississippi than a police station. Except that nobody could miss it, surrounded as it always was by blue-and-white cop cars parked illegally on the sidewalk. The station had a sleepy air, and the round tables of Café Beignet next door spilled out under the magnolia tree shading the entrance.

Gary hadn't told Miss Gertie yet his suspicions about the doctor. She was still flying too high on Labat's arrest and, after all, Gary had been wrong once before. How could he possibly break it to Miss Gertie what Marky's self-proclaimed "brother," who had saved the old lady from whatever that hincty social worker had in store for her, had done to her son? And what was the motive? And the most unlikely part: had the doctor, Mr. Uptown Propriety himself, actually contracted the drive-by with thugs from the projects in front of Labat's funky store?

*A crippled dude with a funny leg.*

That was all Gary had to go on. Yet, after what he found out about Bob White's relationship with both Marky and Labat, it made perfect sense.

Until Marky's murder, Gary always considered himself a real New Orleanian. And was he ever wrong. You never belonged anywhere until someone you loved had died there. Only that kind of loss could nail you in place, and until Marky's death he'd just been another tourist, maybe one with a long lease, but still barely skimming the surface. Until then he had thought that the city was mostly, well, fun. But this murder had sucked him into the dark underbelly of the place, and its guts were much more twisted than he ever imagined possible.

"Hey, Cherry," the lieutenant said, pulling out two iron chairs at a café table. "Look, I'm glad you called but don't waste my time, hear? As if I ain't got enough on my mind, with the parking-lot shooting trial and now this case straight out of some 'Morgus the Magnificent' horror show. Want a coffee?"

Gary nodded.

"Two house coffees," Vinnie shouted to the counter, rattling a pair of handcuffs in the pocket of his stained tan overcoat. "You probably seen the paper today." He waved the headline of the Friday, March 3, *Times-Picayune*. "My chief called me in and said, 'Panarello, what's with all these heads and skulls rattling around in the Eighth District? As if the storm wasn't enough. Talk about scaring off tourists. Gives a whole new meaning to losing your head in the French Quarter.' What's your take on this?"

"I'm sure you know that Labat once sold lessons in mind control," Gary said, feeling menaced by the handcuffs, "based on CIA techniques that could tear a personality down and then rebuild it with hypnotic suggestion. Turn someone into a killer with a subliminal code phrase used as a trigger. Labat's was 'As above, so below.' I tried it on him last week, and it worked. He invited me in."

The cop scribbled in his notebook.

"Thing is," Gary said, "Labat hadn't expected Finn to go apeshit and kill himself after he cut up his girlfriend. He obviously thought Finn would bring him the head to use in some Mani ceremony."

"Yeah, yeah, but what them creeps want with skulls?" Vinnie glanced down at his watch.

"During the Inquisition, the Pope accused the Knights

Templar of worshiping the severed head, among other gross things." Gary had just gotten to that part in Marky's book. "One of the heresy charges was that the Knights used the head in a rite to conjure the spirit of St. John the Baptist before going into battle against the Sacracens, the Arabs in the Holy Land. It was part of their initiation ritual. Finn was probably set to join the brotherhood."

"St. John the Baptist, huh? That's what the doc was saying."

"The doc?"

"Yeah, this shrink working with me on the case. Ever heard of Robert White?

Gary gulped. "Yep." Speak of the devil.

"So I'm glad you've come around and want to help us out. Sorry I had to pull you in last month, but then you was the only lead we had on Naquin." The cop eyed Gary up and down. "So why you want to talk with me today?"

"Have you tied Labat into Marky's murder yet?"

"Not a shred. No skull involved, that's for sure. You got something?"

"Word on the street says someone else did it."

"Who?"

Gary hesitated, studying the bags under the cop's weary green eyes.

"Can make it worth something to you," the lieutenant said.

"I don't want the bread. I just don't know where else—"

"Spill."

"Dr. Robert White."

"Oh, come on," Vinnie sputtered, choking on a mouthful of coffee. "He's the one who. . . ."

"Who what?"

"You crazy. He's a respectable psychiatrist who works with the police. Besides, him and Naquin was friends." Vinnie started to button his coat. "Got a witness?"

"No."

"A motive?" Something was clicking. Gary could almost hear the gears shifting inside the cop's head. Panarello knew more about this than he let on.

"Not a clear one. Except I do know Marky was responsible for Bob White losing his leg in a car accident three years ago."

The lieutenant's brow creased as this sank in.

"How you be this evening, officer?" Gary spotted the palsied hand first, then the rest of J.J. slithered through the gate on a crutch, dragging his dead foot. "What you two jailbirds planning, a big dope deal?" J.J.'s snakeskin face twitched with the joke.

"What you after?" Panarello asked.

"The eagle flies on Friday, don't it?"

"Okay, go pick up your blood money," the cop said, as J.J. gimped up the three steps into the station. Then he turned back to Gary. "You telling me that a crippled white man from the Garden District went down to the projects to contract some drug thugs to do a drive-by?"

*A crippled dude with a funny leg.*

Wait a minute.

Who ever said the crippled dude was *white?* Big Mama's stud in lockup would have said "white boy" if that was what he meant. No black person would have overlooked that particular adjective, just as white people assumed by default that everyone they mentioned was white, unless tagged differently. That was just the tribal way people thought.

Gary had seen J.J. in so many disguises, even in drag zooming around in a motorized wheelchair. Like a chameleon, he could change color, shape, and sex. God knows where he lived, inside walls or under floorboards on Rampart Street, scurrying out with his tongue darting and then disappearing once his vile deeds were done into the cracks between black and white, cop and thug, day and night. He was the go-between in every crooked deal that happened in the Quarter—dealing, pimping, shaking down—and that was why he was so invaluable to the cops.

Was this just a coincidence? How could two crippled men be involved in Marky's murder, one with the motive and the other with the means? But in the event that a white person Uptown wanted to contract a drive-by in the Quarter, who else would set it up but J.J.? Gary never could picture the doctor consorting with thugs, but now the final piece of the puzzle snapped into place with a *click*.

"A crippled dude with a funny leg," Gary said, tugging at the cop's sleeve. "Give me five more minutes. Let me tell you what I know about Marky and Bob White. See, this is the way I think it went down."

The cop listened impatiently to Gary's hurried account. He spilled everything he knew: Big Mama's tip from the queens' tank, Marky and White's past sexual relationship, the car accident, White's rivalry with Labat after the prison experiment at Berkeley, and the doctor's breakdown in Miss Gertie's kitchen. Then he threw in J.J., the middle man.

"Don't you see?" Gary insisted. "The crippled man—"

"Which crippled man?" the cop asked, draining his cup.

"The white cripple, meaning Dr. White—"

"White cripple, black cripple? What we playing, a game of handicap chess?"

"Hired the black cripple J.J. to do the dirty work of contracting—"

"You a real gumshoe, Cherry." The cop stood up to leave, face twisted into a snarl. "Maybe you should give up dealing and write them stories down. Go read your stuff for the open mike at the Dragon's Den. But I can't figure out why you telling me this crap. Where's the *proof*?"

Gary could sense some deep-seated doubt that the cop entertained about the doctor, if only in the way he described their first meeting at what he called the "voodoo confessional" in White's carriage house. But the lieutenant insisted that J.J. worked undercover for the Eighth District, and these days he counted White as a staunch ally of the Police Department, one who had helped him to crack the Hunter Finn case. Did Gary think for one goddamn minute that he, Lieutenant Vincent Panarello, would investigate such an invaluable citizen—one of the few psychiatrists left in the city—on the whim of a hippie drug dealer in the Quarter?

"What you on now," the cop asked him, "some kind of acid trip?"

# Nineteen

BEFORE KELLY'S SNORING WOKE HER, Nicole was amazed to discover a second-hand shop with rack after rack of the exact same clothes she wore in high school. The shop was perched on the wind-swept roof of a Manhattan skyscraper, and the terrier she held on a short leash kept scrambling toward the edge. She didn't even want to peek down—it gave her vertigo—and was terrified the dog would lunge over the edge and pull her with it. So she decided to play it safe, going back into the shop to buy back her favorite skirt from eleventh grade.

Then, still groggy with sleep, she drifted into the kitchen, throwing open the shutters and spooning coffee into a filter. The chilly dawn bathed the kitchen in cobwebs of light, and to dispel the sticky strands luring her back to bed she turned on the portable TV to a whisper, watching images float by that seemed no more real than the dream about skyscrapers and outfits from high school.

Iraqi insurgents in ski masks had beheaded two Canadian hostages in Baghdad, a grim, broken city that reminded Nicole of New Orleans. A black mother was on her knees, wailing behind yellow caution tape as her teenage son's body was lifted into an ambulance. Mayor Blinger was stabbing at the air, saying something about recovery and federal dollars, then Mike Landry, the main challenger in Tuesday's primary, was saying something else about recovery and leadership. In a photo from the storm, Landry was shown in shirtsleeves, an overgrown boy scout helping some drowned-looking people into a boat. An enormous wave crashed against a sea wall, followed by a now familiar aerial pan of the flooded city. Then headshots appeared of four policemen who shot somebody in a parking lot after the hurricane—one of them looked like the cop on Marky's case—now set to go on trial next month for negligent homicide. This was trailed by the latest statistic of residents who had returned to the city: 38 percent.

A Suzuki commercial blared on and, coffee cup in hand, Nicole jumped up to turn off the TV.

She had made some peace with her mother on Ash Wednesday, after Dr. White and Modene Holiday finally left. But this was only following a truly horrendous scene, when she screamed at her mother to put her goddamned pills into a bag that Nicole was going to flush down the toilet. Meanwhile, Kelly was pacing the courtyard, shouting on the cell to his wife in St. Francisville, while her mother sat there nursing a beer with a hurt stare, sulky as a grounded adolescent.

Eventually, Nicole gave up and washed her mother's hair, while they talked about where Gertie's Lakeview neighbors were stranded in other parts of the country and how lucky she was to at least be in New Orleans. Nicole managed to shift the blame for the intervention to Auntie Dixie, and Gertie agreed that it was just like her sister to try some smart-alecky stunt like that. Then the three of them stumbled off to bed, shoulders slumped in Lenten resignation to their fates.

Mardi Gras was definitely over, and Nicole wasn't accustomed any more to these nosedives from manic highs into depressed lows that were so much part of this culture. Even the sight of a stray pair of Carnival beads dangling from a bare branch or lying broken in a gutter could bring her to the verge of tears. Now the city was in an upheaval as the mayoral primary heated up. Nicole, like everyone she knew, took it as a foregone conclusion Mike Landry would win. Senator Landry's brother was down-to-earth and well connected both in Washington and Baton Rouge, in sharp contrast to Blinger, characterized by little more than his prickly ego and a series of grandiose proposals that seemed hatched over some late-night bong.

Nicole wondered how much longer the three of them could camp out this way, and if these musty rooms represented the end of an old life or the beginning of a new one. The French Quarter minted a new brand of eccentric every few years, and perhaps flooded-out suburbanites would now become the new Quarter characters, living like exiled White Russians in Paris between the wars, pinching pennies in peeling shotguns while awash with nostalgia for a lost kingdom of carports and wall-to-wall carpeting. After all, they weren't the first people to lose everything. No doubt it could be done.

The question was: did Nicole want to do it?

They could also sell her mother's house, install her in some seniors' complex across the lake where she couldn't get into any more trouble, and then Nicole and Kelly could make a new life for themselves in Phoenix or Boulder, some place that offered jobs and housing and a future, where everyone wasn't dragging some moldy nightmare behind them like a sodden mattress.

She couldn't count on the FEMA job forever and dreaded looking for employment again in this wrecked city. When she first moved home, she'd worked for two weeks in the accounts payable department of an artificial limb factory across the river. But she soon found out what that entailed. She was the repo lady for false arms and legs. Before she quit, she could picture herself yanking the prosthetic limb off of some poor black grandmother, screaming, "You owe us $263.45, Mrs. Watkins. Gimme back that leg."

"Another day, another dollar." Kelly stumbled into the kitchen in a T-shirt and boxers.

"Going to work on the house today?" Nicole asked, handing him a cup of coffee.

"Me and Geesus almost finished with the kitchen."

"Do you think Lena will finally give in?"

"She don't know what she wants," he said, yawning. "And know something, babe? Neither do I."

Kelly flung open the French doors, taking a deep breath of morning air.

"Home, sweet home," he said to the silent courtyard. "But what price do we have pay to live here?"

"COME SEE, QUICK." IT WAS AS IF Nicole had discovered a sculpted ice swan melting on the doorstep. "A letter!"

She held it between her fingertips like the Shroud of Turin. "From Allstate Homeowner's Insurance, addressed to Mr. Kelly Cannon. This is the first piece of mail since the storm," she said, handing it to Kelly with a flourish.

Every month Nicole had to waste an entire day talking to robots on the phone. This was an established ritual in her new life, pressing one, two, or three, then explaining that because she lived in New Orleans—remember, the hurricane?—where there was still no mail delivery, she hadn't received the utilities bill or credit card summary or bank statement, which had been returned to sender as "undeliverable at this address." Every time it rained, the landline went dead for days at a time, so she couldn't even use the dial-up Internet to pay her bills. So she would spend hours on hold, until sweat had bonded the cell's plastic to her ear, only to wind up yelling about late fees and missed payments to someone who couldn't believe this crazy lady lived in a part of our great country where nothing worked.

So a letter waiting in the mailbox on a Saturday morning. That was a victory.

"Hey, seven months later and finally you got mail." Kelly crossed himself and then tore into the letter.

"Look at this bullshit." He jumped up from the kitchen table. "Wind damage claim accepted. Flood damage claim denied. But the wind brought the water that caused the flooding. It's called 'storm surge,' pal. So if the wind knocks a tree onto your house, bingo. But if the same wind throws some water into your house, nada." He dropped the page into Nicole's hands.

"Can't you appeal?"

"And spend another six months on the phone with those bastards?" Kelly handed her the second page.

Her eyes widened. "This says your coverage is going up 300 percent. Momma's went up 400. What do they want people to do?"

"Drop the homeowner's, so they don't have to insure this swamp any more." He grabbed the letter. "But this may be just the ticket. Let me go fax this to my lawyer. Lena was counting on the insurance settlement to make a profit on the house. But once that Leona Helmsley in a hoop skirt gets a load of this mess, she may settle for far less, like one of my kidneys or lungs."

"But do *you* want the mess?"

"Sweetheart, I come from the mess, know how to jerry-rig it until it works. Let's face it. I *am* the mess."

"I've been thinking," she said, "maybe we should make a fresh start somewhere else. Not selling fish sticks in Mexico, of course, but somewhere prosperous and sane like Phoenix. And Momma would be better off at Mossy Lanes across the lake."

"And leave the mess?"

She nodded. "Leave the mess."

"But New Orleans is the mess you and me have in common. It's the anchor of the past, oyster po'boys, Dixieland, Mardi Gras, the Quarter," Kelly said, slapping the plaster wall of the shotgun. "It's where we were kids together."

"So we don't have a future in common?" Nicole didn't like where this conversation was heading. At all.

"But the future has to grow out of the past, like mulch. I don't want to be an air plant hanging in some climate-controlled condo in the middle of a golf course on the other side of the moon."

"So we should stay on a sinking ship just because it has an anchor?" she asked, incredulous. "Heeello?"

"If I'm going anywhere else, it's Mexico," Kelly said. "Off the grid. To be a painter."

"Here we go again. I'm not about to jump from the frying pan into the fire. The French Quarter is as much of a foreign country as I can take. On the other hand, the job market and real estate values in Phoenix—"

"Now you sound like Lena. I don't give a shit about the job market and real estate values."

"Obviously, since you want to stay in New Orleans."

He took her into his arms. "The city will stay afloat. Wait until after the election."

"I'm tired of waiting," Nicole said, throwing off his embrace. "First people said wait until Christmas, everyone will come back then. Then wait until Mardi Gras, now wait until after the election. Then it'll be wait until after the next hurricane season. I can't wait any longer for my future to begin in this town."

"Your future here began a while ago," he said, folding the letter into its envelope and slipping on his windbreaker. "But you were too busy waiting to notice."

KELLY WAS PUTTING THE FINISHING touches on the lizard's tail when Miss Gertie hobbled into the courtyard with a newspaper under her arm.

Kelly was fascinated by the geckos darting in and out of sight among the vines and banana trees in the patio, and in this painting wanted to capture the viewer's surprise when he caught the scampering motion out of the corner of his eye, like errant thoughts flickering through the mind. When finished, this would be the tenth painting he'd done since moving in with Nicole. The Lakeview Picasso was on a roll.

He grunted a greeting at Miss Gertie, the handle of a fine-tipped brush wedged between his teeth like a bit.

She plopped down in a chair at the patio table and slapped down the newspaper.

"You seen the headline?" she asked.

"Nope."

"Now the cops claim the skulls they found at Labat's house on Thursday came from some anatomy classes at Tulane, just like he said. Something about serial numbers." She held up the front page of the Saturday paper: QUARTER SHOPKEEPER'S SKULLS TRACED TO MED SCHOOL.

Kelly took the paintbrush from between his teeth. "So much for leaving your body to science just to have your head wind up as Labat's toy. They going to let him go now?"

"I hope not. They still think he's an accomplice in the Hunter Finn case."

"And what about Marky?"

"Say he's under suspicion in Marky's case, too, but they

don't have any proof."

"So he's in this thing up to his neck, no pun intended." Kelly chuckled to himself, dabbing on more white light. "Even if the skulls were legit, you were right about Labat."

"And that daughter of mine still owes me an apology."

"Momma," Nicole said, sticking her head onto the courtyard. "I tried calling you all afternoon."

"I was over by the Chinese place," Gertie said, securing her square pocketbook under the chair. "You seen the paper yet, hon?"

Still in her FEMA duds, Nicole stepped out onto the worn, uneven bricks. "I hope they don't let Labat go now."

"Wonder who's taking care of his mama at home," Gertie said. "I feel some sorry for that lady."

Christ, thought Kelly, even skull-worshipping Satanists lived with their mothers in this town.

"The paper says she's blind," Nicole said. "But how could she not know what was going on? Come on, ceremonies with human skulls? It's not like your son having a few friends over to watch the Super Bowl."

"It didn't surprise this mama. How many times I told you Labat hypnotized the Finn boy to do what he done?"

"Too many." Nicole shivered. "I can't take any more of this, FEMA by day, murder by night."

Here it comes, Kelly thought, mixing up a navy-blue wash. He needed to put in more shadows, a bit of definition. Without darkness there was no perspective, exactly what was missing in the featureless landscapes of the places where Nicole wanted to live.

"Kelly and I . . . well, actually, I'm thinking and Kelly isn't sure . . . of moving to Phoenix."

"What in creation would you do there?"

"Lead a normal life."

"Why would you want to do *that*?" Gertie looked genuinely shocked. "After all, you're the only lucky one around here who didn't lose anything in the storm."

"I know, but the whole part of the city that's gone, everyone who can't come back, aches like a phantom limb. It's as if I go to reach for something but my other hand isn't there. Everything that's missing hurts me so much sometimes I can't get to sleep at night."

Gertie nodded, eyes softening. "But what about your poor momma?"

"Once you get an insurance settlement and your house is dealt with, wouldn't you be happier across the lake at some nice complex like Mossy Lanes?"

"That's for old people," Gertie barked, impatient again. "Me, I'm staying here. Oscar says I sing like an angel, and the first Sunday in April I have a gospel solo at Our Lady of Guadalupe. I may be the only white lady singing, but I ain't the fattest."

Nicole sighed. "I don't want to get started again—"

"Then don't."

"Tell me the truth," Nicole said, glaring at her mother's purse stashed under the patio chair, "have you been out dealing drugs again?"

"You've not the boss of me."

Kelly had to admire the old lady's spunk and admit grudgingly that as cuckoo as she'd sounded during the past month, she clocked Labat, whether he murdered Marky or not. And now she was diving into "the community," as black folks called their neighborhoods, through the church. He could picture her carrying her stuffed mirlitons in a casserole dish over to Oscar's house in the Tremé for an S & M potluck. Her upbeat attitude sure beat the bitching and moaning Nicole was doing.

"Tell you what, babe," Kelly said, working more blue into a banana leaf, "your momma and me will stay here painting and singing up a storm, and you skip over to Phoenix to gather your wits at the mall. You can land a fat job to supplement the dope-dealing and find a big house we can evacuate to during the next hurricane."

"*Very* funny," Nicole said.

"Now you talking," Gertie said. "By the way, this morning Dr. White called to see how I was doing, and—"

"So you're finally going to pursue treatment?" Nicole asked.

"I'm not gonna tell that man my business. But listen, he invited us to a shindig at his house next Friday to meet the mayor!"

"Meet Roy Blinger?" Kelly said, laughing so hard he smeared the lizard's eye.

"It's a fundraiser for his campaign," Gertie said, "but he said we don't have to contribute nothing, just eat and drink. He wants to introduce me to his wife."

"I can't believe someone so intelligent is supporting The Great Blinger." Nicole mimed sticking a finger down her throat.

"Send White over to Labat to have his head examined," Kelly said. "I'm game. You?"

Nicole shrugged. At the moment, she struck Kelly as looking almost as old as her mother.

"The doctor told me to please invite any black friends," Gertie said, "so I'm going to ask Sweet Pea and Oscar. And some of the choir ladies. Guess he don't want the party to look so Uptown people will think the mayor is a bartender. Oh, and Gary, of course. Wait till I tell him we going to hobnob at the Garden District home of Dr. Robert White." She puffed out her bosom, wiggling a pinkie. "He's going to be *so* excited."

# Twenty

ALL WEEK NICOLE'S MOTHER HAD been in a tizzy about the Blinger fundraiser at Bob White's house but complained she didn't have a thing to wear. Which, as Nicole knew, she really didn't. Since her house flooded, she'd been scraping by with Salvation Army bargains and too-small hand-me-downs from Dixie. No department stores had reopened in the city, so this afternoon Nicole shepherded her mother and Kelly to a mall in Jefferson Parish to shop for what Kelly called their "Blinger gear." Gertie insisted that her two choir-lady friends would dress to the nines, and then there was Sweet Pea! She had already nixed his rhinestone tiara.

While the shopping areas of the city still looked like a war zone, Nicole was bug-eyed at the booming suburban malls. It reminded her of Austin, where the efficient Mrs. Doctor had known exactly who she was and what to do. After the shopping spree, while they unloaded her double-parked car on Dauphine Street, she felt like a Cuban returning to Havana after a week in Miami. The Saturn was filled with plastic bags bulging with fresh produce, art supplies, discount linens, electronics, flowering azaleas, and, of course, the objects of the excursion, a lilac organdy dress with a shawl collar for her mother, a navy-blue blazer for Kelly, and for herself, a wool-blend jacket on sale to match that dressy charcoal skirt.

After the inevitable fashion show with her mother, the floor strewn with wrapping paper and tags, Nicole sank onto her sofa bed, thinking about Phoenix. Of course, she'd never set foot there but knew just what to expect. That reassuring, one-size-fits-all formula was the real allure of the prosperous and sane America she daydreamed about: the stucco malls with Barnes & Noble and Pottery Barn, the morning ritual of laptop and frappuccino at Starbucks, the neat subdivision lawns, the fussy fusion restaurants decorated in a regional theme—Phoenix would be sandstone tones and Navaho weavings—and the perky neighbors and co-workers who would bring her a fruit basket when she moved in and celebrate her birthday with a Dutch-treat lunch and worry with her about carbs at the mirrored health club. She would giggle with them about the square-jawed personal trainer, fifteen years her junior, whose bedroom eyes would meet hers for a moment over some syrupy pink concoction at the local fern bar on a Friday night, and then she would drive a million miles alone on the freeway to her condo with the Berber carpeting to watch CNN, missing her mother and Kelly and the sassy accent and greasy food of this doomed city so much that she would cry herself to sleep on the Santa Fe-patterned pillowcases.

"This the last darn outfit I'm trying on," Gertie said, appearing with an expectant gleam in her eye at the pocket doors in her lilac dress and tangerine pumps, with a green vinyl belt and matching nylon scarf. Nicole burst out laughing. It was the most hideous combination she'd ever seen.

"That's just perfect," she said. "You'll be the belle of the ball." Then she jumped up to throw her arms around the dolled up old lady with smeared lipstick, reeking of some sample from the Dillard's perfume counter. "I miss you so much."

"But I'm right here," Gertie said, glowing.

"Then stay here," Nicole said. "Just the way you are."


KELLY SAT BEHIND THE WHEEL OF his SUV, wondering what the hell he'd gotten himself into. With their brimmed hats and eighteen-wheeler hips, Miss Eola and Miss Ranell took up the entire back seat. After stopping to pick them up in the Tremé, Nicole had made a big fuss about helping the choir ladies into the car. It was just as well that Gertie had joined the rowdy crowd riding to the party with Sweet Pea and Oscar in Gary's Chevy van.

"Yes, indeedy!" Miss Eola said, straightening her fuchsia jacket around the straining seat belt buckled over her hefty paunch.

"Isn't this something?" said throaty Miss Ranell. "I hope to tell you."

Kelly bet these two were never at a loss for words.

"So," he said to the back seat, "you ladies big Blinger supporters?"

"Well," said Miss Eola with a girlish giggle, "not exactly. He don't always do what he say he gonna do for the community, know what I mean?"

"That right," added Miss Ranell in a rich contralto. "I didn't vote for him the first time around—he too smart-alecky—but now I not so sure about that other one, Landry. About what he do to bring all those people home, hear what I saying?"

Now Blinger and Landry were squaring off after the circus of the primary election, which ended on Tuesday. Thirteen candidates had jumped into the primary, including the zookeeper, the gay owner of Labat's bookstore, a fire-and-brimstone preacher, a shrill neighbor of Dixie Rosenblum's who wanted to abolish local taxes, and an obese man famous for his mattress commercials. Blinger had barely uttered a peep. He spent his time flying around the country visiting the enclaves of poor black evacuees, warning them that if those rich white folks took over City Hall, they wouldn't be welcomed back. Now an absentee voting system had been set up in major cities—Kelly heard buses were being chartered to bring them to town to vote—although most of these people hadn't supported Blinger during his first term because he was "in the pocket of Uptown." He was, as they put it, just "too white" and recently cut an unlikely figure as a racial rabble-rouser.

"Blinger sure blew it after the storm." Kelly cut a look at Nicole, who was listening with an arched eyebrow.

"Oh Lord, ain't that the truth," said Miss Eola. "My sister from Gentilly spend three days walking up and down that hot overpass, and she seventy-two with diabetes. She not coming back, no siree. She happy in Houston where her grandbabies got good schools."

"Unh hunh. Bernadine daddy die in a wheelchair in front of the Superdome, praying for help," said Miss Ranell, clucking. "Atlanta suit her fine."

"Isn't that something?" said one.

"I hope to tell you," said the other.

Both cars pulled up to the Seventh Street address at the same moment, where a group of snowy-haired gentlemen suited with impeccable tailoring were smoking and poking each other in the ribs on a wide veranda under Doric columns. Miss Gertie was the first through the iron gate, the round pie-pan of her face beaming with the splendor of it all.

She introduced herself to the pair of surprised security guards—obviously off-duty cops—as if they were the evening's hosts or club doormen she had to talk her way past. She then

presented the choir ladies, Miss Nida Mann, Mr. Oscar
Batiste, and finally Mr. Gary Cherry, giving him a squeeze
around the waist. Oscar was dressed like an undertaker and
Sweet Pea like a casino hostess, his backless heels clopping
along the brick walkway. Kelly lingered at the back of the
group, embarrassed that these rubes saw fit to mingle with the
stone-faced security guards, one short and stout as a tea kettle,
the other dark and thin as a licorice stick. The snowy-haired
gentlemen had frozen in mid-conversation, studying the scene
as if perhaps they were the ones at the wrong party.

"Me, I got to find the lady room fast," Sweet Pea announced,
straightening sparkly panty hose over his meaty calves. The
choir ladies tittered, cupping hands over their mouths. The
stout guard, who as everyone soon found out was married
to Miss Eola's brother-in-law's niece, finally cracked a smile,
looked Sweet Pea up and down, and shook his head as if to
say—mayor or no mayor—*this still crazy New Orleans.*

ONCE INSIDE, KELLY STEERED NICOLE by the elbow past clusters
of bejeweled ladies balancing porcelain hors d'oeurve plates in
one hand and cocktail glasses in the other. His gaze swept the
salmon expanse of the high-ceilinged salon, over the balding
pink pates and highlighted blond flips, as if searching for
someone important he was supposed to meet.

What he was really looking for was the bar.

No, it wasn't where a group was gathered around a rectory
table writing checks and pinning on campaign buttons ("Roy's
Our Boy!") or where a line snaked along the candle-lit banquet
table at the center of the dining room, silverware clinking
around a huge slab of prime rib. There it was, an actual oak bar
probably shipped over from a village pub in Ireland, manned
by an elfin-faced old deacon with a generous hand, the only

other black person in the room except for Kelly's posse. He could understand why the doctor had been anxious for Miss Gertie to invite her friends to color-coordinate this Botox clinic of aging debutantes and their ruddy-faced escorts. Kelly just hoped that Sweet Pea didn't rifle through any of these ladies' purses, or Oscar wasn't caught in the bathroom with one of their baby-faced hubbies, who seemed a little light in the tasseled loafers, if you asked him.

"So, where's the doc?" Kelly asked Nicole, knocking back a slug of Jameson.

"Over there," she said, pointing with her chin.

"Why you think," he asked out of the corner of his mouth, "this bunch of Uptown über-ofays going all out for The Great Blinger?"

"He may be black," Nicole said, fingertips over her lips, "but he's *their* black. They want to hang onto the power they have in this town. Blinger is almost a Republican, and to these people Mike Landry's father was, well, the Viet Cong. Don't you remember? He was that hotshot civil-rights lawyer who integrated City Hall while we were in high school. And they'll never forgive him or his family," she said, wagging a finger. "Never."

"So rather than vote for the nigger-lover, they'll vote for the nigger? Now that, Miss Scarlet, is what I call prejudice."

"I'll pretend I didn't hear that. But I bet the doctor has political ambitions. I can tell you more about that after I meet his wife." Nicole craned her neck to peer over heads. "There's Blinger now."

A caramel-colored dome sailed above the crowd, followed by the same two muscle-bound goons Kelly remembered from the art party on Royal Street. Guests applauded as Blinger camel-walked to the center of the room under the massive crystal chandelier, where he clasped his hands over his head like a prizefighter. He looked distracted, as if only going through the motions, anxious to get on to the next event. Kelly figured he already had this room sewn up and was just here to pocket checks from rich white people before he jetted to Texas and Georgia to scare poor black people that they could never come home unless they voted for him. What a fucking shuck.

Kelly drained his glass in one gulp.

Strike one, the hurricane. Strike two, FEMA. And strike three, Blinger. Kelly had to admire somebody from the projects who had worked his way up to become the CEO of a chain of electronics stores. This Blinger blow-hard had wooed a bunch of Uptown Republicans into financing his first mayoral campaign, promising them sweet deals, the black vote, and smooth sailing. As far as the sweet deals and the black vote went, he delivered, but then the ship sank. His only project to revive the economy after the storm had been to propose that gambling casinos line Canal Street. Who would vote for him?

A fashionably emaciated woman in a blood-red silk blouse, Tibetan jewelry layered around her neck, held up her hand like a traffic cop. Her imperious gray eyes sought out those still chattering and silenced them with a severe glance. She smiled, ever so slightly, and her lustrous black hair, pulled back tightly from her Roman profile, glistened under the hundreds of bulbs in the chandelier.

"As most of you know, I'm Margot Carondelet White. And I'm proud to introduce the man who will move this city forward after the storm, our mayor Roy Blinger, who seeks your generous financial support in his bid for a well-deserved second term." She threw her arms heavenward, an ecstatic expression on her pinched face. "Roy's our boy!"

At the applause, the mayor shifted from one wing-tip shoe to the other, flashing his diamond cufflinks.

Nicole cupped a hand around her mouth. "I can tell you right now, it *is* political ambition."

"That dame's a piece of gristle in a skirt," Kelly stage whispered.

"Mark my words," Nicole said *sotto voce*, "Lady Macbeth."

"New Orleans coming back!" Blinger shouted to cheers and whistles. "This is a new day, and we're here to rebuild this city better than ever," he said, grabbing the air as if he planned to do so with his bare hands. He went on to count the billions of dollars that "any day now" would be pouring in from the federal government due to his deft diplomacy and recounted with a heartwarming smile his personal ties to the President, who always kept his promises, no matter what.

"Need to find a john," Kelly said, gagging with mock dry heaves.

"I'm right behind you." Nicole was already squeezing along the side of the room.

At the climax of Blinger's speech, he vowed to tumultuous applause to close "those incubators of violent crime, the storm-damaged housing projects." When the hubbub died down, Margot White scurried around the room rounding up Miss Gertie and her friends to introduce them to the mayor. As soon as she gathered them around Blinger, she signaled to the *Times-Picayune* photographer. Nudging Gertie out of the way, Mrs. White grouped herself and the doctor next to the mayor, flanked on one side by the choir ladies and on the other by Sweet Pea and Oscar. As the camera flashed, Kelly was grinning from ear to ear at this maneuver.

Bingo! White money, black faces. These spin doctors didn't miss a trick.

"Where's Gary?" Bob White asked, looking around. "Didn't he come with you?"

"Haven't seen him since we walked in." Miss Gertie looked at Kelly. "You?"

Kelly shrugged. Leave it to Gary. He was probably smoking

a number in the backyard with the caterers, the wily scamp.

Sweet Pea was eyeing the mayor with a come-hither look, fluttering spidery false lashes. He reached over to flick a piece of lint off the lapel of Blinger's Armani suit with a crimson fingernail extension, smiling so hard his peach lipstick cracked.

"Lemme ask you something, Mr. Mayor," Sweet Pea said in a fluty falsetto. "I come up in the project like you. Now you say you wanna close the project. But then you go around the country promising poor people you gonna bring them home. Now *where* you gonna bring them back *to*, hear what I saying? Where they suppose to *live*?"

The choir ladies harrumphed, nodding.

Sweet Pea should have worn that shiny tiara after all, Kelly decided. It would have matched his brass balls.

Wide-eyed, the mayor stepped back. "My position on housing issues has always been consistent."

Sweet Pea's voice dropped to a baritone. "That your answer, bro?"

Margot White wedged her way between Roy Blinger and his plucky little constituent, swiveled the mayor around and marched him toward the check-writing table. She turned her head back to the circle of black faces with a strained smile, gold fleur-de-lis earrings flashing. The photo op was over.

"Then you be a consistent fool," Sweet Pea thundered at the mayor's back.

Silver prongs were suspended mid-bite as heads turned.

"You go, girl," said Miss Eola.

"Isn't that something?" said Miss Ranell. "I hope to tell you."

# Twenty-One

PROOF.

That was what the lieutenant had said he needed, *proof.* Gary was relieved that he wouldn't need to use the screwdriver tucked in his back pocket. The front door to Bob White's carriage house swung open. He beamed the palm-sized flashlight around the musty hallway. It sure smelled like proof was moldering in here somewhere.

Gary had been planning this break-in ever since last Saturday, when with great fanfare Miss Gertie invited him to the Blinger fundraiser. At first he panicked at the prospect of chitchatting with Marky's murderer, but then a light popped on. This could be the perfect opportunity to scope out the carriage-house office that the cop had mentioned, the doctor's lair.

Jesús, who bragged that Purépecha Indians could see in the dark like cats, padded closely behind. He turned around at the door to whistle a whippoorwill call. His roly-poly cousin José Luis, stationed as a lookout behind a ginger plant on the brick path leading to the carriage house, answered with a higher pitched bird call. Contact was established. Gary and Jesús were safe inside.

# Higher Ground

Everything was going according to plan.

Gary hadn't encountered any problems in sneaking the two aproned Mexicans past the security guards, explaining that they were last-minute reinforcements for the caterers. The chuckling guards remembered exactly who Gary was— the one with those big ladies and that funny little queen— which is why he'd asked Miss Gertie to make such a show of introducing everyone to the off-duty cops. Of course, Miss Gertie didn't suspect a thing. So Gary informed her that out of *noblesse oblige*, people in-the-know chatted up the security guards at society bashes. It worked like a charm. Gary told the guards that Dr. White sent him to show these two kitchen helpers to the side entrance by the pantry, which he then did in a display of his backpacker Spanish.

Once on the path winding through tropical foliage, well past the tall windows sparkling with crystal chandeliers and laughter, the Mexicans tucked the aprons into their back pockets and followed Gary to the carriage house. Thanks to Kelly, Jesús was now working part-time at Hewitt's gas station, doing so well that he'd sent for Rosalinda, his pregnant wife from Playa Azul. And José Luis would be using Gary's van next week to buy supplies for his new taco truck. They seemed glad to do him the favor.

Gary shone the flashlight around the cluttered office, backing into a precarious statue of Shiva dancing on a pedestal. At the last minute he caught the Hindu god by one of his six waving arms.

"*No entiendo*," Jesús said. "Explain me what we look for."

Gary put a finger to his lips.

While Jesús's dark features melted into a murky corner of the room, Gary moved straight to the desk, yanking open drawers and pawing through stacks of stapled papers and rubber-banded files: Jung Center . . . In the Shadow of the

Shadow . . . Notes for New Book on Murder/Suicide . . . Invoices, Private Patients. Gary went back, flipping through the patient files. Could this be true? Invoices for four sessions with Lieutenant Vincent Panarello. Diagnosis: Acute Post Traumatic Shock Disorder. So the cop was actually one of the doctor's patients. That put everything into perspective. Here was the doctor's deposition dated just this past Monday, March 6, verifying the lieutenant's episode of "temporary insanity" on September 2. And a long typed account signed by Panarello about a shooting in a parking lot.

Gary pulled open another drawer.

Then another. Flashlight in one hand, he frantically clawed through the contents with the other. Wads and wads of scribbles on yellow legal paper, scrawls underlined, starred, scratched out. In spite of the doctor's crisp demeanor, what a secretive, obsessive squirrel he really was. Wait, these next pages weren't in the same squarish handwriting. More spidery. With a shudder, Gary recognized Marky's penmanship. "Love is the LAW, but vengeance is MINE. So ordered, so be it." Rows of Egyptian hieroglyphs were followed by a dripping heart with a knife through it.

The most sacrosanct pact between brothers, sealed by blood, semen, tears, is broken. You are POLICING my thoughts and must be brought to JUSTICE. Those who follow the Left-Handed Path of the prophesying BAPHOMET, those who worship the severed head must be exposed to the LIGHT OF DAY. You of all, who walked with me down the Path for many years. You of all, who studied with me the secret doctrine of the Brotherhood. You of all, who instilled in me the spirit of the

226

Mystery, have betrayed the truth and joined the great Satan in his quest for POWER. Labat shall not triumph. And you my brother, tender twin, shall meet the same FATE. So it is written. So shall it be.

The next piece of paper really blew Gary's mind. It was a restraining order issued against Marc Rousell Naquin, who was advised to keep five hundred feet from the person and property of Dr. Robert White, signed and dated October 28. So the battle had been going on for some time now. This went beyond an ex-lovers' spat and seemed more like blackmail. Was White involved in the Left-Handed Path with Labat, his old nemesis? What was Marky going to expose to the "light of day"? He paged back through the papers. Here was a letter—or the rough draft of one—in White's hand. Through the scratched out words, he could make out "warned if you go to the press or police about my former patients" and "most dire consequences."

"I'll take that," a voice said.

Gary jumped, waving the flashlight around the room. Its beam reflected first off the metal crutches, and then spot lit a silver-plated pistol.

The dark figure creaked forward, the oval orbs of eyeglasses shining like luminous mirrors.

"How did you—"

"I used the back door, Gary." Bob White's voice sounded weary, slurred with drink. "I came to pick up the caterer's check, but when I saw a light in the study window, I circled around through the rear. Put whatever you're reading back into the drawer." White raised his arm, aiming the gun. "I'd be quite within my rights to shoot an intruder."

Gary flicked off the flashlight and, at the same instant, slid under the desk.

Jesús tiptoed behind the doctor and grabbed him around the waist with a wrestler's grunt.

"Let me go," the doctor groaned, trying to twist around in the pitch darkness to face his attacker.

The crutches clattered to the floor.

The Mexican attempted to pry the gun out of White's hand, but the doctor tightened his grip on the handle. Jesús grabbed the bronze statue of Shiva from the pedestal next to him and whacked White on the wrist with it, then wrestled the pistol out of his limp fingers.

"Goddamn," shouted White. "Gary, are you still there? Get this goon off me."

Shaking, Gary crept from beneath the desk and snapped on the lamp. The gun in one hand, Jesús was holding up the swaying doctor like a huge rag doll with the other.

"*¿Estás bien?*" the Mexican asked, flashing two silver front teeth in a wide smile.

"Put him in this chair." Gary shoved a leather-upholstered chair next to the desk. "*Y átale por las manos.*" He yanked a ropey tie from the curtains and tossed it to Jesús. "No, tie the hands in front of him. *Por delante.* And hand me that gun."

"I know it's not cool to barge in here." Gary dropped into the swivel chair behind the desk, aiming the pistol at the doctor. "But I need to find out something about Marky."

"I'll tell you anything you want to know." Rubbing his wrist, Bob White glanced at the Mexican. "But no witnesses."

"*Pónte de guardía un ratito en la puerta.*" Gary pointed Jesús toward the front of the building and struck a sentry pose. "This will only take a minute."

"So," said Gary, after Jesús had left the room.

"How much do you charge?" Bob White asked with a drunken giggle. "It looks like you're the doctor and I'm the patient." He glared at the gun. "Or once again, the prisoner."

Gary bundled up the letters he'd been reading and stuffed them into his pocket.

"Hey, that's private!" the doctor said, lifting his tied hands.

"Let's start with J.J. How do you know him?"

"We had the same physical therapist at Veterans when I was learning how to use my new leg. Birds of a feather," the doctor said with a hiccup.

Gary could barely believe his luck. Here he had Bob White seated before him, soused to the max, tied up, and menaced by a pistol. If only he'd thought to come wired.

"How much did you pay him to have Marky killed?"

Dr. White tilted his head. "What puts such horrid ideas into your spacey-lacey mind?"

"These letters sound threatening. And what the fuck is 'Baphomet?'"

"Baphomet," said the doctor, voice rolling into orotund lecture mode, "is the severed head of St. John the Baptist, invoked in the rites of the Knights Templar. Some say the name is a corruption of 'Mohammet.' This oracle prophesized about the Crusaders' battles in the Holy Land and the fate that awaited each newly initiated warrior. Many of them were decapitated, a quaint Moorish custom reserved for infidels. Sometimes the Crusaders used real heads for these rituals. Even the ridiculous Masons in my daddy's lodge had a plastic skull on the altar. Pirates turned the same symbol into the Jolly Roger, supposed to be St. John the Baptist's skull and crossed leg bones, and brought many of the Templar ceremonies to St. Domingue, the island now known as Haiti. . . ."

Bob White halted mid-lecture, searching Gary's face. His eyes were tearing.

"In this light you remind me of him," the doctor said. "Marky."

"So you and Marky were involved with Labat and the Mani."

"Marky, never." The doctor shook his head violently. "But Eli and I go way back."

"I know."

"He's always had a certain power over me, but I've got him where he belongs. In jail. And now he's the prisoner. You see, when we were poor undergrads, we volunteered for this paid psychology experiment—"

"I'm hip. There's a book out about it, *The Torturer Inside*." Gary wondered what had turned freedom-loving flower children like Bob White into the uptight monsters they eventually became, worse than the parents they once rebelled against. Far worse.

"Eli was the torturer in the title. And I was his prisoner."

"Looks like you're still a prisoner." To Gary's surprise, Bob White seemed to be enjoying this.

"So I am." White looked down at his hands, cackling, and then up into the muzzle of his own pistol. "Say, do you know how to use that thing? Bet you wouldn't dare."

"Try me." Now Gary felt like the cop and was amazed at how much he was getting off on it. During those years in San Francisco when half of his friends dropped dead, he'd become inured to blood, catheters, and cadavers, to pulling a sheet over those he loved after endless bedside vigils. Gary's index finger caressed the trigger. After their deaths, this one would be so quick and easy. "Tell me about Labat."

"We first met when we were fourteen in a chapter of De Molay, the boy's branch of the Masons. My daddy was a 32nd degree Mason and forced me to go to that kind of crap. But Daddy only used the Masons to sell insurance policies on the golf course to fellow lodge members. But Eli, ha! He was a true believer."

"In beheading people?"

"His family goes way, way, *way.* . . ." White rotated his head, as if spiraling back in time. "That's the first thing you learn about Eli, what a Creole aristocrat the bastard thinks he is. To him, his blood is the very force of history and everyone else is just straws in the wind. The mighty Labats escaped to Louisiana from Haiti during the slave rebellion. Eli claims the last thing his family saw when they sailed out of Port au Prince were the bloody heads of their cousins that rebel slaves had mounted on stakes. The Labats brought with them the 'Lodges of the Rite of Perfection,' created after the Scottish Rite of Perfection by their uncle, Étienne Morin. Slaves used those decapitated saints as symbols in voodoo, but the sugar planters from St. Domingue kept the rites alive as part of a secret brotherhood, a left-handed path of the Masons that has survived only in parts of Louisiana and the Caribbean. Arcane doctrines that everyone in Europe had forgotten about festered here in the heat, violence, and isolation. And took on a horrible new life, like some spent hurricane regaining force over the torrid Gulf. It's no coincidence that the severed heads of slaves were speared on stakes along the Mississippi levee after the 1811 uprising. Eli's family put down that slave revolt, the same people who after arriving a few years earlier had named the area—what else?— St. John the Baptist Parish. Eli didn't make all this up. He has Morin's original documents in French and showed them to me."

"And he sucked you into it."

"I would never, *never* have had anything to do with Eliphas Labat after what happened between us during that prison experiment at Berkeley. Except for Marky. He dragged me kicking and screaming to those Mani discussion groups at the bookstore. It was three years ago, right after the accident, and I was vulnerable, not used to being a cripple. You know, when people meet after a long time, even after changed circumstances, they often fall into old patterns. And once again, Eli was the jailer, and I was the prisoner." The doctor's pale face flushed. "It's all Marky's fault," he spit out between clenched teeth. "After the accident, Margot warned me—"

"So you had him killed and Labat arrested for it."

"Wait, it's not that simple."

"He was going to expose you. For what?"

White averted his face, whispering into a darkened corner. "Sending sick souls like Hunter Finn to Labat."

"You encouraged Finn to behead his girlfriend?" Gary couldn't believe his ears.

"No, no, *no*. Although Eli must have. It was his dream to initiate a *real* Crusader, to ratchet up his ceremonies from symbolic skulls to the next level. Look, Marky—I mean Gary—this is hard for me. Here I am, tied up in my own office, telling you this incriminating stuff, which no one would ever believe, especially from the likes of you."

"Of course nobody would believe an old hippie like me." Gary flashed a guileless smile. He had Bob White right where he wanted him. "This isn't for the cops," he lied, "but for me." And for Marky, and every other lover he'd buried.

"Okay," White said, taking a deep breath, "Eli tricked me into sending him some of my patients from Veterans' Hospital. They were troubled young men who he claimed the Mani could set straight. He called them 'those wounded Crusaders' and ended up using me as a recruiter for the Mani. It must have been the lunacy after the storm, but Eli finally went psycho and programmed Hunter to prepare for what they call the 'Rite of the Incarnation of St. John the Baptist,' to use a freshly severed head for the initiation ceremony instead of the med school skulls."

"Aren't you afraid Labat will blab about your role in this,

and when the fuzz finds out who sent him Hunter and the other vets, they'll come after you."

"Oh, you don't know Eli, my friend. To release the initiates' names would be heresy. Besides, the patient records at Veterans were washed away in the flood. Without exception, the initiates were ex-servicemen just back from Iraq and Afghanistan. Don't you see why the Mani would appeal to them? The Knights Templar mounted the first crusade against the Muslim world, and this American war, in their twisted minds, is the second. Yet their country let them down, dragging them through a slaughterhouse without any rhyme or reason. But Eli fed them a transcendent purpose for the violence they carried around inside, the brotherhood of the Crusaders, the Mani!"

"So Marky knew what was happening?"

"He wanted me to stop Labat when he saw how Eli was manipulating those vets. Or Marky threatened to go to the police. I would have lost my license for funneling patients into a gruesome cult. He started stalking me with nonstop phone calls, letters, and visits. When we came home in October after the evacuation, he'd spray-painted *witch doctor* on our house. That's when I got a restraining order. His invective was scrawled on the clapboards next to the $X$ made by the National Guard, with a zero at the center. It looked exactly like a Jolly Roger, which I thought Marky had left there as a Mani symbol. I freaked."

"Then you had him killed."

"Do you have any idea how much this torments me?" White shouted, attempting to stand. He collapsed back into the chair, beating the armrest with his elbows. "After the storm, Marky stopped taking his meds and snapped, obsessed with me turning in Eli before someone was killed. My hands were tied."

Hiccupping, the doctor looked down at his hands.

"Marky showed up at Touro when the clinic first opened, screaming 'Baphomet, Baphomet!' at me. Of course, everyone took him for another storm victim acting out his stress disorder. Initially, getting rid of him was Margot's idea. She's a bit high strung, overbred, you might say, and is well connected in this town. Marky's horrifying tirades were getting in the way of . . . well, her political plans. At first I was amused by her idea of making Marky disappear. As things got worse, I wasn't so amused."

"How much did you pay J.J. to have your soul mate bumped off?"

White's shoulders slumped. "Three thousand."

"You know that Latrome Batiste—his uncle is standing in your house right this minute—was a seventeen-year-old student at St. Aug. who was practicing the clarinet to march in Carnival parades. He got in the way of the gunfire you paid for and was also killed. Latrome's blood is also on your hands."

White stared at Gary with red-rimmed eyes. "Marky always knew it would end in murder."

"His own?"

A whippoorwill sounded in the distance, answered by another from outside the door.

"Someone's coming." Gary jumped from behind the desk, untied the doctor's hands and then tossed the pistol inside a desk drawer.

Somebody rapped along the side of the house.

Footsteps creaked along the corridor.

Then the door squeaked open on rusty hinges.

To Gary's relief, it was only Mutt and Jeff. The stout security guard entered the room first, followed by his licorice-stick partner.

"Hey, doc, they looking for you," the stout guard said with a broad grin. "Your wife say go look in the house out back. That his hideaway," he said, snickering. "Every man need him a hideaway. Know I got mine. Except my wife ain't found it yet."

"I could tell you I've been kidnapped by Mr. Gary here," the doctor said, "but I know you wouldn't believe it, would you, gentlemen?"

"Looking for you, too," grunted the skinny guard, turning to Gary. "Them big ladies. Say that little thang in the sparkly drawers riding back to the Quarters with you."

"Officer, would you hand me my crutches?" White said, pointing across the room to where the Mexican had grabbed him. "My friend and I have been telling stories nobody would ever believe. Ghost stories."

"Bet this place full of haints." The stout guard glanced around wide-eyed at the Buddha heads and dancing Hindu gods, the desk lamp casting elongated shadows along the walls. "Give me the willie just standing here."

"If Mr. Gary would kindly return those . . . manuscripts we were discussing to the drawer where he found them," the doctor said with a tight smile, "we can repair peacefully to the house for a final libation." The doctor's look said it even more eloquently: *Put those letters wadded up in your pocket back in the desk, or these two cops with pistols strapped to their belts will escort the thieving intruder to Tulane and Broad.*

"Go tell the kitchen help to wrap up some of that prime rib for you," Bob White said to the guards. "Take it home to your families."

"Much obliged," said the stout one. "Think I'll take it to my hideaway, know what I mean?" He slapped the doctor on the back.

As the three stepped along the brick path behind the tipsy

psychiatrist wobbling on his crutches, Gary vowed that as long as he was alive, Bob White wouldn't get away with what he had done. But for the moment, as the supporters of Mayor Roy Blinger trailed out of the columned house on Seventh Street, he had to slip back into the skin that allowed him to survive in this city. High-pitched laughter rang from the front gallery, and through the windows, Gary spotted caterers clearing tables. Inside, a vacuum cleaner roared, and a uniformed maid collected glasses. On the other side of the fence, stragglers were lingering on the brick banquette, braying their endless Creole goodbyes.

A whippoorwill warbled from a fig tree inside the garden.

Another answered from down the street.

That must be Jesús and José Luis, waiting for him. Gary raced down the path and out of the gate, rubbing his eyes as if trying to wake from a terrifying dream.

"YOU ASLEEP?" KELLY ASKED.

Nicole rolled over, squinting. "What time is it?"

"About 3 a.m." He grabbed Nicole by the waist, pulling her closer.

"I was having a nightmare." She yawned, hand on his chest. "I was under the spell of this magician. He was an alchemist and could combine different potions to make the people he wanted. He was trying to create the perfect person."

"What did he look like?" Kelly traced a circle around her pert nipple.

"Actually, like Labat." She stroked the hair on his chest. "Pretty scary. We were in a poor village where people were speaking French, somewhere like Haiti. The magician's rooms were filled with vials and beakers of herbs, powders, and liquids. And word got out that he was dealing in illegal substances."

"Here comes your momma for her cut." He traced his fingertips along the inside of her thigh then slipped a hand between her legs.

"So a policeman paid him a visit. And the magician sprinkled brown powder in concoctions that fizzled and then foamed over. He looked at the cop taking out his handcuffs and was, like, astonished. His mouth was hanging open. The perfect person he'd been trying to create all these years was the one standing right in front of him."

"The one going to arrest him?" His fingers were inside.

Nicole moaned, biting his ear lobe. "Yeah, the cop was the perfect person."

"Wasn't a New Orleans cop then, was he?" Kelly said, sliding on top of her.

"How would I know?" She opened her legs, wrapping them around his. "But the magician scared me. So I woke up."

"I'm glad you woke up," he breathed into her ear, entering her.

"Me, too." She squeezed him closer. "Glad I woke up."

## Twenty-Two

CONFEDERATE JASMINE WAS BLOOMING in the courtyard of Croissant D'Or, perfuming the outdoor tables with its scent. It would have been a serene April morning over coffee and pastry except for the Sunday newspaper opened on the iron table in front of Nicole. All of the grisly details about the "head-worshipping Mani cult" were recounted in an investigative report, knocking mold remediation and the mayoral runoff from the front page for a change. Nicole was shocked to find her brother's photo on page six, right under Deckie Hall's, both captioned as "cult victims." The blood drained from her face as she read.

"Want another cup?" Kelly asked, pushing back his patio chair.

"Better not. We'll be late for Momma's solo at Mass."

"Hell, we been listening to her rehearse for a week." Kelly covered his ears. "I know the lyrics to 'Higher Ground' by heart."

"Here's the part I don't understand," Nicole said, screwing up her face. "The article claims that 'Eliphas Labat is charged as an accessory before the fact in Hunter Finn's murder of his girlfriend.' What does that mean, 'accessory before the fact?'"

"Means Labat sharpened the knife then waited in the next room. An accomplice."

Nicole shivered. "Then the paper says that 'Homicide Detective Vincent Panarello filed charges that Labat hypnotized Finn to murder the young woman, and the bookseller has been transferred for psychiatric evaluation to Jackson, the state hospital for the criminally insane near St. Francisville.'"

"Great," Kelly blurted out. "Now Labat and Lena can pal around yammering about the good old days of the fourteenth century."

Nicole continued to read out loud. "Dr. Robert White has testified as to the psychotic nature of Labat's homicidal impulses and connected the bookseller to the January 28 drive-by shooting that ended the lives of Marc Naquin and Latrome Batiste. White maintains that Naquin frequented Labat's Rampart Street bookstore, and the two had fallen out. The police are looking for corroborating testimony from other cult members, ex-servicemen living in the Marigny and Bywater who have disappeared without a trace."

"Your mama was right." Kelly reached for the newspaper and folded it.

"Wait a minute. What does White mean by 'other cult members?'" Nicole stood, studying her watch. "My brother was never a member of Labat's cult. Gary could tell them that."

"Every time I bring up Marky's murder, he changes the subject." Kelly rose from the table and slipped into his new sports coat. "He's not saying much these days. Looks like he's tripped out on some pretty bad shit. Wonder what could be wrong."

As Nicole and Kelly hurried along Rampart Street, bells

were tolling in the distance from Our Lady of Guadalupe. They lingered for a moment in front of the darkened storefront of Minerva's Owl. Nicole cupped her hands to peek through the window at books half-packed in crates and felt sullied by even looking at the place. The word in the neighborhood was that Duffy Bordelon, a former candidate for mayor, would rent the Minerva's Owl's storefront to his boyfriend, a bipolar hairdresser just out of rehab. As Nicole leaned against the window, she noticed a homemade sign taped to the door: COMING SOON—HEAD TRIPS SALON!

THE TEN O'CLOCK MASS HAD ALREADY begun when they slipped into a rear pew. Two pews ahead sat Auntie Dixie, her gnarled fingers petting the expensive pelt of some dead rodent slung over her shoulder, obviously trying to work her way back into her sister's good graces. Next to her was a diminutive lady whom Nicole recognized from the society pages as Bitsie Landry, and to the right sat her son Mike Landry, Blinger's opponent in the runoff election. Worshippers seated ahead kept stealing looks over their shoulders to make sure it was him, then turned to whisper to those at their side. The election weighed heavily on everybody's mind, and many felt that the fate of the city hung in the balance.

It didn't surprise Nicole to spot Mike Landry's beaming Eagle-Scout face at this service. The congregation was an eclectic mixture of residents from the Iberville projects on one side of Rampart Street and of eccentric Quarterites from the other side of the divide. The checkerboard mix of parishioners around her was close to the image of racial harmony she had once entertained in high school, when Landry's father was trying to integrate the city and so many idealistic blacks and whites shared a dream. Unfortunately, the city's white middle class was then fleeing en masse to the suburbs while tens of thousands of displaced black sharecroppers were pouring in from the hardscrabble countryside of the new Sunbelt. Demagogues of both races had since polarized everyone into a steely mistrust. But in this setting, even Nicole's bigoted aunt, with her tireless support for Harvest House, somehow fit into a rosy nostalgia for a united city. Nicole wondered where this dream had gone wrong, and as a basket piled with crumpled dollar bills was shoved past her on its long handle, figured that it probably had something to do with money, too much in one place and not enough in the other.

Father Anthony was a short, stocky Sicilian who paced the altar like a rock star on a concert stage. Nicole could tell that nobody nodded off during his Masses. The First Reading was from Genesis, Chapter Four, the story of how Cain rose up in the field to slay his brother Abel. "'And now,' as God told Cain, 'you are cursed from the ground, which has opened its mouth to receive your brother's blood from your hand.'" And then the priest turned to Chapter Six, about Noah and the flood. "'Now the earth was corrupt in God's sight, and the earth was filled with violence'." After a Psalm and the Second Reading from St. John, Father Anthony concluded, "the Gospel of the Lord."

"Praise to you, Lord Jesus Christ," the worshippers murmured.

Rather than deliver his homily from the pulpit where he stood, Father Anthony stepped down into the aisle, from which he worked the congregation like a stand-up comedian. He seemed to be talking directly to Nicole, although she suspected that everyone there felt the same way.

"You can't just sit inside behind locked doors and feel, *whew*, I'm safe, none of this evil will taint my life. Every murder in this city is a blow against us all," the priest said, raising his arms to take in the entire church, "and diminishes who we are. We can't discount this as black against white, have-nots against haves, downtown against uptown. This isn't a football game, with winning and losing teams. And any way we choose to divide ourselves up into two teams—by race, color, language, creed, or income—comes up short, because we're all on the losing team. Cain's blood still courses through our veins, and his mentality of brother against brother is the source of our original sin. 'For the imagination of man's heart is evil from his youth,' scripture tells us."

Father Anthony paced the aisle, green stole flying, winking at people he recognized and smiling at children.

"As in Noah's time, those of us who have survived in this city after the flood form a most holy ark protected by a covenant with God. And after those nasty floodwaters disappeared, we saw His rainbow of forgiveness on Canal Street and on St. Charles Avenue and here on Rampart Street, and that covenant is to respect the ties of brotherhood and sisterhood that unite us in God's eyes. But yet we still have brother who murders brother on a Saturday night over a rock of crack cocaine, we have a monster up the street who hypnotizes young veterans to serve Satan, and we have the gnawing shards of fear and envy in each of our hearts that cut down those we most love, and we think nobody knows. But guess what? God *knows*. Do we need another flood to remind us what God knows?"

"No!" the congregation roared. Hands raised heavenward rippled through the church, spilling into isolated "amens" and "hallelujahs." The old latté-hued lady seated next to Nicole, swollen feet stuffed into worn bedroom slippers, pulled out her handkerchief and wept, as the congregation's *No!* reverberated to the rafters.

Then the choir rose in a flutter of burgundy robes, ladies in front, gentlemen to the rear. Although Nicole did notice several white men with earrings, her mother was the only white woman, wedged between the pleated burgundy bosoms of Miss Eola and Miss Ranell. Oscar, dressed in the same undertaker's suit he wore to the Blinger fundraiser, was seated at an upright piano. At his signal, the choir's voices rose, punctuated by the funky thump of his full-chorded churchy keyboard.

> We climbing
> Lord we climbing
> higher
> higher
> HIGHER
> climbing up to higher ground

Tambourines rattled, keeping time with the rhythmic clapping that soon caught fire among the congregation. Even the weeping lady next to Nicole tucked away her handkerchief and set her slippers to tapping. At each repetition of "higher," the key shot up an octave, until only Gertie's crystalline soprano filled the nave before the baritones surged from below in a crescendo of "climbing up to higher ground."

Then Gertie lifted her head, gray corkscrew curls glowing in a nimbus of light. Nicole could tell by the faraway look in the old lady's eyes that she wasn't singing to anyone in particular seated in the pews before her. She was singing to the whole city's sense of loss and to her dead son Marky riding a tricycle in front of an abandoned house in Lakeview.

> The Lord said to Noah
> this ark cannot go down,
> I'll take you to the mountaintop
> where you'll find higher ground.

# James Nolan

So Noah led his family
from the valley of despair
where Pharaoh rules
a land of fools
with murder everywhere.

The chorus came crashing back, everyone in the congregation swaying as they clapped.

We climbing
Lord we climbing
higher
higher
HIGHER
climbing up to higher ground

Nicole's eyes watered. Some strangely iridescent butterfly had emerged from the brittle cocoon of that crabby old lady she called Momma, the one who used to polish furniture and weed flowerbeds and fight protracted battles with the electricity company and water-delivery man. Her new wings vibrated with savage life above the rhythmically bobbing heads around Nicole. Although she prayed her mother would stop dealing drugs and causing scenes in gay bars, this transformed creature before her certainly wasn't ready for Scrabble and yarn crafts at Mossy Lanes. Nicole had never witnessed suffering transform a person so. Except, she thought, glancing at Kelly, for the man at her side, who had just been invited to hang five of his lizard paintings in a group show at the Hanson Gallery on Royal Street. The former accountant and suburban dad now painted half the night, long after Nicole went to bed, and the more focused and polished his paintings became, the more of himself he gave her, as if the two went together.

# Higher Ground

And Noah said to Pharaoh
these sands we leave behind
to search the sea until we see
God's beacon or His sign.
So Noah led his family
from the valley of despair
and Babylon
came tumbling down
with water everywhere

Her mother's clear soprano moved Nicole in ways she didn't think possible. It unmoored her from the Phoenix fantasy on which she sailed off to sleep many nights. Now that she wasn't Mrs. Doctor any more, she doubted that moving her Beautyrest mattress to some hollow facsimile of an ideal life would help to recapture the world she had lost. For somebody, somewhere, that collie might still be racing across the St. Augustine lawn, but the fleecy dog wasn't bounding toward her anymore. If and when she and Kelly moved back into his house in Lakeview, she would have to start from scratch, living in an abandoned neighborhood with one working street light and no mail delivery or garbage pickup. No, it wasn't a Phoenix life, but it was her life. Maybe that was why she so often found herself involved with married men, because she was afraid to create her own life and always preferred some other woman's, as if she could slip into the Pottery Barn window display of a perfect room and actually live there. But here she was, stuck with her own mess, and this was her last chance to make the best of it. She could always go back to school and get a Master's degree in social work at Tulane so she could help people like her brother not to get murdered. She couldn't do a worse job than Modene Holiday. Staring at her mother shaking a tambourine—where in the world had she learned to play that thing?—Nicole acknowledged that no, she hadn't found her mountaintop. She slipped her arm around Kelly's waist. But at least she wasn't drowning.

> We climbing . . .
> climbing up to higher ground

When the Mass was over, Nicole caught up with Auntie Dixie, standing at the edge of a circle of people around Mike Landry, campaigning until the last minute. She threw her arms around her aunt, avoiding eye contact with the beady peepers of the dead fox draped around her neck, and tried to forget whatever Dixie had called her—was it a "spineless milksop"?—when she stormed out of the intervention.

"Was just telling Bitsie how much your mama's voice improved since she used to screech on the radio," Dixie said. "My sister got some soul left in her yet. Don't know where she gets it, after what she been through. If I lost everything, I'd just set down on the banquette and bawl."

"She's high on her mountaintop," Nicole said, her voice quiet and serene.

"Either that or she high on them goofballs she pops. Don't forget, hon, the runoff is this Saturday, and I don't have to remind y'all," Dixie said, patting Bitsie's shoulder, "who to vote for. Everybody I talk to say they calling the long-distance moving van if that Blinger wins."

"Don't worry," Nicole said. "We're registered in the Quarter and will be there when the polls open."

Nicole was scooting away from Dixie toward the gothic arches of the front door, where Father Anthony was shaking hands, when she almost collided with the cop.

At first she didn't recognize Lieutenant Panarello. He was sidling out of the St. Jude altar with raccoon circles around his bleary eyes, the skin on his face hanging like an old bulldog's. She'd heard that his negligent homicide case stemming from the Walmart parking-lot shooting was scheduled to be tried early this week. His face was often in the news these days, but he never looked this bad. Could he be drunk?

"Officer," she said, extending her hand, "I'm Nicole Naquin, Marky's sister."

"Good to see you," the cop said, averting his eyes as he offered a sweaty palm.

"I saw the paper this morning and want to tell you how much my family appreciates everything you've done to find Marky's murderer." Nicole stepped back from the lieutenant's stale breath and sickly demeanor. "We're really pleased that Eliphas Labat will pay for this."

The cop nodded, eyes searching the tiled floor as if for a lost button.

"You do think Labat did it, don't you?" Nicole asked.

Panarello shook his head. "We don't have a solid case yet, but. . . ."

"Dr. White has one thing wrong." Nicole's shrill voice echoed in the vaulted sanctuary. "My brother was *not* a member of Labat's cult, as the paper implies. Marky opposed the cult. You need to speak with his friend Gary Cherry, who can confirm this."

The cop winced. "I'll check it out. Excuse me, but I got to talk with Father Antnee."

Panarello scampered past Nicole, racing down the steps to tap Father Anthony on the shoulder. The cop was hiding something, Nicole decided, unnerved by the encounter. As soon as she turned around, she fell into the fleshy embrace of Miss Ranell and Miss Eola, trailing burgundy robes on wire hangers.

"The Lord spoke to us in your mama's voice this morning," Miss Ranell said.

"I hope to tell you," said Miss Eola.

"That woman staying with us," Miss Ranell said, "on the mountaintop."

## Twenty-Three

SEATED AT THE BAR OF HARRY'S CORNER, a Quarter joint at Dumaine and Chartres, Vinnie ordered another Seven and Seven. He rubbed his eyes, as if waking from a dream. It was Saturday, April 8, the evening of the runoff election, and he was still a homicide detective at the Eighth District. Nothing had changed, except he was drinking too much.

That, and—thank you, St. Jude—he wasn't going to jail.

He glanced up at the blue glow from the murmuring tube over the bar. With only 35 percent of the precincts reporting, Landry maintained a wide lead over Blinger. That was a relief, because to Vinnie's great surprise, he was still a cop. A friend at the station had taken a straw poll, and at least three hundred officers citywide vowed to leave their jobs if Blinger were re-elected mayor. Another hurricane was coming, if not this summer, then the next, and nobody wanted to be put back in the same chaos they found themselves in eight months ago. Yet no matter what happened on the TV screen tonight, Vinnie wasn't going anywhere. He took a slurp from his Seven and Seven.

Nowhere at all.

White's expert testimony at the trial this week, when he questioned Vinnie's ability to distinguish right from wrong at the moment of the shooting, had swayed the jury in the defendant's favor. If Vinnie had been conscious that he'd done wrong, the doctor argued, wouldn't he have tried to run, to cover-up any evidence, to justify his actions? No, Lieutenant Panarello, in fact, called for help, then ran to the side of the wounded man to stanch the bullet wounds. His befuddled, sleep-deprived consciousness in that scorching parking lot corroborated a technical state of "temporary insanity." And as for motive, why would he have wanted to shoot a deaf man after a storm? Certainly not out of premeditated malice. If out of delusional self-defense, didn't that then prove that his ability to judge right from wrong had been impaired by the inhuman circumstances under which he was operating?

Based on the doc's testimony, his case had been brilliantly argued. The family of the slain man wasn't happy and threatened to bring a civil damages suit against the cop. But that could take years. Maybe by then Vinnie might be retired.

But he wasn't right now. His application for an early retirement, accompanied by the doc's diagnosis of post-traumatic shock disorder, had been denied. As a matter of fact, based on his work with the Eliphas Labat case, as of yesterday, he was being promoted. He was now Captain Vincent Panarello. And he couldn't walk away from that. Not with three kids in Catholic school. Now his wife wouldn't have to work part-time as a waitress at the IHOP just so they could pay the new sky-high insurance premiums on the house.

So cheers, he thought, emptying his glass. He owed this to Dr. Robert White.

The very man he suspected of contracting the murder of Marky Naquin.

And what was he going to do about it?

Vinnie eyed the bartender, pointing at his empty glass.

Not a damn thing.

Nothing, in spite of what Father Anthony had counseled him to do after Mass last Sunday, which was to turn over every shred of evidence to the D.A.'s office, no matter how incriminating it may prove to that unnamed person he owed a favor to.

"What if your son had been murdered?" Father Anthony's brown eyes blazed. "Wouldn't you want the police to catch the right killer?"

The father was a *paisano* and had a point. It was like talking to Nonno. But Vinnie had to face it: he'd rather go to hell than to jail. Hell might last longer but it came later, and nobody would be watching. But jail would destroy his family, his only reason to be on this earth. And, come on, no son of his would ever have gotten mixed up with a crackpot cult in the French Quarter. Vinnie couldn't confide in his wife about any of this—she wouldn't tolerate a single word about murder cases, not even his own—and he only wished that his first wife were still alive. Nobody guessed it, but he still talked to Janice, and at bedtime couldn't get to sleep until he bid goodnight to an image of her face.

White's name had surfaced during Vinnie's long interrogations of Labat, but the cop always steered the responses in another direction and whited out any mention of the doctor in his reports. Okay, so he had to beat up on Labat a bit, but soon the jagged pieces of a puzzle fell into place, a story not too different from what that Cherry clown told him weeks ago. Vinnie wasn't sure to what extent White had gotten his hands dirty in the Mani cult but did know that from his V.A. practice, he sent Labat a bunch of flipped-out GI's from Iraq. But Labat wouldn't release the names of the others involved, and the V.A. records had been washed away eight months ago, like every other important piece of paper in this town. Forget trying to solve any crimes committed before the storm hit. The evidence was now fattening crabs at the bottom of Lake Pontchartrain.

It seemed that Naquin raised a big stink about White's involvement with Labat's creepy scene and had been harassing the doctor night and day. Or that was how Labat remembered it. The clincher was what the bearded man said about J.J.

"During the last week in January," Labat had said, "whenever I'd peer out the shop window a crippled Negro with a palsied hand would be passing by. I'd never seen him before. One afternoon, it must have been around the 27th or 28th, Bob's black Mercedes roared up to the curb on Rampart, where the Negro was standing. They spoke to each other, and something was passed through the window. I couldn't make out what. It struck me, because I couldn't imagine what Bob and that street person would have in common. And why in front of my shop? In retrospect, it looks like I was being set up."

Naquin and Batiste had been murdered at 9 p.m. on January 28th.

This juicy tidbit hadn't made it into the police report. Of course, any minute Vinnie wanted to, he could pick up J.J. and crack him open like a rotten pecan. The cops and J.J. owed each other, big time, and the little snitch knew he could get away with almost anything. Even murder. Slip enough dough into his twisted fingers and he'd come clean.

But where would that leave Vinnie?

Of course, nobody would ever believe Labat—straight out of the cuckoo's nest at Jackson—if he claimed that the very psychiatrist who pronounced him psycho was the real culprit in the Naquin and Batiste case. *The doctor who said I'm crazy did it.* Vinnie could picture the jury rolling their eyes at that one. But even Naquin's sister smelled something fishy about the shrink. The only person who could point an incriminating finger at White was the dope dealer. He could corroborate everything, and Labat must realize that. What if the bookseller's lawyer subpoenaed Cherry to testify when the case reached trial? The last time he saw the doctor, Vinnie had felt compelled to mention that distinct possibility.

"Gary's already taken care of," White said, looking away.

Vinnie didn't ask what he meant but suspected it might be another job for J.J.'s thugs.

He glanced up at the screen. Suddenly, with 65 percent of the precincts reporting, Blinger had galloped ahead of Landry by 7 percent.

Then the lead was 8 percent.

Nine.

Harry's Corner fell silent.

"You believe this shit?" the bartender asked a sunburned man in a baseball cap three stools down.

"They say Blinger had busloads of New Orleans people in Texas to bring in if he needed they vote." The sunburned man spit. "Bet them the votes just got counted."

"He ain't gonna help them people come home." The bartender swiped the counter with a sour rag. "Three-hundred-dollar apartments now renting for a grand. Where poor people supposed to live?"

"Politics, politics," slurred a beat-up iguana of a broad at the other end of the bar. "Who wants to buy me a drink?"

Vinnie eyed the bartender, shooting a finger at his glass and then at the dame. Words failed him.

The screen cut to the Blinger victory party at the Hyatt, the same hotel where the mayor had holed up after the storm. Balloons were bouncing and confetti swirling in the ballroom as a triumphant Roy Blinger shook hands with a group of snowy-haired gentlemen in beautifully tailored suits. The camera caught Dr. Robert White beaming next to a skinny dame who Vinnie took to be his wife.

In his victory speech, Blinger thanked his good friend the President for his promises kept. "And tonight I have a few promises to keep myself. We're going to run this city with an all-new dream team. Here at my side, we have the new Director of Public Health, Dr. Robert White, a strong and honest man with the gargantuan task of bringing back this city's medical facilities to their pre-storm level."

Vinnie jumped up, throwing a few greasy bills on the bar.

The pasty regulars had turned mute, staring at the TV with the same grim looks on their mugs as if they were watching home videos of their daddies' funerals.

Outside the streets were deserted.

Vinnie swung a left onto Chartres, heading back to the station to pick up his car. He staggered under a row of wrought-iron galleries that sheltered him from the fine drizzle now slickening the street. His own haze blended with the misty gusts blowing in from the river as he floated along in a boozy cloud of memory and oblivion. His skin prickled as Janice's gaze caressed the back of his neck. She was leaning over a balcony railing in a bloodied lace nightgown, shaking her head. *Now you're dead, too, sweetheart, or might as well be. Who have you let yourself become?*

Tonight Captain Vincent Panarello might well have lost his way except for the footprints he followed, tracks tattooed onto this brick banquette a century before. Nonno, that tired old grocer, trudged ahead, as he always did whenever Vinnie walked these streets. The old man was fingering a St. Jude medal and mumbling a Pater Noster under his breath to ward off the evil eye that peered at him from between jalousied shutters. He swore that hookers and sailors, murderers and thieves were waiting for him in the shadows of every crumbling doorway.

"Keep your head up, son, and walk right," Nonno always told him. "You'll be safe in God's love."

Only now Vinnie had gone and done it. Nonno's good-luck spell was broken for good. He had managed to cross forbidden Rampart Street and was marooned in a menacing world that he no longer recognized. The old man would be furious at him, and now he'd never find his way home to those kind eyes twinkling over the dusty antipasto jars at Angelo's. Vinnie's fate had been decided, and he knew it. He had no choice but to keep walking in the wrong direction, toward wherever this shadowy path might lead. And when he got there, the darkness would swallow him without a trace, as it had so many good cops before him.

GARY WAS SURE HE WAS BEING FOLLOWED. Every time he glanced back, out of the corner of his eye he caught a flash of long white T-shirts, always the same two guys with dreadlocks vaporizing into the dim light. The Creoles had a superstition that the weather was always gloomy on Good Friday. He looked up. Sure enough, the sky was a galvanized gray, humid air hanging heavy to the horizon.

It was about to storm.

He shoved open the blackened door of the Aftermath Lounge. Strange, but at six in the evening on a holiday weekend, the bar was almost empty. People here didn't go out much during Lent, and it was considered in remarkably bad taste to go cruising on Good Friday. Something about Christ on the cross.

The streets had been particularly quiet since Blinger won the election, as if everybody were locked inside wondering what to do now. During the next four years, Gary suspected that the city could expect only the same brutal reality, nothing more. No gallant knight was poised to charge in on a steed to save New Orleans, to make the place anything like what it used to be before the hurricane. The whole city was home alone with Stanley Kowalski. Now Gary understood exactly how Blanche DuBois felt at that moment when she realized that her phantom boyfriend Shep Huntleigh wasn't coming to rescue her. Stripped of any illusions, she broke the neck off a bottle and turned to face the big ape lunging at her in red silk pajamas.

Yet still the star-struck groupie, Gary kept a tight grip on his illusions, brittle scrapbooks that they were: musicians like Mick Jagger and Iggy Pop, writers such as Allen Ginsburg and William Burroughs. They were his Shep Huntleigh and would always save him. Even though at the moment the music sounded faint, wasn't he still with the band? Couldn't he just pick up the phone? *Hello, Mick, this is Gary Cherry. You remember me, don't you? We smoked a joint together at Altamont and then fooled around backstage. I have this hot picture of us. Listen, I'm in New Orleans, and things are getting sort of strange. . . .*

"Somebody was in here looking for you," the bald bartender shouted over the factory-like drone of tech music. "Crippled guy."

Bob White hadn't returned any of his phone calls.

"White?"

"No, black. With a shriveled up hand."

"What did you tell him?"

"Said you were at church," the bartender said with a snicker.

Gary peered through the tinted window. The white T-shirts had disappeared.

During the past couple of days, Gary had been so unnerved

that he stopped carrying any drugs or money and didn't answer the doorbell. Then it hit him with a sock to the gut. It sure would be convenient for the new Director of Public Health and Captain Vincent Panarello if he disappeared, wouldn't it? It might be months, even years, before Labat was released from Jackson to stand trial for Marky's murder. Yet it was uncanny how time had a way of eventually squeezing out the truth, especially if somebody were walking around who was still capable of telling it.

This Sunday Miss Gertie would bury her son's ashes, believing the murderer was behind bars. At last she was at peace, and how could Gary roil her up again with what he knew about White? Gary finally had finished *The Torturer Inside*, and that twisted prison experiment White participated in at Berkeley said a lot about what made the sicko doctor tick. The tortured eventually became the torturer, and the victim, the victimizer. How else to explain the horrors of Abu Ghraib and this vengeful war? Gary was blown away by the book's epigraph, lines from a war poem by Auden: "I and the public know / What all schoolchildren learn, / Those to whom evil is done / Do evil in return."

When Gary slipped back onto the street, thunder was rumbling and the sky had blackened. He craned his neck to the right then left. He was tired of hiding inside his slave quarter like a nervous Nelly, and besides, he needed new headphones for his iPod. Even as the first drops of rain sprinkled his face, he was sure that he could make it to the Radio Shack on Canal Street before the downpour.

Once on Royal, he scooted past the Eighth District station and disappeared onto a quiet side street where no one would bother him. Exchange Place was an alley filled with trash, abandoned restaurant freezers still packed with maggoty meat from after the storm, and the looming hulks of overflowing dumpsters that blocked the sidewalk. Nobody came here unless they had to.

Gary scurried along, staring straight ahead through the drizzle. The streetlights were still out here, but in the distance lights flashed on Canal Street with a welcoming glow. He cocked an ear. There it was again. A creak, followed by a dragging sound. He glanced over his shoulder. Nothing. Another creak. The drag.

Then two patches of white darted behind a dumpster.

He spun around. A white T-shirt was standing with J.J. at one end of the alley, and another white T-shirt at the other.

A gunshot ricocheted off a lamp post.

Gary dove between two garbage cans, and the squeak of slick rubber soles hitting cement followed him. Then he sprang for the iron door in front of him. He yanked. Miraculously, it swung open.

The lock clicked behind him as the door clanged shut.

He raced through an empty passageway, leaned his shoulder against a double door, and then caught his breath.

His Converse hightops were sprinting through the parking garage of the Monteleone Hotel. Panting, he bathed in the reassuring fluorescent glare, then maneuvered a winding hallway that led to the glittering lobby. An ornately carved grandfather's clock was chiming seven as he entered, freaked out of his head.

"May I help you, sir?" asked a desk clerk with a German accent.

"Just waiting for my friend to come down." Chest heaving, Gary grabbed a worn copy of *Time*, one from the August before the storm. He collapsed onto an oval velvet settee near the door, under a huge Victorian vase brimming with Easter lilies.

He was winded and shaking. If he reported this shooting to

the Eighth District now, guess who he'd run into? That police snitch picking up his Friday pay envelope. Gary could just picture the pigs' amusement at that confrontation, no matter what he said. Who could he tell? Certainly not Miss Gertie and her family two days before the burial. No, for as long as he could, he'd just sit here, pretending he was a tourist with the time and money to explore this crazy city, a tourist who would be jetting out in the morning, back to one of those dull, sane places where people actually lived. Later this evening, he could slip through the crowds on Bourbon, where no savvy hit man would ever take out a mark. That way he would probably make it home in one piece.

Heart still racing, Gary flipped backward through the dog-eared magazine pages. A deafening clap of thunder boomed overhead, and at once the faces in the hotel lobby looked up, exchanging glances as if to reassure each other that, yes, they were still alive and safe. While torrents of rain pelted the sidewalk on the other side of the brass-framed glass doors of the Monteleone, Gary stopped at an article about Mick's sixty-second birthday bash in London.

And as if he still had all the time in the world, he started to read.

# Twenty-Four

FOR THE FIRST TIME IN MONTHS, Kelly felt flush. So after Mass on Easter Sunday, a white stretch limousine adorned with blinking lights swerved into Lafayette Cemetery, its long tail almost catching on the ornate gatepost supporting the arch. Under a bright sky enameled cobalt blue, tires crunched over the shell walkway as the limo pulled up in front of the vacant shelves of the Naquin tomb. The uniformed driver popped out and waltzed around to open the back door with a flourish. First to emerge was an enormous spray of lavender mums hoisted by Kelly, dressed in what he still thought of—never without a shudder after the election—as his Blinger blazer. Then Nicole stepped out, a bouquet of yellow tea roses in hand, followed by Dixie, crimson fingernails wrapped around a go-cup of gin and tap water. High-pitched giggles issued from inside of the tinted windows, followed by a sharp *yip* and then a slap.

"I told you not to poke me there no more," squealed a falsetto voice. "Miss Ross about to meet her public."

Wig on crooked, Sweet Pea stepped out wearing Jackie O. sunglasses, right into the blinding flashbulbs of the paparazzi. Kelly could tell this was Miss Nida Mann's moment of glory as she exited a real chauffeured limo, lips posed in a saucy moue, to greet the throng of her adoring fans, unfortunately all dead. Oscar Batiste followed, still rubbing his cheek, carrying Schnitzel in the crook of his arm, chariot wheels spinning. Then with trembling hands and a hunted look in his eye, Gary slid out, pale and translucent as a ghost. To Kelly, he resembled some spooked out rocker touring with the Procol Harum, grooving on an eerie mixture of glamour and death. *Lighten up*, Kelly wanted to tell him, *it's Easter, not Halloween.*

Finally one of Miss Gertie's puffy ankles appeared. Then another.

"Here, somebody take Marky," she said, "so I can get my big behind out this contraption."

Kelly received the urn of ashes with one hand while helping the old lady out of the limo with the other. The limo rental was his treat, not only to honor the burial of his friend Marky, whose spirit had guided him back to his true life as a painter, but to celebrate the new accounting gig. Of course, those motherfuckers with the deepwater oil-drilling contracts in the Gulf of Mexico were screwing him royally. The job was part-time so they didn't have to give him benefits, and his contract was month-to-month, in case the limeys hit oil somewhere even cheaper and more corrupt than Louisiana. Although the whole conniving deal made Kelly see red, it would pay the bills, and Nicole was thrilled. "How could you not trust British Petroleum?" she asked. "At last something safe and solid to build a future on in this town."

At the moment, the future of this town wasn't looking so hot. After Blinger's shocking win in the runoff last week, Kelly had a sinking feeling that New Orleans, long buoyed by the false hope of new leadership, would continue to rot. Miss Dixie had been right: after the election, long-distance moving vans were revving up all over town. But today he had a personal victory to celebrate and made a concerted effort to block that out. Here you had to strap on blinders just to make it through the day. People didn't call the still habitable part of the city the Isle of Denial for nothing.

The real reason for putting on the dog—something of a surprise for Nicole—was that the house was finally finished, and it was his. As he'd explained to Nicole, Leona Helmsley in a hoop skirt balked at the paltry insurance settlement and resale value of a flooded house in Lakeview. So in the divorce she settled for half of his future retirement benefits, which at fifty seemed like a distant abstraction to Kelly. After all, in fifteen years he didn't see himself teeing off in Palm Springs living on a BP pension but lugging his easel around Mexico dressed in a faded T-shirt. How much dough would that take? Nicole looked shocked when he informed her that Lena had quit her job at Sundown Plantation and was moving alone to a condo in Boulder.

"No, I don't know a soul there," Lena had confessed, "but after New Orleans, I just want to be normal."

To Kelly, that sounded like a slippery slope: *normal*.

"My sister still hasn't dealt with Latrome's ashes," Oscar told Gertie. "They setting on the mantel at her house. Says she wants to scatter them over the lake. He loved to go fishing there whenever his dad happened to be around."

"I couldn't bear to scatter my Marky." Gertie took Oscar's hand. "That boy was scattered enough while he was alive. Besides, he'd want to be with me when I go."

Dixie ambled over to the open tomb, sticking her head inside to survey the two empty shelves.

"Where you moved Mama to?" she snapped at Gertie.

"Her bones down below, with Mémère and Pepère." Gertie put her arm around her sister's waist. "We couldn't leave her casket in there all these months with nothing to cover it. Honey, you don't know what I been through with them cemetery people. Finally they picked up the tombstone to repair it and engrave Marky's name. Soon as we leave today, they gonna bolt it back. His name is the last one on this marble tablet, you know. We at the end of the line here and will have to turn over a new leaf when one of us go."

"Don't look at me," Dixie said, untangling herself from her sister. "I'm not going in there."

"Where you going, sugar?"

"I told you a million times, I'm going with Abe over by Hebrew Rest, right across the street from Langenstein's Grocery." Dixie knocked back a gulp of her drink. "What if I get thirsty?"

"You mean you don't want to be with me and Mama and Marky?" Gertie said, pouting.

"Okay, you two." Nicole marched over to the tomb in her wool-blend jacket and charcoal skirt. "You've been having this conversation about who's going to be buried with who since I was ten years old, and it always leads to trouble."

"Nicole," Gertie whined, "where you gonna go?"

"Momma, stop it."

"Tell your aunt you want her to be with us."

"Lord have mercy," said Sweet Pea, sucking his teeth. "Nobody gonna shove my sweet ass in one of these brick boxes. It mess up my hair. Me, I going straight to the Aftermath Lounge in heaven to hang with the other sissies."

"Was Marky a sissy?" Gertie asked him.

"Momma!" Nicole said, reddening.

"Well, I want to know everything about my son before we say goodbye."

"Naw," said Kelly, staring down at the urn in his hands. Before Marky got sick, he would hump anything in sight. He had been so in love with life, like that wild, good-looking hero from *On the Road*. One night Marky had picked up a drunk redheaded chick at La Casa on Decatur Street, who brought along some lisping coke-dealer dude. Somehow Marky, the chick, and the dealer wound up in the back seat of Kelly's car, and feeling like a chauffeur driving down Canal Street, he glanced back to see both of them giving his friend a blow job while the dealer held a coke spoon to Marky's nostril.

"Is there anything else I can get you, sir?" Kelly asked Marky in an English accent. And they roared. The question became a tag greeting that cracked them up every time they saw each other.

Kelly held up the urn as if addressing Yorick's skull. *Hey old buddy, is there anything else I can get you?* Then he handed it to Miss Gertie. "Time to say good night, Gracie."

"I been saying goodbye to Marky every night on top that utility cart in the kitchen." She kissed the urn and placed it on the top shelf of the tomb. Each of them pulled out a lavender mum or a yellow rose to place next to the ashes. Finally Gertie covered the urn with a palmetto branch blessed at Mass last Sunday.

Sweet Pea started to clap in a mournful rhythm, hoop earrings jangling. Then his falsetto soared, joined by Gertie's soprano and Oscar's bass.

> We climbing
> Lord we climbing
> higher
> higher
> HIGHER
> climbing up to higher ground

Even Nicole mouthed the words, tentatively, and toward the end Kelly chimed in with his Irish tenor. Dixie pursed her lips, a tear running down one cheek.

# Higher Ground

Chariot wheels creaking, Schnitzel ran yipping across the dead grass. The ferocious dachshund stood his ground, barking at some distant threat that Kelly figured only the dog could sense.

He swung around in time to see a man in dark oval glasses glaring at them. Their eyes met, Kelly blinked, and then a pair of metal crutches disappeared around a tomb. It was that doctor, Marky's friend who had staged the Blinger fundraiser. After all, this burial had been announced in the obituary pages of today's paper. What was that Beatles' song about Eleanor Rigby's funeral? "Nobody came."

"Say, wasn't that Bob White?" Kelly turned to Gary. "The doctor who Blinger just appointed the city's new Director of Public Health?"

"Yep."

"Why you think he didn't want to join us?" Kelly asked, mystified.

"Now it looks like he's the stalker."

"Stalking who?"

"Me."

"Why?"

"You don't want to know." Gary averted eyes wide with panic. "After Sweet Pea comes down from his celebrity buzz with the limo, he needs to talk with another crippled guy I know, one who owes him a big street favor. Maybe Sweet Pea can fix it so I'll be alive next week."

"Don't go paranoid on me, man." Kelly scratched his head. Why would a tough customer like Gary be so weirded out by a cemetery? "But sure is odd the doctor would be watching alone."

Gary glanced over the heads gathered around the flower-decked tomb, as if mapping out the nearest exit. "I've never met a lonelier man."

"Wonder what a rich, powerful guy like him saw in crazy Marky?"

"The one thing he couldn't buy. Freedom." Gary moved toward the people huddled around the tomb. "He's a born prisoner, and Marky was his only hope for parole."

"Back into the limo," Kelly announced, clapping. "Time to pop the corks on the bubbly."

"Now we gonna second line in style!" Sweet Pea snapped his fingers, flicked on the shades, and with a lingering wave, took leave of the silent rows of his adoring fans.

THE MOOD TURNED GIDDY INSIDE the limo as iced bottles of Freixent were dug out of the bar and poured into crystal flutes. Sweet Pea unearthed a CD from his voluminous leather drag bag, and the luxurious yellow submarine began to rock as it glided through the lunar landscape of a devastated city.

"Those poor trees," Nicole sighed as they passed City Park. The majestic groves of live oaks now stood bald and stunted, branches mutilated to mere stumps of the long gracious limbs that once shaded the park under a canopy of Spanish moss. "I remember how as kids we'd climb them. I was so scared of falling and could never keep up with Marky, always calling down to me from somewhere higher, higher, higher. Then I'd look up and he'd have disappeared, and I'd slide down the trunk to wait for him at the bottom. And he'd always drop something of his for me to hold—a yo-yo or penknife—just to let me know that even though I couldn't see him, he was still up there, climbing." Fighting back a sob, Nicole slipped her hand into Kelly's. "Thanks, Marky. This guy you sent me is better than a yo-yo."

Kelly got goose bumps. "How freaky is that? After twenty-eight years, we ran into each other on the day Marky died."

"Makes sense," Gary said. "Marky always said his last act on earth would be a magic one. Looks like you two are it."

"My brother never let me down," she said, squeezing Kelly's hand, "no matter how high he climbed."

Gertie was still studying the trees outside. "You know, those oaks are three-hundred years old, and if storms didn't come around to prune their heavy branches, they'd topple over and die. They been through worse winds and lost lots of dead wood over the centuries, and that's why they still standing. You watch, if a storm hits a healthy tree, it'll sprout back lickety-split. Of course, a storm hit a rotten tree, that's it, but it would've died anyway. So this hurricane just been a necessary pruning so one day these trees will be a thousand years old."

"So, which are we?" Nicole asked. "A healthy tree or a rotten one."

Gertie raised her glass. "Just look at us!" Sweet Pea snapped a garter while Oscar was fighting with a champagne cork. "I didn't know most of these people eight months ago, and now they like my family. Blinger or no Blinger, let me tell you something: we the new New Orleans."

"Get a load of that pile of gawbage." Eyes widening, Dixie swung around in her seat to take in the five-story mountain of trash piled on the neutral ground of West End Boulevard, surrounded by house-gutting advertisements.

"That's everybody's Christmas presents from the past twenty years," Kelly said.

"All that retail," Dixie said in a mournful tone.

"Why are we taking a limo through Lakeview?" Nicole complained. "As if Marky's burial isn't depressing enough."

"Pull over here." Kelly tapped on the Plexiglas partition. "We got to pick up Hewitt from his gas station."

"Hey, Hewitt," Kelly yelled, jumping out of the limo door. "Get your butt in here. Champagne getting warm."

Hewitt shuffled over to the limo, dressed in a rumpled white shirt and bolo tie.

Kelly rushed up to pump his hand. "Like I was saying on the phone," he said, slapping him on the back, "so sorry I acted like such an asshole that day my supplies were looted. Come on, man. Hop in and have some bubbly."

"Still recovering from the José Cuervo Geesus give me last night after he finished his shift at the station." Hewitt stepped inside, beaming. "Hey there now, Nicole. And my old customer Miss Gertie, who I ain't seen since the storm."

"Hewitt!" Miss Gertie pecked him on the cheek. "How's your momma?"

Nicole cut an eye at her mother. "I still don't understand where in the world we're going."

AFTER THE WHITE LIMOUSINE PULLED up next to the weeping willow tree on Mouton Street, everyone filed out to stand at the very spot where Kelly's trailer was once parked. He certainly had a story to tell, but he winked at Nicole, letting her do the honors.

"On the day Marky was shot," she said, "my Zoloft was just kicking in when I rammed my car into this filthy lunatic's FEMA trailer—"

"Which, after months of hassles, I'd just gotten set up—"

"And then we both collapsed right here on the sidewalk, and I was in shock until it dawned on me this pissed-off jerk was Marky's friend Kelly Cannon, who I'd been in love with in high school, and I told him he could take a shower at my place if he'd drive me home, and then—"

"Soon as I took my clothes off, she raped me."

"I did *not*."

"Isn't that romantic?" Dixie said, lighting a Kent. "Now

don't go around saying FEMA ain't done nothing for the city. It even gets people laid in the French Quarter."

"*¡Felicidades!*" Jesús leaned out of the front door, salsa music blasting from inside. Then out stepped his wife Rosalinda, a kangaroo of a pregnant woman clutching a wooden cooking spoon, followed by pudgy José Luis in an apron.

"Do everybody like *cabrito*?" Jesús asked, flashing his silver-toothed smile. "Barbecue goat?"

Kelly nudged Nicole. "Come see the house, babe."

While everyone made halting introductions standing around the limo with champagne flutes in hand, Kelly took Nicole on a grand tour of the restored house. It would be ready to live in as soon as the polyurethane on the bedroom floors dried. In spite of the stolen building materials, Kelly and his Mexican crew had actually done it, and he was bursting with pride and excitement. Lena and the hurricane be damned.

He was home.

"Look." He opened the refrigerator door. "An icemaker! And over here, antique marble countertops that Jesús cut to size from slabs we found at the salvage company. And this," he said, waltzing with arms akimbo around the huge living room floor, "real heart of pine floors. All Lena and I ever had was hundred-year-old shag carpeting."

"It's gorgeous," Nicole said, pointing at the paint job. "Peach is my favorite color."

"Got a great deal on the drywall." Beaming, Kelly pounded the wall. "This sturdy stuff from China will last forever. Wanna shack up with me here, starting next week?"

"But what about my apartment on Dauphine, and Momma?"

"Oh, no, we not gonna give up that place. Want to keep it as a painting studio. And the best part is Jesús and Rosalinda," he said, rounding a hand over his stomach, "want to rent your mama's place, restore it, and then buy it, now that he's on full time at Hewitt's gas station."

"I don't know if she'd go for that."

"Go for what?" Gertie tottered in, carrying a paper plate piled high with salad, beans, and what looked like the charred leg of a small dog.

"I was telling Nicole how Jesús and Rosalinda want to lease-to-buy your house while they restore it."

"Was just talking to that nice Spanish man Geesus about it," Gertie said with her mouth full, a lettuce leaf working its way out of the corner of her lips. "Sounds like a jim-dandy idea to me. I raised my kids there, and that's what they want to do. And the rent would pay my expenses until the place is fixed up and they buy it. His wife Rosalinda asked me to help them bring back the garden."

"But, Momma, don't you want to move back in once you get a FEMA trailer set up?"

"And leave my friends in the Quarter? And the choir?" Gertie waved her hand dismissively. "To be the old lady who lived in a shoe in an abandoned neighborhood? And then fill up a big lonely house with a pile of new stuff that gonna float out the door the next time the wind blows? You must be crazy. Like my boys say at the Aftermath Lounge, 'Girlfriend, I'm over it.' Let them sweet people raise their kids there. Me, I'm moving to higher ground."

"Kelly and I are coming to live here next week."

"But keeping our love nest on Dauphine as a painting studio," Kelly added.

"Good. Won't have to put up with you spying on me." Gertie held up the goat leg. "Now will somebody show me how to eat this thing."

"Don't go making a big mess on our good floors," Nicole said, pointing. "Outside with that."

# Higher Ground

Sweet Pea had cranked up the limo sound system, and while Jesús taught his boss Hewitt how to scoop up beans with a tortilla and Kelly freshened flutes with champagne, Sweet Pea and Oscar discoed under the fluorescent carport light, next to the smoker filled with grilled goat. After a while, they managed to pull a brooding Gary onto the oil-stained dance floor. Then Miss Gertie put her plate on the hood of the limo and joined in, jigging like a peasant under the harvest moon, fluttering her fingers as if all the molecules in the universe were exploding.

> And I was there not dancing with anyone
> You took a little, then you took me over
> You set your mark on stealing my heart away
> Crying, trying, anything for you
>
> I'm in the middle of a chain reaction
> You give me all the after midnight action . . .
> We talk about love, love, love
> We talk about looove . . .

"What are the neighbors going to think?" Nicole stood under the weeping willow, eyes scanning the forlorn block as the sky blushed pink with sunset. On either side, knee-high weeds choked the front yards of decaying brick ranch houses, dark windows gaping. Across the street, a leafy sapling was sprouting from the top of a sagging carport.

"Relax," Kelly said, draping an arm around her neck. "We don't have any."

# Acknowledgments

As New Orleans restaurant owner Leah Chase once said, "I owe so many people I can't afford to die."

I would like to acknowledge with gratitude Julie Smith, who first put me up to writing this novel and later served as its expert editor. I also thank Michael Murphy for his valuable editorial suggestions, and the staff at the University of Louisiana at Lafayette Press, James D. Wilson, Jessica Hornbuckle, and Melissa Teutsch, for so carefully and enthusiastically bringing this project to fruition. For their helpful readings of the manuscript, I am grateful to Harriette Grissom, Christine Wiltz, Lisa Brener, Amy Conner, M.T. Caen, and Todd Bottorff. I also acknowledge the indispensable background information provided by Lamont Dubose, Jerry Cullem, Ellie Rand, Ulysses D'Aquila, Valerie Borders, and Maurice Ruffin. For their support of this novel, I also thank Rosemary James and Joseph DeSalvo of the Pirate's Alley Faulkner Society, and Marian Young of the Marian Young Literary Agency in New York.

The first chapter of this novel previously appeared in *Crab Orchard Review*, Volume 15, Number 1, Winter/Spring 2010.

UNIVERSITY OF LOUISIANA AT LAFAYETTE PRESS
# LOUISIANA WRITERS SERIES

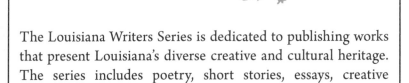

The Louisiana Writers Series is dedicated to publishing works that present Louisiana's diverse creative and cultural heritage. The series includes poetry, short stories, essays, creative nonfiction, and novels.

## BOOKS IN THE LOUISIANA WRITERS SERIES:

*The Blue Boat* by Darrell Bourque (out of print)
*Amid the Swirling Ghosts* by William Caverlee
*Local Hope* by Jack Heflin
*New Orleans: What Can't Be Lost* edited by Lee Barclay
*In Ordinary Light* by Darrell Bourque
*Higher Ground* by James Nolan

FOR MORE INFORMATION VISIT:
WWW.ULPRESS.ORG